The Magdalen Laundries

Copyright © 2017 by Lisa Michelle Odgaard

All rights reserved. This book or any portion thereof may not be reproduced or used in any manner whatsoever without the express written permission of the publisher except for the use of brief quotations in a book review.

Printed in the United States of America

First Printing, 2017

ISBN 9781546932390

This is a work of fiction. Names, characters, places, events and incidents are either the products of the author's imagination or used in a fictitious manner. Any resemblance to actual persons, living or dead, or actual events is purely coincidental.

The Magdalen Laundries

a novel

Inspired by True Events

by

Lisa Michelle Odgaard

Dedicated to my children:
Selah, Erick, and Brynjar.
I have never been prouder of anything
than to be called your mother.

Prologue

Nova Scotia, Canada: August 1994

The scream yanked Brigid from sleep, but didn't frighten her. She had heard it too many times before.

Staring blankly, she lay in the dark, her eyes fighting to focus on the hazy expanse of ceiling above her bed as she listened to the agonized sound coming from two rooms away. This was the third night this week, she realized. It was happening more often. Whatever it was that terrified Mum enough to cause those gut-wrenching screams must be getting worse.

Not for the first time, Brigid wondered what it could be that frightened her mother so often and to such great extent. The screaming continued, gradually ebbing into soft whimpers and echoed by her father's soothing tones, which became audible to Brigid's ears as the noise that had cloaked them died down. Now only gasping sobs and sniffles interrupted the constant calming flow of Dad's crooning. Brigid could imagine them as clearly as she had seen them that first night, the first time the peace of sleep had been interrupted by a scream in the dark. She had been only a few years old, but she vividly remembered bolting upright in her small bed, her eyes round with fear, and throwing back the quilt to run into her parents' room. There they had been, Mum rocking slowly back and forth in Dad's arms, her arms bent at the elbows and her shoulders hunched in self-protection. Her wrists were pressed tightly to her eyes as Dad held her loosely, whispering words of love and reassurance in a steady, calm stream. Brigid had braced herself in the doorway and watched them, a study in contradiction: where her father was relaxed, the very essence of tranquility, Mum was tightly wound to the point that she shook. Brigid had never seen anyone so tense. Shutting her eyes briefly, she saw the memory etched on her lids, knowing that if she walked into their room at that moment she would see that contrast playing before her once again.

    Brigid's heart ached with a familiar longing to protect her mother. She was suddenly aware that her hands were clenched into fists, held stiffly at her sides as she lay on her back in the bed, and that her nightgown was clinging to the cold sweat that had erupted the moment the scream wakened her. Her apprehension had risen in the room in the form of tangible heat, taking the chill from the walls and air. Consciously Brigid tried to relax her hands, flexing them at her sides. She could feel the bones creak and settle as she fanned her fingers; she must have been clenching them hard.

    She rolled to her side, pulling the damp clutch of the nightgown away from her skin, and strained to hear what her father was saying. His murmurs had succeeded in calming Mum down enough that she was quiet, only occasionally emitting a small sigh. Brigid could imagine her mother relaxing into her husband's arms, finally feeling safe, feeling protected. He would loosely enfold her softening body in the comfort of his arms before gently lowering her to her pillow. In the early years, when Brigid would still run to their room, she would be snuggled with her mother as Dad tucked them in, having immediately put her tiny arms around Mum's taut neck and held her, lending whatever support she could. Dad would wrap the soft flannel blankets around them as she held her mother tightly, believing that she lent strength to rival her daddy's.

    She had long since stopped going into the bedroom when it happened, having learned as she grew older that it upset Mum to know that she had frightened her only daughter. Torn between wanting to reassure and wanting to spare her mother embarrassment tangled with worry, Brigid forced herself to pretend that she slept through the bloodcurdling screams. Donal never mentioned Mum's nighttime disruptions, so Brigid assumed that he remained unconscious throughout, which astonished her. Then again, he was only twelve, and a boy at that. The five years' difference between Brigid and her brother accounted for many of their differences, but she believed that it was his innate apathy as a male that allowed him to sleep soundly while she tossed and turned with concern. She had brought it up several times over the years, wondering why he never seemed to notice their mother's red-rimmed eyes some mornings or wake when the entire household was disrupted in the night. Donal had given her the classic boys' shrug, muttered something and run off to play whatever game interested him at the moment. Brigid had decided that boys simply didn't have the sensitivity of girls, with the exception of her wonderful father and his understanding of Mum's anxiety. Perhaps Donal would grow into it, whereas Brigid felt she had been born taking care of her mother.

All was now quiet in the other room. Brigid could feel the nighttime chill reclaiming the air in the house, replacing the fleeting warmth as silence reigned once again. With a deep breath, Brigid settled into her pillow and pulled the quilt up around her shoulders, closing her eyes to shut out the dark, and the trepidation with it.

Brushing her teeth and whipping a stick of lip gloss across her mouth, Brigid gave herself an encouraging grin in the bathroom mirror and headed downstairs to where she knew her mother would be sitting looking out over the water.

Sure enough, Maren Adair was sitting at the kitchen table and looking out the window, the fingers of both hands wrapped tightly around her deep blue coffee mug as she watched the sun start to come up over the sea. Brigid smiled as she came into the kitchen and caught the last few moments of the sunrise her mother had been watching. It was a beautiful view, and she heard Maren sigh as the golden rays turned the sky from its dark night black into a burst of color. The reds, oranges and pinks spread slowly across the sky and faded away leisurely into a lovely, bright blue as she looked up and noticed her daughter. With a smile of welcome, she pulled out the chair next to her and gestured for Brigid to sit. Brigid waved a hand and looked toward the countertop, where the coffee sat in its pot, still hot. "Hang on a sec, Mum; I'll just get myself a cup and join you."

Brigid could feel her mother's eyes on her as she made her way efficiently around the kitchen, and she reached for the silver-rimmed glass coffeepot with one eye still on the view through the windowpane. The water was calm, its waves barely moving, but small ripples of pink and orange played across its surface as the sun rose higher into the sky. Bright blue surrounded it, and the few clouds that floated gently past were white, fluffy and not at all menacing. Brigid knew that her mother had grown up in Ireland, where no town was more than seventy miles away from the sea coast. The town where she had lived was very near Dublin, right on the eastern coast of the country, but every morning found Maren like this, sitting by the large bay window with her coffee and watching the sun rise in the sky over the water. Brigid supposed it reminded her of her youth, but as her gaze moved back to her mother, she saw on Maren's face a look almost akin to hunger as she stared out over the sea.

With her short-cropped dark hair and deep brown eyes, Brigid's looks were as different from her mother's as they could be. Maren had worn her blond hair long and curly for as long as Brigid had been alive, and her eyes were as blue as the sky and the rippling waves beneath it. Yet they were both tall and slender, with a proud, regal bearing, and when outsiders looked more closely into Brigid's younger face they could see that the shape of her jaw and her eyes and mouth were very like that of her mother.

As Brigid poured her coffee into a cartoon-emblazoned mug and walked over to the table, she saw Maren's eyes following her, filled with fondness. *It looks like she's in a good mood*, she thought. *Maybe I shouldn't ask her. I don't want to ruin this beautiful morning by reminding her of her nightmares.*

Reaching across the table to where Brigid had settled herself, Maren grasped her daughter's hand in an affectionate squeeze. "Good morning, darling."

Brigid smiled as she dumped a spoonful of sugar into her coffee. "Good morning to you, too, Mum." She looked at her mother, shaking her head slightly with an affectionate laugh.

"What?" Maren responded immediately, looking wary.

"Look at you, Mum. You're not even dressed!"

Giving her worn orange robe a cursory downward glance, Maren chuckled. "*You're* the strange one, Brigid, not me. How a child of mine can wake up and be instantly cheerful, I can't understand." She shook her head. "I need some more coffee before I'll be ready to face the day."

"How long have you been up?" Brigid couldn't refrain from asking.

"An hour," Maren answered, her tone defensive, and gave another quiet laugh. "Look, I don't have to answer to you, young lady! I'll bet you've even brushed your teeth, haven't you? What self-respecting girl brushes her teeth before she eats her breakfast?" Maren herself still sat with sleep-mussed hair and the coziness of her winter robe wrapped around her. Brigid looked fresh-faced and alert, with her damp hair neatly combed back from her face. She couldn't keep the expression of amusement from her face as her mother closed her lips tightly against her own unbrushed teeth. "When did *you* get up?"

"Maybe ten minutes ago." She gazed out to the water and sighed. "It's beautiful, isn't it? I never get tired of looking at it."

Maren nodded. "You didn't appreciate it so much when you were younger. Maybe turning seventeen has sharpened your appreciation for life." She smiled to show she was teasing and took a long draught of her coffee. Brigid gave her a brief grin and poured some milk into her coffee, stirring it briefly before taking a small sip. She frowned at the bitterness and added another heaping spoonful of sugar, seeing Maren shake her head with a grimace. Brigid knew that Maren never put more than a few grains of sugar into her coffee, and Brigid's cup was easily smaller than her large stone mug. "You're going to rot your teeth."

"I'll brush them again afterward." Satisfied with the next taste, she relaxed into her chair, her sock-covered feet balancing on the edge of the table and her knees drawn up. "Aaah. Nice."

She gazed again out the window, knowing that her mother was studying her. Although she believed she looked tranquil, she knew Maren could tell that there was something she wanted to say. Brigid had never been able to hide her feelings from her mother, and it had been the same from mother to daughter. When Brigid was small, she had always been able to sense when Maren was upset or unhappy, and she would always draw close to give her a comforting hug and ask what was wrong. She remembered fondly how, as early as when she was two years old, she had snuggled into her mother's lap and wrapped her pudgy arms around her, content to just hold her as she cried. Their relationship had become closer each time they had needed to console one another, as though by reassuring each other, they were increasing their strength. Now Brigid sat staring out over the water with her mug held close to her chest, trying to decide how to phrase her many questions, when Maren's voice broke the silence. "What is it, Brigid?"

Brigid shook her head with a small grin and reached forward to put her mug back on the table. "I can't hide anything from you, can I, Mum?" Her voice was slightly tinged with a Gaelic inflection, evidence of the Irish heritage she had observed in both parents, although she herself had never been out of Canada. "I've just been thinking about a few things. Wondering, actually."

"Well, if it's a question I can answer, fire away," Maren invited. Her features were calm and encouraging.

Grabbing her teaspoon and stirring her coffee again, Brigid began awkwardly. Her heart beat furiously in her chest. "You—always used to say...that is, you would never tell me..." Unable to find an easy question to start with, she sighed in frustration.

Maren leaned forward to grasp her daughter's hand once again, saying gently as she did so, "Go on, honey. You can ask me anything."

Keeping her eyes locked on her coffee, Brigid said forcefully, "It's about what happened last night, Mum. When I was younger, you said there were things...that you would tell me when I got older. Like whatever it was that happened to you...that makes you so—sad, whenever you remember it." Refusing to look up, and hearing the way Maren's breath caught, she rushed on. "I heard you crying last night. I hear you every time. All these years, every time it happens, I lie awake in my bed, waiting until the screaming stops and hoping and praying that it won't happen again. I've told myself that someday everything will be all right, and that you'll finally have peace with whatever it is...but it's been getting worse lately. More and more often I wake up hearing you scream and cry." She took a deep breath. "I don't know if I can help you, Mum. I wish I could; I want to more than anything, but I don't know what to do about it. I just think that, now that whatever it is seems to be getting harder for you, maybe...maybe I should finally ask the things I've been wondering about all my life." She ended abruptly, and stole a quick glance at Maren.

Maren wasn't looking at her daughter. Her face was pained, and Brigid cursed herself for making her mother feel whatever varied emotions were causing that expression, but she was glad she had asked. Though her face was red and her breathing felt labored, her heart had ceased its panicked racing. Now that the words were out, she sat quietly, waiting for Maren to respond. After a few moments, she did. Giving her daughter a weak smile, she reached again for Brigid's hand, and began.

"I'm so sorry that this has caused you pain. I had no idea...I didn't know that you were lying awake so many nights, my darling girl. I suppose, considering that my troubles began at sixteen, and ended when I was near your age, that it is right for me to tell you this now." She exhaled deeply and continued, and Brigid leaned forward in her eagerness.

"It was 1961. I was living in the village of Somhairle, a very small place, and your grandfather and grandmother were raising me to be a good, proper Catholic girl." She smiled again, but sourly. "My father had started the farm with almost nothing, and he did a good job of it. By the time I was twelve we were supplying milk and cheese to almost everyone in the village, and in Dublin, which was nearby. In 1961, I was sixteen, and my life was fairly sheltered. I did help out with the farm, but not much. The only great mysteries in my narrow existence were whether my father's farmhand would ever notice me, and the secrets of the convent laundries."

Brigid listened closely, the coffee forgotten on the table, as Maren began her story.

Chapter One

Somhairle, County Dublin, Republic of Ireland: Spring 1961

Maren Bradigan awoke later than usual on a fine June morning, jumping out of bed to pull on a soft blouse and a skirt. She went to the fresh water her mother had set out in the washbasin near the bed, and gasped at the cold as she splashed her face. Grabbing a brush to detangle her hair, she looked out the window to where her father was working and waved to him. "Good morning, Da!"

    He stretched his neck up enough to see his pretty blond daughter overseeing the yard work as she dragged a brush through her thick curls, and gave her a mock salute and a wide grin. It was early in the day, but Oran Bradigan had already been at his work for a full hour. Farming was his livelihood, and he worked hard to make sure the dairy ran well and the farming chores were always up to date. Maren's older brother, Rian, came into sight, leading his favorite horse, Stepper, and tilted his hat back in order to see the girl framed in the window two stories up. "Hey, you little scamp!" he called to her. "Get your little bottom out of bed and come help me round up those cows for milking!"

    She grinned and stuck her tongue out at him. "You go on, Rian Bradigan," she yelled back. "I'll be down as soon as I finish making myself pretty."

    Rian shook his head at his father. "She thinks of nothing else but," he complained good-naturedly. Oran gave him a smack on the shoulder with his hat, then used it to wipe the sweat from his forehead.

    "Ah, give her a break, will you, Rian? You know there's no one else except your mother who does it better."

    Rian smirked. "I know it, Da. If only she'd been a boy."

Oran laughed. "Don't think there's a single one of us who *really* thinks that. Get to work." Rian's laugh was an echo of his father's as he passed him and went into the barn.

Oran Bradigan had grown up in nearby Dublin, and had left as soon as he was old enough to make his way. He and his wife Naomh settled just outside the village and embraced the farming life, starting with a single milk cow. Oran had worked hard to establish their business over the following years. When Rian was born, they were barely surviving, but by the time of Maren's birth in 1945, they had accumulated a large herd of jerseys. For as long as Maren could remember, her family had been hardworking farmers, supporting themselves easily while supplying all the villagers with milk, cheese and other necessities. Maren enjoyed a relatively easy life as their only daughter, but even as a little girl she was up at dawn with her family every day to tend to her chores. Without Maren's and Rian's help, the farm could not have run as smoothly as it did; Oran would have needed to hire more workers on top of the three he already had employed. Of those three, only two were strictly necessary, but Oran considered the third a good investment in his daughter's future. Faolán Ó Ciarmhaic, a young boy from Dublin, had come to the village as a youth and headed straight for the Bradigan farm. Oran had been hunched over his prize cow, gently coaxing lightly steaming milk from her udders into the bucket he held carefully between his legs.

Cap in hand, the boy nervously asked Oran for work, his pre-pubescent young voice wavering slightly as he struggled to keep it masculine and deep. Giving young Faolán the once-over from his perch on the old wooden stool, Oran sized him up as young, strong, and perhaps most important, willing. His father had been one of Oran's closest friends, Faolán claimed. Oran had smiled to himself, putting the bucket of warm milk down on the dusty ground and leaning his arm on one knee as he watched the young boy. Faolán moved in an unconscious echo of his father, who Oran indeed remembered from his youth in Dublin.

"I don't know about that, young man," Oran rumbled at the shy lad, "but I suppose I could find some work for you to do. You'll be needing a place to stay, anyway, seeing as you've brought yourself out here on your own, and I can't be giving away lodging for free, now can I? Follow Gormghiolla there"—he gestured toward the old cowhand, who looked up and nodded—"and get yourself washed up at the house. He'll get you settled into the way we do things around here. We'll talk wages later."

Faolán nodded eagerly. "Yes sir, Mister Bradigan. I'll work hard for you, I promise." He gave a short bow in Oran's direction as Gormghiolla hustled him away toward the house, and Oran gave a gruff reply, smiling as soon as the boy had scrambled out of sight.

"That one there might be a good match for young Maren, one day," he murmured under his breath before turning back to his work underneath the jersey. The cow snorted and took a step back, nearly knocking over the bucket. Oran caught it neatly, patted her rump with his rough palm to soothe her, and resumed his work.

This fair morning, Faolán was nowhere in sight. Oran looked about as much as he could, but he could not spare the time to leave any of the milk cows to go on a search for the young man. Oran shook his head, but he was not worried. Faolán knew his way around the farm; he had been there for a few months now and had never shirked his work. Perhaps he was in the house, talking to Naomh about an addition to his breakfast; he was a healthy fellow and always complained about being hungry. Oran grinned to himself as he remembered himself at that age. Four meals a day hadn't been enough for him then. Ruefully he patted his round stomach; now he tried to keep it down to less than three.

Maren's giggle came floating back to him from behind the barn, and he strode over to give her instructions for the day. He was on his way to deliver milk and cheese to some of the patrons in the village, and he wanted her to take care of the chickens while he was away. As he drew closer, however, he realized that she wasn't alone. Faolán Ó Ciarmhaic was sitting on an overturned bucket, his eyes on Maren as she talked happily about her school and her work around the farm, her fingers twisting one long blond lock of her hair. Faolán was grinning at her, and Oran felt his own face quickly turn to a scowl. Sixteen years old was not nearly old enough for Maren to be flirting with the opposite sex. Regardless of how highly he regarded Faolán, he wasn't about to lose Maren to him just yet.

"Cassán," he called roughly, and Maren looked startled. She pulled her fingers out of her hair and walked quickly toward him.

"Yes, Da," she said meekly. "I was just about to get on with my chores. I'm sorry if you were looking for me."

"I was looking for both of you," Oran growled, his eyes on Faolán. The boy's cheeks heated and he almost bowed. "I've got work for you to do, Faolán."

"I'm sorry, sir. I was just having a little chat with—"

"Yeah, yeah," Oran grumbled, waving a hand. "Just get on with it. Maren," he spat out, making a quick decision. She leaped forward, looking guilty. "You're coming with me on the deliveries. Faolán can take care of the chickens this morning."

Maren's face suddenly became animated. "Yes, Da," she said. "But what about school?"

"Don't worry about the morning. You can make it up later. Now get in the truck."

"Yes, Da," she nodded. "I'll meet you there."

Oran looked satisfied as Faolán went about his business in the barn with Rian, and he watched Maren eagerly running to the truck. It had been a while since he had allowed her to come along on a delivery, and she was obviously elated. She was definitely not worried about how Faolán saw her; she tripped in her excitement and nearly landed face-first in the mud. With a snort, Oran headed for the truck to start into the village to make his deliveries. If Faolán had seen Maren flailing to regain her footing like she had, he would have fast been reminded of how young she was. *That ought to hold him off for a while,* he thought, and slammed the door. Starting the engine, he gave Maren a little grin, and started off toward the village.

Chapter Two

Somhairle itself was in the shape of a diamond, with the large, steeple-topped church framed by a cluster of shops marking the upper half. The lower half consisted of several homes, the houses of the "town folk", as the occupants of the nearby farms referred to them. The middle section of the diamond was a bare, grassy field, the "town square" if such a tiny village could be said to have one. Here, in a throwback to days of old, the young children often played with hoops and sticks and balls, delighting the milling townsfolk with their happy cries. It was a peaceful center to a peaceful existence.

Branching off from the top portions of the diamond to the northeast and northwest were two long roads of heavily trodden, densely packed dirt that could better be called paths. Dotted along the "V" that was formed by these two roads were numerous farmhouses, where the "country folk" lived with their families and made their living. To the northeast, at the very juncture where the road met the diamond-shaped center of the village, lay the school, which instructed children from grades one through ten. The dirt stretched for miles in either direction, the farmhouses becoming fewer and farther between until they reached the outskirts of the city of Dublin. At the very farthest point of the northwestern path lay the orphanage, and the high stone walls that bordered the convent laundry that was owned by the Sisters of Grace in Dublin.

It was along this northwestern road that Oran Bradigan's yellow Ford F-100 pickup rattled on this lovely June day. Maren hung out the window on the left side of the old milk truck and stared as they approached the menacing sight of the laundry walls, and as her father brought the truck to a shaky halt, she clambered from the cloth-covered seat and stood on the path in mute excitement. It wasn't often that she got to visit the place that brought whispered words of awe and terror from the throats of the young girls back home. As Maren's father disappeared inside one farmhouse down the road, Maren walked quickly and easily down the path toward that forbidden place. Its high stone walls had been visible from the road as her father had driven the milk wagon toward the farmhouses, and Maren had pressed her nose against the foggy window glass in curiosity as they approached. "Stay close, Cassán," her father had admonished in his thick brogue, as he always did when she came along on his deliveries to the farms. "You've got to be extra careful around here. I wouldn't go wandering off the way you tend to do."

Maren's mouth broke into a smile at the familiar nickname. *Cassán*, he always called her. *Little curly-haired one.* It was a name he had called her since soon after her first birthday, when the downy hairs on her head had begun twisting into ringlets that framed her tiny face. No one else called her by the name, and the affection in Oran's normally gruff tone when he used it warmed her heart every time. "I'll stick close, Da," Maren agreed obligingly, but by the time they had gotten into sight of the farmhouse, she had already planned her escape. She would sneak close to the walls, try to find an opening, and peer in as best she could. Maren did not know the name of this convent, and had never seen the front of it, which was only accessible by going directly into Dublin proper. All that was visible on the Somhairle side were the tall stone walls that bordered the convent and held their secrets deep within. The convent laundries were mysterious places, and disobedient or rebellious young girls were often threatened with being sent to work in them. Maren had never been worried that her family would send her to the laundries; her father was as close to her as any man could be to a daughter, and her mother would never dream of sending her only daughter away. In response to Oran and Naomh Bradigan's loving way of raising her and Rian, Maren was a thoughtful and obedient child, and it usually would not occur to her to disregard her father's warning.

Today, however, she had given into the sudden surge of mischievousness. The curiosity that had drawn her to the tall stone wall now blended with terror and anticipation; Maren could feel her trepidation as she drew close, but her heart pounded with excitement. These forbidden walls contained within them a secret that had the whole village whispering. Maren and her two best school chums, Orla and Saraid, often whispered in quiet awe about what happened in the laundries, giggling with the delight of frightening each other as though the tales were ghost stories. And to a point they were; no one knew much about the girls and women who lived within the walls, only that they had gone astray from the restrictions of the Church and had lived sinful lives until the priests, nuns or the girls' own families had, in desperation, secluded them within the place in order to work for their penance. The air of mystery that the place held kept the town youngsters in their place: no one knew exactly why the threat of being sent to the laundries was so horrible, but none of the young girls Maren was associated with wanted to find out. The thought of washing other people's laundry was enough to scare Orla and Saraid into staying on the straight and narrow path. The laundries always brought to Maren's mind Old Mr. Bannon, the butcher who owned the meat market in the center of the village. Bannon wiped his bloody hands on his large white apron with such relish that the girls shuddered whenever they saw it. His large, hairy knuckles streaked with blood and flecked with bits of bone marrow and sinew tarnished the fresh white of his apron five minutes after opening every day. Maren was always in a hurry to do the milk delivery to Bannon's as early as possible in the morning, just to avoid the glint in Old Bannon's eye as he hacked away at fresh meat, the warm red liquid squirting up with every stroke and splashing down upon the wooden block. Remembering this now, Maren grimaced with distaste. No, she wouldn't relish cleaning his dirty linens. She felt sorry for anyone who had that awful job.

The gray stone was icy against her hands, and she felt its chill slowly seeping into her, infusing her with the coldness of the early morning. Maren shuddered, but continued her search for an opening, welcoming the sunlight as it slowly crept toward her from the horizon. She stopped for a brief moment to glance toward the orange glow in the sky. "Good morning, sun," she said in a soft voice. "Come to aid me in my search, have you?" Her fingers moved in an incessant horizontal slide across the ripples of stone, feeling for a dip that was larger than the others, or a hole that would only become visible once her sensitive fingertips found it. She glanced toward the farmhouse; her father was nowhere in sight, but she knew she didn't have much time.

"Blast," she muttered. The wall was longer around than it was high. Maren knew that she would never have enough time to thoroughly scan it in its entirety, and her father would come walking out any minute. Giving up, she turned and slumped down to the damp ground, her back pressing against the hard rock. Some adventure this had turned out to be. Oh, well, perhaps another time she would be able to get her father to bring her out with him again, but it was usually difficult to convince her father to take her along. Maren didn't quite understand what had persuaded Oran to bring her on the rounds this morning, but she was not about to let this chance get away without trying to assuage her curiosity in some way. Oran had been aware of Maren's interest in the tall stone wall as they drew near, and she had felt his eyes boring into her as she watched the place approaching from the truck's window. "You be careful while I'm working, missy," he warned her in his deep growling voice. "I don't want you traipsing around those farmhouses. It could be dangerous out there. You just stay close to me and we'll be out of there in no time." Oran smiled at her and ran a hand through her curly blond hair, suddenly recognizing the coarseness of his tone. "Careful, my Cassán, you hear?" he repeated gently, and Maren had nodded eagerly. She was sure that this one trip along with her father would be enough to discover the secrets of the laundries. Now she was running out of time, and nothing to show for her daring.

The moisture of the ground was beginning to soak through the thin fabric of her skirt. In sudden realization, Maren jumped up with a muttered exclamation, brushing in vain against the wetness on her derriere. "Oh, great," she hissed. "This will be comfortable all the way home." She continued trying to dry her skirt between her two palms, rubbing furiously but doing nothing more than creating new wrinkles in the sodden fabric.

As she worked, slowly she became aware of a sound breaking through the constant chirping of insects and birds. She cocked her head to one side to hear better, the motion of her hands stilling, the wetness all but forgotten. A light, sweet sound rose up on the morning air, fading in and out through the slight wind, but definitely recognizable as a melody. *Someone's singing*, Maren thought in amazement. She dropped her skirt and it fell with a gentle damp slap against her upper thigh as she pressed her ear to the wall. As she moved from spot to spot, trying to catch the sound, the singing suddenly became clearer. *This must be a thinner part of the wall,* she reasoned. *I can almost hear her like she's right beside me.* Maren closed her eyes to shut out the distractions around her and focused on the voice.

"Lord Jesus, my King...my sins purged away; In thy loving embrace...I endureth each day." The sweet soprano rose into the air, filling Maren's head as she concentrated fiercely on the words. *"O Jesus, my Lord...I serve Thee to find; Your promise of rest...And quiet of mind."* The girl's voice was filled with emotion; Maren wanted to laugh and cry at once as she heard the loving, heartfelt quality of the song. Without even thinking, she began humming a counter-melody to the song, harmonizing unconsciously with the girl on the other side of the wall. Her body relaxed against the stone as she joined in the sweet song along with the mysterious person singing it, and her hands sagged against her knees as they pressed into the dirt and grass beneath her. Her skirt was once again saturating through with wetness as she sat on the dewy ground, but she didn't notice. *"Lord Jesus, Thy Son...Nailed high on a tree...Through darkness and shame; Be known Thee to me."*

"Maren! There you are! Get up off that wet ground!" Maren's eyes snapped open as she heard the crunch of leaves beneath her father's feet. She scrambled to her feet as he strode down the path toward her.

"Sorry, Da, I—"

"Just hop on," he interjected coarsely. "We've got several more deliveries, and you're keeping people waiting." Oran turned abruptly and made his way back to the yellow Ford, and Maren brushed the leaves off her wet skirt and hurried after him. His long strides carried him quickly to the driver's side, and his irritation floated back to Maren as she hurried to keep up. "I told you not to go off wandering, didn't I? I trusted you, Maren, and you're making me feel as though I've misplaced my trust."

Maren hung her head. "I really am sorry, Da." They had reached the truck by this point, and as Maren opened the passenger door and swung herself in, Oran reached for the rope that tied the packages of milk and cheese for delivery into the truck bed and yanked to make sure it was secure. Giving a small grunt of satisfaction, he leapt up into the cab and started the engine. The old Ford gave a leap and started trundling along the path. Maren leaned against the window pane, the wetness of her skirt not bothering her in the least as her mind drifted off with thoughts of the girl on the other side of the wall. She hummed the tune again with a small smile on her face as they made their way to the next farm.

The girl on the other side of the wall was abruptly cut off in her singing as the wooden door to her small room banged open and another girl poked her head in. "Be quiet!" the younger girl hissed. "Someone will hear you and make you get back to work. If you're well enough to sing, you're well enough not to be in your room at all."

The girl let out a sigh. "I can't help it, Amy. I just needed to sing. It feels like the angels are singing with me this morning." She leaned her dark head against the stone of the wall that served as her headboard and drew her knees up, wrapping her thin arms in a circle around them. She looked at Amy, who stood framed in the doorway with a scowl on her face, and smiled. "You'd better get back. I promise, I'll keep it down."

Amy nodded. "Just remember that if you get sent back to work, it's not my fault. I did warn you at my own risk."

"I know, Amy. Go on. I'll keep quiet."

Amy closed the door quietly and walked down the hallway, and the young girl on the narrow cot leaned forward once again, placing her chin on top of her knees and straining to hear the voice she had heard a moment before. Nothing. She sighed and, deep in thought, began to whisper the last verse of the song under her breath:

"Lord Jesus, my King...Inspire in Thy sight; My yielding to Thee...From darkness to Light."

Chapter Three

Maren was quiet all the way home from the last delivery. Oran looked at her with a quizzical expression as she leaned back against the window frame, a faraway look in her eyes. "What are you thinking about, Cassán?" he inquired, reaching over to put a loving hand on her shoulder. Maren looked at him with a sigh.

"Da, what do you think about the laundries?"

Oran frowned. "You mean the convent laundries?"

Maren nodded. "The walls we were driving by back there...what do you think *really* goes on inside them?"

Oran struggled with his thoughts. As a young man, he had been only vaguely aware of the laundries, but as he had grown older and traveled in wider circles, he had heard a few things about the convents all over Ireland that ran such laundries. Nothing he had heard had been good, but it was considered to be a hush-hush topic, and no one in Ireland would willingly talk about what really happened behind the high stone walls. Although outwardly people seemed disgusted at the thought of the rehabilitation centers, even the most outspoken of those who were against the laundries would make use of them if they felt it was justified or necessary. One of his friends had sent his own daughter to live there after it was discovered that she had been sleeping with her stepbrother and had become pregnant. Oran tried not to think of what had happened to that little girl and her baby. "I don't know, Cassán. Just regular woman's work, I suppose. Nothing you should concern yourself with."

Having noticed her father's hesitation and the pained look in his eye, Maren was not satisfied with his answer. Unwilling to pry, however, she used a different tack. "You would never send me there, would you, Da?"

Oran pressed his foot down on the brake as he pulled the truck over to the side of the road. Almost roughly, he grasped Maren by the shoulders and pulled her toward him. "Cassán, don't ever, *ever* suggest such a thing! I would sooner feed you to lions than see you in that place." Seeing his daughter was taken aback, he loosened his grip and sat back. "Besides, the laundries are not the place for your type of girl. You're one of the good ones, Maren...just keep that way."

Maren leaned against the seat again, her heart beating frantically in her chest. She could tell that there was fear and loathing behind her father's words, but she didn't quite understand why. She was content to sit back and keep quiet as her father started for home again, and decided that she would not bring up the topics of the convents or the laundries again.

The type of girl who would belong there...no, I'm not. The thought of Faolán crossed her mind, and she allowed herself a reluctant smile. *Just thinking about him is not the same thing as what those girls have done.* Still, a niggling sense of doubt stayed with her as the old truck bounced down the path. Was she doing wrong by dreaming about Faolán? Now that she thought of it, her father had certainly seemed anxious to drag her away from him this morning. And it had been their first real attempt at communication!

At the thought of Faolán's smile greeting her as she arrived home and added her hands to the chores, a grin broke over her own face in response. For the time being, anyway, she wouldn't think about the laundry or the girls inside, or worry about what she should or shouldn't be thinking about Faolán. No; today, she would just enjoy it.

Two days later, Maren left the little church in the village with a light heart. After two days of worrying and anxious moments, she had confessed her attraction to Faolán and now, it was over. She had no reason to fear her father sending her to the laundries, she knew that, but she still felt better knowing that she had made a conscious effort to curb her affinity for the young farmhand.

Going to the church for confession had been a difficult decision to make. Maren had always been thought of by the townfolk as "the good little Bradigan girl", and indeed, she thought of herself the same way. Of course, as a dutiful Catholic, Maren had made confession a part of her routine, but never before had she had anything to really confess to the priest who always sat, one wrinkled hand on his cheek, on the other side of the grate in the booth. That morning, Maren had shaken with fear as she thought of telling the old priest all the thoughts she had been having about Faolán. Since the boy had come to the farm to work for Maren's father, she had found herself not able to do her regular chores with as much focus as she normally put into them. The tall, strong young man with the wavy chestnut hair gave her a smile and a nod each morning as she walked from the house to the barn to begin her morning chores, and from the first, Maren had found herself smitten.

Never before having been a girl to concern herself with her looks, she found herself rising early every morning to brush her hair with the one hundred strokes her teacher at the little farm school had stressed were required to maintain beautiful locks, and begged her mother for shiny ribbons to tie her unruly curls back with. Several times Naomh Bradigan had to chastise her young daughter for wearing school dresses in which to do her chores, and although Maren groaned at the rebuke, she was certain that the few times Faolán had seen her in the pretty frocks he had been suitably impressed.

The two years of difference in their ages mattered not to Maren. She was certain that her maturity shone through her youthful appearance, and after all, at sixteen she was certainly old enough to be courting. Faolán didn't seem to have a steady girl; no strangers showed up at the farm seeking him out. Maren knew that she was the only girl he saw on a consistent basis, and although the only other females he saw—besides her mother, whom she didn't believe counted—were her school chums, she didn't want to take any chances and continued to pretty herself up before sunrise every morning.

It seemed to be working; Faolán always looked up as she passed, no matter how busy he was with splitting firewood or moving the cows out to pasture. Sometimes he would have his sleeves rolled up, showing the youthful length of muscle in his arms, and Maren would stop to stare before he noticed her. It had gotten to the point where nearly every night, as she retired to bed, Maren would wrap her arms around herself, closing her eyes tightly as she imagined Faolán's warm, tanned arms encircling her. Her dreams were filled with his laughing face, his long limbs, and his warm, dancing eyes, and the promise of finding him in her sleep each night, combined with the early mornings, gave her deep, restful nights.

As the sun rose the morning before, she had walked into the kitchen in a daze, still caught up in the memory of a wonderful dream, and Naomh had scowled at her daughter. "Maren, you had better stop thinking about that boy so much." She moved to the table and loudly dished some oat porridge into Maren's bowl, glancing out the window to see if Oran was about. As Maren sat down and poured some fresh milk over the porridge, she continued. "I know he's an attractive boy, but you must be careful not to let your imagination—or your feelings—get carried away. You're a little too young to be focusing on one lad so entirely." She gave her daughter a warning glance and joined her at the table.

Maren shrugged and lifted the spoon to her mouth. Through a mouth full of the hot cereal, she tried to reassure her mother. "Mother, I like him a lot, but I'm not getting carried away. It's just nice to have someone my age around all the time." She avoided her mother's eyes, knowing that Naomh could see right through her.

Naomh snorted. "He's *not* your age, Maren. He's the same age as your brother, and you have *him* around all the time." She folded her arms on the faded linen tablecloth and squared her shoulders. "No, there's a difference, and don't think I don't see it. He is a nice boy, but all the same, I would ask you to keep your emotions reined in, especially right in front of him." She gave her daughter an affectionate look and reached over to smooth the curls out of Maren's eyes. "I hope for so much for you, Maren.

I just don't want to see all those opportunities fly away when you are yet so young."

Maren did not quite understand all her mother's words, but they troubled her just the same. "Even if I do like him, Mother, why is that so bad? I haven't done anything wrong, and I'm not likely to, but is it a bad thing to dream a little? Am I not allowed to look at him, or him to look at me? I don't quite understand."

Naomh gave her daughter a long, appraising look before replying, leaning forward with an intensity in her eyes meant to underscore the importance of her words. "Sins of the heart are as bad as sins of the flesh. Whenever you look at a man with lust in your eyes, it is a disappointment to the Lord. And what it can lead to will condemn you if you give in to it."

Those words had brought Maren, troubled in her spirit, to the little church on this bright spring morning. Suddenly feeling consumed with guilt over the way she had looked at Faolán, she found herself worrying that she was on the road to hell, and only a priest could restore the grace of her salvation back to her. Father Seanán had listened quietly as Maren confessed to looking at a man with lust in her eyes, and in her heart.

"Father, I have *tried* to stop looking at him. I really *don't* mean to do wrong, but he's always around...and I can't seem to stop myself." She kept her eyes averted from the little screen to her left, but out of the corner of her eye she could see the old priest nodding. When he stayed silent, she continued, assuming he wanted her to go on.

"Nothing has happened between us, and I know nothing would, but I find myself looking at him and dreaming about things..." Maren sighed heavily, her eyes floating dreamily to the top of the booth, not seeing the heavy curtain hanging on its gleaming metal rings, or the paint flaking off the wood above her head. "...I keep thinking about what it would be like to be married to him...to have his babies...Just to belong to someone forever would be the most wonderful, romantic—" Suddenly realizing that she was babbling, and worried that she had said too much, Maren cut herself off and gave the shadow of the priest a startled glance.

"I'm sorry, Father." She gave a small, self-deprecating laugh. "You see? I can't seem to stop thinking about him. I can't even stop *talking* about him."

"You must, wee one." His voice was gruff, as if the long silence while waiting for her to finish rhapsodizing had rusted his vocal chords. Maren hung her head and nodded into her lap. Her gaze fell on her fingers, which she had been twisting nervously without realizing what she was doing. Surreptitiously, she wiped her sweaty palms on her skirt and looked back to where the priest sat waiting for her answer.

"Oh...Yes, Father. I know, Father. I *will* try harder." When his silence continued, and his shadow didn't move, she began to grow anxious. "Father?" He turned slightly to face her. "What is my penance, Father?"

What she could see of his face made her uneasy. The small diamonds of the grating between them cast strange shadows on his old cheeks, and she drew back as she saw the disapproving frown pulling his skin into tight hollows over his bones. After a long, queasy moment in which she was afraid to say anything, he spoke, and she nodded, her mind elsewhere, as he instructed her in how many Hail Marys and Our Fathers she was to say. Then with another brief last look through the grating, she thanked him softly and left.

As Maren hurried down the aisle and out the heavy wooden doors of the church, her mind already filling again with thoughts of Faolán Ó'Ciarmhaic, Father Seanán exited from his side of the confession booth and watched her leave. He shook his head sadly. *So many of these girls come to ruin so young. It fills me with despair.*

Wearily, he walked into his private chamber and moved to the small recess in the back wall where he kept a large black book under lock and key, a book filled with names and addresses of young girls he had seen over the years. *I suppose it will soon be time to contact Sister Líadan again. I had not thought young Maren to become so ripe for the sins of the heart, and so quickly.* His gnarled hands fumbled with the lock as he opened the old book; it creaked slightly as the binding bent, sending a new crack across the aged leather of its cover. The pages crinkled with their many years of use, the paper made thin and delicate by the many names covering it—spidery scrawls written in many different hands, most of the ink dulled by time.

    Seanán sighed again as he flipped through the last few pages, thinking of the young women whose lives the few notations represented. Many of these girls he had known, and most he had not seen for many years. He had no idea how few of them still lived, or which ones now survived only in memories, and his old heart was pained as their sweet young faces floated through his mind. Maren's voice came back to him as he had just heard it, full of hope and yearning, and a frown came over his face. He closed the old book and laid it heavily back in the small stone chamber in the wall, snapping the lock shut with his thumb and giving it a slight shove to the back of the recess as he mused. *I will keep an eye on that Bradigan girl over the course of time...but I will not call Sister Líadan just yet.*

Chapter Four

Two weeks later, Maren rushed home from school, her face aglow with excitement, and hurried through her chores. As soon as she finished her supper, she raced into her room to debate what she ought to wear. Naomh Bradigan walked up the stairs behind her and laughed at her daughter's frantic attitude as she pawed through her wardrobe.

"Calm yourself, Maren. It's only a *céilidh*," she admonished lightly, referring to the communal dances that Somhairle held once every few months. "You've been to many of them."

"But not while Faolán has been here, Mother! I want to show him what they're like. I've heard they don't have *céilidhs* in Dublin very often."

Naomh nodded in agreement. The *céilidhs* were more popular in the western and southwest areas of Ireland, but old Ultán Bannon, the butcher, was from Killarney, and had brought the traditional dance with him when he had arrived in Somhairle many years before. Most of the younger generation had grown up with the dances and were surprised to find that they were not well known in the "big city next door". Maren herself had been attending them since before she could walk. "He might not even know what it is, Maren. What if he doesn't come?"

Maren shook out a long dress with a faded flower print and held it up in front of herself. "Of course he's heard of a *céilidh*, Mother. Orla and Saraid have been talking about nothing else their past few visits!" She grimaced, remembering with embarrassment how her two friends had placed themselves in close vicinity to Faolán to discuss the *céilidh* in overly loud voices. She knew that they were trying to help her to get to know him better, and that they only wanted to make sure that he would show up, but she worried that Faolán would think she herself had put them up to it.

She shook her head and tried not to let herself worry about it. "Why wouldn't he come?" She scrutinized the dress as it draped against her body, then threw it on her bed with an unsatisfied groan and reached for another one. Naomh sighed and moved to the closet, bringing forth a dress from the top shelf of Maren's wardrobe. Maren gasped with pleasure as her mother shook out the folds and smoothed it down gently. "Mother! Where did this come from?" she cried happily, feeling the soft material between her fingers.

The dress was a beautiful shade of green, ruffled at the bottom and covered with a delicate ivy print. Maren held it up with delight, picturing herself in it and knowing that it would perfectly complement her blond hair. "I've had it up there for a while," Naomh said, "just waiting for you to grow into it, but I'd forgotten about it until just this minute. It looks like you should fit into it now." She smiled as Maren stripped out of her school clothes and pulled the dress on over her petticoat.

"It's perfect, Mother!" she announced, turning around so that Naomh could fasten the hooks that ran down the back closure of the dress. Naomh stood back as Maren examined herself in the long mirror that was mounted to her bedroom wall. The dress fit beautifully, with its long sleeves that floated as Maren raised her arms, and the fitted waist emphasized her slenderness before falling into masses of pleats and ruffles to just below her calves. Maren was delighted. "Thank you so much, Mother," she whispered happily, turning to hug Naomh tightly. "Tonight will be *perfect*, absolutely perfect. I'm sure of it." She was already picturing Faolán's face when he saw her in this breathtaking dress.

Naomh opened her mouth, then shut it again. She knew that she was fanning the flames of Maren's attraction to Faolán Ó Ciarmhaic, but Maren was so happy with the dress that she decided not to give any more warnings. Besides, the dress was perfectly modest and very becoming. Certainly there was no harm in letting her dress up a little for the evening.

The sky was beginning to blush with the evening sunset when Father Seanán stepped out of the church and observed the celebrants participating in the *céilidh*. A merry fiddler sat on a box near the edge of the town square, while nearby a plump, sweating man dutifully squeezed away on the *uillean* pipes, pumping the bellows under his elbow and laughing at the sounds he produced. Ultán Bannon played the *bodhrán*, the little goatskin drum held tightly between his legs as he pounded on it, and his son, Gobán, strummed a banjo furiously. Laughing girls swirled around the roaring bonfire in their long, full skirts, clacking spoons together on their thighs or blowing on simple tin whistles to the beat old Bannon set. Both the older men of the village and several teenage boys danced a jig around them. Father Seanán smiled at the general air of gaiety in the village square, and set over to where young Noel Brosna sat clapping his hands and smiling at the girls. Seanán noted wryly – and not without satisfaction – that not a one of them returned the adolescent lad's smile.

"How's it been going tonight, lad?" he asked Noel cheerfully, patting the youthful man on the shoulder. Noel glanced up and then quickly back to the girls in the square.

"Fine, Father. It's a beautiful night, and the *céilidh* looks to be quite a success."

Seanán glanced around, but didn't see the face he sought. "Have you seen young Maren Bradigan tonight, then?" he asked casually, and Noel nodded.

"Oh, aye, Father. She's been spending most of her time in that corner over there, with that new farmhand her father's hired, Faolán Ó Cianáin or whatever his name is."

"Ó Ciarmhaic," Father Seanán corrected gently, sending Noel's head into bobbing assent again.

"Yeah, that's the one. They've been dancing all night. He seems quite taken with her." Noel shook his head and sighed. Having known Maren all his life, he had never looked at her as an attractive girl, merely a buddy, but tonight, in that fancy new dress, she fairly glowed. Suddenly he had found himself wishing that he were the one dancing with her.

Seanán peered into the corner Noel had pointed out, seeing two silhouettes but unable to make out their faces until the musicians changed their tempo and began to play a slow air, which was when the taller one reached for the other's hand and began to lead the shadowy figure forward toward the fire. He could see Maren's face as Faolán brought her out into the open, and there was no mistaking the flush to her cheeks as she and Faolán came closer together and began to dance slowly around the fire. Many other couples had joined together for the dance, but Father Seanán looked only at Maren and Faolán, his senses alert to any danger.

Certainly there were sparks flying between them, and knowing how Maren felt about the boy, he watched closely for any signs of a deeper intimacy. They danced at a respectable distance from each other, and as he glanced at the crowd he saw Oran and Naomh Bradigan standing nearby with small smiles on their faces, but he was not satisfied.

Seanán leaned back and observed them as casually as he could, sure that things were progressing too quickly for this young girl. With a sinking heart he watched as Faolán reached forward to gently brush a tendril of hair away from Maren's cheek, and her cheeks flamed. Faolán smiled down at her with a look that could only be described as affectionate, and spoke soft words that only she could hear above the noise of the crackling fire and the instruments. The spots in her cheeks only brightened, and she lowered her eyelashes demurely.

There was definitely something going on between the two of them that could not continue without drastic consequences. Father Seanán closed his eyes in sorrow. It was obvious that there would have to be something done about this...before it was too late.

The cold draught coming in through the window near Maren's seat bothered her very little as she sat in the hard wooden desk, her chin in her hand and her eyes dreamily unfocused in the general direction of the teacher. Her eyes were on him as he spoke on and on about Silken Thomas Fitzgerald and his revolt against Henry VIII in 1537, but she heard not a word. Her mind was filled with thoughts and memories of Faolán and the last few days since the *céilidh*. That night had been so wonderful, the definite beginning of the fulfillment of her fantasies. She and Faolán had conversed for hours on end, about everything and nothing. And he had been the perfect gentleman, dancing with her at the proper distance, requesting her parents' permission to see her home, and delicately kissing her hand as he left her on her doorstep. The next few days, they had spoken every moment they could find, and she was falling for him more each day. Her eyes glazed over and she let out a long sigh.

"Miss Bradigan!"

A voice rudely interrupted her thoughts and she jumped. Her teacher was standing over her desk, tapping the palm of his left hand with the long pointer he held in his right. "Yes, sir, Mr. Leary?" she gasped, her cheeks flooding with color. Across the room, Orla giggled and hid her smile behind her hand as she elbowed Saraid, who sat in the desk next to her with a grin plastered across her face. Maren struggled not to look in their direction; she knew she would laugh if they started making more of the kissy faces they had been directing at her the past few days, and Mr. Leary did not look as though he would appreciate her laughter at that moment. She did her best to look interested as she gazed up at Mr. Leary's angry face.

He sighed heavily. "I asked you, Miss Bradigan, the result of Fitzgerald coming up against Henry VIII. Can you answer me?"

Maren drew a complete blank. "They...went out for a pint together?" she suggested timidly, and the class erupted in laughter. She allowed herself a brief grin before seeing that Mr. Leary's countenance was definitely not showing amusement; indeed, it was growing ever redder with suppressed anger.

"Miss Bradigan!" he practically shouted at her. "Silken Thomas Fitzgerald *revolted* against Henry VIII in 1534 *and failed*. As you will do, young lady, if you continue to insist on having all our famous historical war figures re-unite over a glass of Guinness!"

Maren cringed as he pointed to the front of the room, and stood up from her desk with an air of trepidation. She knew she deserved the whipping that was about to be given her, and the waves of laughter coming at her from the students was not helping her composure. She made her way timidly to the front of the room and braced herself against his desk, squeezing her eyes shut as she waited for the blows.

They never came. Instead, a timid voice came from the doorway. "Excuse me, Mr. Leary, but is there a Maren Bradigan here today?"

Maren opened her eyes in surprise and swiveled her head around to see a young, scruffy boy standing at the entrance to the classroom. He looked very nervous, his face streaked with dirt and his eyes darting every which way. His cap was clenched tightly in both hands in front of him. "I'm here to deliver a message for her," he added timidly.

She stood up straight as Mr. Leary made his way to the entryway, his anger rapidly replaced by suspicion and concern. He walked out of the classroom and held the door nearly closed behind him as he spoke in a low voice with the boy, looking back once and giving Maren an anxious glance as he listened and nodded. Maren looked at Orla and Saraid, who both shrugged, their faces worried.

Mr. Leary made his way over to her and took her by the arm, bringing her swiftly up to where the boy stood. "This boy has a message from your farm, Maren. You may go with him."

Anxiety filling her mind, Maren nodded, giving her friends one last look as she left the classroom and retrieved her coat and scarf from a peg in the coatroom. She followed the boy out of the building to a car that stood idling by the dirt road, where Maren was surprised to see Father Seanán waiting. He gave Maren a slight smile as he gave a few pennies to the boy, who raced off through the woods and disappeared. Beside the priest stood a very tall, very pale nun whose eyes glittered as she scrutinized Maren. Her hands were clasped together in front of her, and her long black skirts ended just above sturdy, black leather shoes.

Maren's eyes were wide with worry as she stared up at the two black-clad messengers. "There is an urgent matter we must attend to together, Maren," Father Seanán said softly. "Please come with me." The nun watched silently.

Father Seanán opened the back door for her and indicated that she was to get in.

Maren climbed in without question, eager to get this matter settled. She noted without curiosity the dark paper that was taped over the rear window, and settled into the hard leather as Seanán got in on the driver's side and the tall nun folded herself into the passenger seat.

Without another word, Seanán shifted into first and started off.

Chapter Five

Maren had not been able to keep track of what ground they had covered on the long journey. Father Seanán had often turned around from his place behind the steering wheel to make sure that she was doing all right, but the thin nun with the pinched face who sat stiffly in the passenger seat did not glance in her direction even once. Maren wished she had been able to ask more questions, but any time she ventured to speak, she was met with only silence or a terse, "Questions will be answered later."

She leaned back against the hard leather seat of the ancient vehicle and tried to keep her fear from rising to overcome her. *Questions will be answered later!* she thought in disbelief. *These people come and take me from my school, telling me there is some urgent matter I must attend to, and then stuff me in a car and drive for hours to who-knows-where, and they refuse to answer my questions?*

She shook her head, refusing to permit herself to become frightened. There would be a simple answer, she was sure of it, and if she allowed herself to give in to worry, she would put herself in a panic for nothing. The fact that her father and mother were not with the priest and the nun worried her most of all; what if they had been injured, or killed? What if the only reason her questions were not being responded to was because the answers were too horrible to bear? Or Faolán; Father Seanán knew of her feelings for him. What if something had happened to him, and Father had taken her away from the school so that she would not break down crying in front of her classmates when she heard the news?

The thoughts whirled through her head, but stubbornly she shook herself and looked out the window. The dark paper that had been taped over the glass gave her no view at all for the first part of the journey, but after a while she had picked at the lower edge enough to make a small hole she could look through. There had been nothing spectacular or even interesting in the view; Maren could have been looking at any part of

Ireland that was not in the middle of a city. Several times they had passed through parts of towns, but none that she recognized.

The long-faced nun glanced at her and suddenly snapped, "Keep away from the window!"

Maren jerked upright and hastily put her finger over the hole she had made. "I'm sorry...I was just trying to see where we were."

"Sister Líadan has told you already, Maren," Father Seanán said patiently. "We will answer all your questions later. Please, just do as you are told." The nun resumed her position of staring stiffly forward, and Father Seanán tossed Maren a warning look that said no more would be tolerated.

She closed her eyes. *Oh, what am I doing here?* she wondered sadly.

After another hour, the car came to an abrupt stop, and Maren's eyes popped open. She rubbed at her face, surprised that she had been able to fall asleep. Father Seanán had gotten out of the car and gone around to open the woman's door for her, but the nun pushed the handle before he could reach it and stepped out, her long legs hidden beneath her voluminous black skirts. Father Seanán's matching black cast an ominous air about the pair.

"Okay, little lady. Up and out." Seanán opened the back door for her and reached in a hand to help her step forth from the car. The nun watched sullenly, her air of impatience signaling that she believed Maren needed no help.

The instant her feet touched the ground, she swayed and nearly lost her balance. Rubbing her eyes again, she looked up at Father Seanán with a wry grin. "My legs have fallen asleep, Father," she said with an embarrassed laugh. "I'll be all right in just a minute." She started to stamp her feet on the ground, feeling the tingles in her legs and feet as the blood rushed back to her extremities. The nun gave her a disgruntled look and began stalking away down a long stone path.

Maren's eyes followed her. They had parked beside a large stone building, and the iron gates above the entrance proclaimed it "Convent of the Sisters of Sacred Mercy". Maren looked at the large statue of the

Virgin Mary and crossed herself automatically, though she had to lean on the car to keep her balance. Father Seanán looked thoughtful, and then took her hand. "Come, Maren. We need to show you to your room."

She looked at him in shock. "My room?" He strode ahead, obviously expecting her to follow, and she did, loping along beside him as her eyes searched his face for answers. "What do you mean, Father? What room? Why are we here?" He did not reply, and frantically Maren gazed around, looking from the neat sections of packed dirt that would be obviously be filled with glorious blossoms in the springtime to the long cobblestone walks. A slight movement caught her eye and she glanced upward, to see the small, pale face of a young girl watching her from one of the many windows lining the walls. As Maren's gaze fell on her, the girl jerked her head away from the opening and disappeared, her wrinkled, blanched hand pressing against the rippled glass for a fraction of a second.

Her hand... With a start, Maren realized she must be at one of the Laundries. "Why have you brought me here, Father?" she cried, panic filling her voice. "What am I doing here?" When he didn't respond, she planted her feet squarely on the stone and called to him. "I will not move another step until you tell me why you have brought me here!" she called in what she hoped desperately was a commanding tone.

Inside, she felt anything but commanding. Her heart raced frantically as she realized the implications of her presence here. They were going to force her into washing other people's laundry, like old Mr. Bannon's bloody aprons! "No! I won't stay here! I won't!" She turned and began to run back to the car, urgency pushing her to get away, to anywhere she possibly could. Before she had taken two steps, however, Father Seanán had grabbed her around the waist, pinning her arms to her sides and yanking her back down the long path with him. The nun, who was waiting at the large wooden doors, stood with her arms crossed and a look of annoyance on her face.

Maren kicked and screamed, her long blond curls flying and her skirt swinging around her flailing legs as she tried in vain to make the priest let go of her. His face was a study in concentration, but she could see the hurting in his eyes. "Father, please! Let me go!" she begged, trying to pull her wrists out from under his strong arms. "How can you do this?" Tears began to fall from her eyes, and she tried to make him look directly at her. "Father...please..." Maren began to sob, no longer worrying about how it would look for her to be afraid.

There was no accident, nothing "requiring her attention". Her parents were fine, at home, waiting for her to return from school, and most likely worrying that she had been gone for so long. The thought of her mother's anxiety filled her with anger. "You can't do this! Leave me be! I need to go home to my mother! Let me see my parents!" She kicked at Seanán again and again, not bothering to try to control her tears as he forced her through the doors where the nun had been waiting.

By the time they had walked through the foyer and down a long hallway, Maren's cries had diminished to an occasional whimper. It was useless to try to resist Father Seanán's strong arms around her; he would have her where he wanted even if she had continued to protest. The nun had been joined by another one, with a figure much rounder and a face much gentler than the first one's. She laid a hand on Maren's arm and lifted her chin to look into her downcast face. "Let us help ye, little one," she whispered. "I am Sister Grania, and this is Sister Líadan." The dour-faced woman gave a short nod and kept walking, until they reached a large door that led into some type of office. The room was sparsely furnished, with a large desk sitting in front of a worn leather chair. Two other chairs, ladder-backed and looking extremely uncomfortable, sat placed in front of the desk. Líadan walked in and held the door for the other three. Maren sniffled and furtively glanced around, reminded of a principal's office.

Sister Grania helped Maren out of Father Seanán's strong embrace and led her to one of the stiff-backed chairs. "Here, now: you sit down and relax for a moment. We've just got a few things to say, and I suppose you've got a few questions yourself you'll be wanting answers to. Well, now's the time." She settled her motherly figure into the other chair, while Líadan crossed behind a desk to sit in the large leather chair. Father Seanán closed the door behind them and stood with his back to it.

Líadan was the first to speak. "Do you know why you are here, Miss Bradigan?" she asked coldly. Maren shook her head. "Answer: 'No, Sister,'" the nun snapped.

"No, Sister," Maren mumbled into her lap. Líadan scowled but chose to ignore the annoyance.

"Then perhaps Father Seanán would be kind enough to explain to you." She gave Seanán a nod, and he took a step forward, discomfort written all over his features. Wringing his hands in front of him, he smiled awkwardly down at Maren. She stared up at him with tears running down her cheeks.

"Maren, it has come to our attention that you were perhaps getting a little too – friendly – with a certain young man your father has working on his farm." He looked into Maren's eyes, which widened in alarm.

"Do you mean Faolán? We haven't—" Líadan cut her off.

"I suggest that you do not complicate matters by speaking," she stressed in chilly tones. Maren hung her head again and waited for Father Seanán to continue, her mind racing and her pulse quickening at the thought of Faolán. What could he have to do with this?

Seanán cleared his throat. "No one is saying that you've done anything, Maren. But at your age, we must be careful not to allow our young girls to get themselves into situations where they might – well, situations that might be dangerous to them. It has been noticed by others in the community, and your mother herself, as you have told me." Maren shook her head numbly, knowing that nothing she could say would change things. "In these situations we have often found it necessary to remove the girls from the sources of temptation, so that they do not end up as many of the other girls who reside here." She looked back up at him, and he nodded. "Many of the young women you will live with here in Sisters of Sacred Mercy have conceived babies out of wedlock, some having given birth, others in early or late stages of pregnancy. It was my decision"—he cleared his throat again—"to remove you from the enticement of Faolán Ó Ciarmhaic, in order to spare you the difficulties that many of these girls are now going through."

Maren jumped out of the chair. "But I haven't done anything! I never even told him—" Another look from Sister Líadan silenced her, and she sat back down. Her mind was confused with all the thoughts raging within. Father Seanán had *decided* to bring her here, to escape the fate of pregnancy out of wedlock? But she had never even *thought* of such a thing with Faolán. She had dreamed of marriage, of someday having his babies, of loving him and being loved...

Her mother's voice drifted back to her: *"Sins of the heart are as bad as sins of the flesh...what it can lead to will condemn you...it is a disappointment to the Lord."* For a moment, her heart sank. Was she really as guilty as Sister Líadan's glare seemed to assert that she was? She shook her head in frustration. No, it wasn't the same thing! She didn't believe that looking at Faolán the way she had was a sin. How could Father Seanán even think that she could end up in that situation?

Here she was, though, in a strange place where she would be treated as though she was a sinner, as though she had committed indiscretions she couldn't even have dreamed of. Well, she would have to show them that they were wrong. Maren lifted her chin stubbornly. "What will I be doing while I'm here?" she demanded.

The two Sisters exchanged glances. "You will earn your keep," Sister Grania said slowly. "We have rules here, which we expect will not be disobeyed. You will wake at five, attend Mass, and then come to breakfast. After breakfast you start work in the Laundry." Maren shuddered, but listened as Grania continued. "After work you will attend supper in the dining hall, and then retire to your room for the night. Lights out is at nine o'clock."

Maren thought about her options, and decided that fighting would only worsen her predicament. Deciding that what Grania was saying sounded none too difficult, she looked up defiantly and tried to smile. "I think I can manage it," she whispered, her voice trembling despite her resolve.

Father Seanán looked down at her with a semblance of pride, and then put a strong, wrinkled hand on her shoulder. "It won't be too bad, Maren," he soothed. She looked up at him, and his eyes were kind.

"When—when will you be back to take me home?" she managed.

Glancing away for a moment, he looked back into her eyes with a weak grin. "When it is time," he said consolingly. "Maren, we all must do penance for the wrongs we have committed. Here you will learn how to guard your heart against the evil that all men possess. You will learn the sanctity of your body and your womanhood. When you have learned the right way to go about your relationships, you will go home."

It was a small comfort, but Maren thought that it wouldn't be too difficult to convince the nuns that she had learned her lesson and would no longer look at Faolán Ó Ciarmhaic like a hungry dog looks at a bone. She squeezed the priest's hand as she asked in a trembling voice, "And...do my parents know where I am?"

He stood up and came to her side, kneeling before her. "Don't worry about anything any more, Maren," the old priest comforted her. "I will take care of everything." Smiling at her for a long moment, he said, "It is time for your confession, Maren. We are ready to hear of your need for forgiveness, and then you may receive the Sacrament of Reconciliation."

Maren fought the rage and panic that welled up inside her at the priest's words. She had to remind herself forcefully that she had decided to cooperate with Father Seanán and the nuns, and that objecting to her first confession inside the convent walls would definitely not be a good start. She heaved a deep breath and nodded.

Seanán stood and walked back to the chair he had left, sitting down and facing at a slight angle from Maren. "You may take your time for Examination of Conscience and Silent Reflection, and let us know when you are ready." The nuns stepped back a respectful distance, but their eyes missed nothing as they darted from one to the other of them.

Maren steadied herself, squeezing her eyes shut. She was quiet for a few minutes, knowing that she was expected to mentally go over all her sins since her last confession and pray heartily before confessing. The nuns watched closely. After a moment of wondering what in the world she should be reflecting on, she opened her eyes and nodded, signaling that she had examined her conscience and was ready for confession.

Father Seanán came to her side and put his arm around her, helping her to her feet and moving her across the room to where a bright red curtain hung on a wall. She allowed him to lead her as he lifted the curtain to reveal a small antechamber, where candles burned dimly and a large wooden crucifix stood prominently displayed. Maren recognized that this room was one specially set aside for the Sacrament of Reconciliation, and she must be respectful.

She made the sign of the cross over her chest and said automatically, "In the name of the Father, and of the Son, and of the Holy Spirit. Amen." When Father Seanán nodded, she began the familiar routine of ritual confession that she had done many times before in her young life.

"Forgive me, Father, for I have sinned. It has been..." For a moment she paused, wondering what time it was and unsure of how long they had actually been traveling in the car. Deciding that they couldn't possibly have been gone long enough for it to be Thursday already, Maren continued: "...three days since my last confession."

"How have you sinned, my child?" Father Seanán asked softly, his fingers moving to his cheek.

She hesitated, working to concoct the best confession she could in order to appease the three who listened so intently. "I have sinned with my heart and with my mind, Father. I have looked at a young man with lust in my eyes and delighted in the feelings I was having. I have desired him to hold me and...touch me." One of the nuns gave a derisive snort of disgust, and Maren winced. She hated the pictures her confession put into her mind. It made the feelings she had for Faolán seem so dirty and sensual, instead of what they were: pure and loving. Tears filled her eyes.

She had wanted his love, not his lust, and she knew that he felt the same. It was these three who were making it a crime to feel fondness toward someone of the opposite sex.

She began to cry, and the two nuns looked at each other with satisfied faces, believing, she supposed, that she was so overcome by the severity of her sins that she could stand it no longer. Knowing that her tears were helping her with her confession, Maren didn't try to keep back the sobs as she continued. "I have done wrong, Father! I know I have. I desire to rid myself of the filth inside me." She cried harder, despising her words and feeling as though she was betraying Faolán. Putting her face in her hands, she rocked back and forth on the chair, crying uncontrollably.

She was vaguely aware of Father Seanán reading a passage from the Bible, but did not try to listen to what he was saying. He waited until she was finished crying, and when she looked timidly up at him, smiled. "You have done well, Maren. Your penance is to work here, at the convent laundry, until such time as it is determined that you are ready to go home."

Maren nodded, knowing she was to accept the penance and thank him, but she couldn't bring herself to speak. Father Seanán seemed to understand, for he stood up and gave her absolution, saying, "God, the Father of mercies, through the death and resurrection of his Son, has reconciled the world to himself and sent the Holy Spirit among us for the forgiveness of sins; through the ministry of the Church may God give you pardon and peace, and I absolve you from your sins in the name of the Father, and of the Son, and of the Holy Spirit." He genuflected as well, and Maren's right arm automatically made the motion.

Maren sniffled back, "Amen."

"Give thanks to the Lord, for He is good," Seanán intoned.

"His mercy endures forever," Maren mumbled in reply.

"You are dismissed in the peace of Christ." Seanán placed a hand on her forehead, and then stood back as the nuns appeared on either side of Maren to escort her from the room. They each took a candle from the

desk and walked out. As they led her down the long hallway, Maren's thoughts were jumbled, but she did manage to form one clear thought:
"*If I have been 'absolved from my sins' like he said, then why am I still here?*"

They made their way down the long hallway slowly, not speaking a word. Maren gazed dully at the intimidating dreary walls as they passed door after door, not a sound coming from behind any of them. When they reached the end of the hallway and opened the last door, Maren gasped at the sight that was before her.

Even in the dim light from the moon shining in the windows, the room was huge. It seemed to stretch for a mile in each direction, and its ceiling was low and covered with pipes running in every direction. There were large metal basins in each corner, and through the dank silence the constant, hollow sound of water dripping filled Maren's ears. Rows and rows of washtubs, their metal sides bent and pockmarked, stood lined up on wooden stands that were anchored to the concrete floor, and a long line of pumps stood against one wall, their faucets rusty and worn from age. A small puddle of water collected beneath one of the dripping faucets and raced along the uneven cement to where they stood, veering off at the last second to empty itself into a large drainage hole on the floor a few feet away. Maren's mouth hung open. *The laundries.* This was what she had wanted to see for so long. This was what she had always been so curious about. It might have even been interesting for her to see.

If only it weren't real.

She noticed a large storage bin, perhaps eight feet across and five feet high, open at the top and with a large opening in the side that was facing her. Through the opening, she saw piles and piles of filthy linens jumbled against each other, and grimaced without thinking. A swooshing sound suddenly became noticeable, and another large pile of dirty cloths fell from an overhead laundry chute into the bin as she watched. Sister Grania and Sister Líadan stood beside her and allowed her to glance around before either one of them spoke. Finally, Líadan broke the silence.

"This is where you'll be working," she stated crisply. Her voice echoed loudly through the room, and Maren jumped slightly at its timbre. "There's no time for a proper tour today, but someone will instruct you in your duties tomorrow morning when you start. Now, it's off to your room to get some sleep. It took us altogether too long to get here, and completely unnecessarily, too." Her mouth tightened as though she were stopping herself from saying something, and she nodded to Sister Grania. "Sister Grania will show you to your room. I bid you good night." She turned and was gone before Maren could reply.

Grania turned to her, candle in hand, and almost smiled. "Your room, then," she stated, and began walking back down the hall from where they had come. For such a round little woman, she walked quickly, and Maren struggled to keep up. They passed the room where they had first had their meeting, and made their way to a tall, steep set of concrete stairs halfway down the entire length of the hall. Grania mounted them and strode up efficiently.

Stopping outside a door on the third floor, she turned to Maren with another half-smile and opened the door. Maren automatically stepped back against the safety of the wall as she was ushered into the cold, unfamiliar room. It was darker inside than even the dim light of the hallway, and she remained shrunk into the nearest corner as the nun moved past her and laid Maren's newly acquired apron down on the bed closest to her. "This will be your bed," Sister Grania said shortly, and then walked purposefully out the narrow door into the hall, pulling the heavy slab of wood shut behind her with a loud scrape against the cement floor and a decisive, hollow slam.

Maren waited until her eyes adjusted to the miniscule sunlight that struggled to shine past the heavy draperies that concealed the tiny window, finally taking a cautious step toward the bed.

"A new one, are you?" The voice came from the other side of the small room. Maren gasped at the unexpected sound and sat down heavily on the bed, turning to face the darkness where the voice had come from. Slowly a figure became visible on another bed a few feet away. The girl was lying flat on her back, her hair framing her face in a ghostly halo as the light touched her features. She didn't move an inch as she contemplated Maren's stiff body.

"They...brought me here today," Maren began hesitantly. When it became obvious that the other girl was waiting for her to continue, she reached out a trembling hand. "My name is—"

"No names," the other girl interrupted her. She sat up slowly, every movement pained as she moved stiffly into a half-sitting position. She glared at Maren through the darkness. "We don't use our real names here," she stated. The hardness in her eyes suddenly softened into sadness as she continued to stare at Maren. "It...makes this place seem a little less real." Her hand reached out to shake Maren's, and as Maren grasped it she could feel the roughness of the other girl's skin. It reminded her of holding her grandmother's hand as a little girl. "You may call me Étain. And you'd better think of a name for yourself. After a day or so here, you won't want to remember who you used to be."

On that ominous note, Étain rolled over and left Maren to contemplate in the darkness.

Chapter Six

After her first day in the laundry, Maren could barely drag herself down the hallway and up the three flights of stairs to the room she shared with Étain. After a grueling ten minutes, she managed to make it to her door, and practically threw herself on the narrow bed, her gasp of relief echoing in the small room. The girls had been led down to the dining hall and given a small supper, but Maren had barely been able to lift the spoon to her lips. Étain had leaned over from her seat at the next row of tables and whispered, "Eat up, young one...it gets worse!"

Maren lay on the bed, grateful to be alone and working hard to control the shaking of her shoulders. She had never dreamed it could be this difficult; after all, it was only washing clothes and linens! Closing her eyes, she let a tear trickle down her cheek. *I thought I could be tough...oh, God, what am I doing here?*

Sister Grania had climbed the stairs to awaken her that morning, and although Maren was used to waking early, she had been shocked at the sudden sound of the bell for Mass tolling loudly right outside her window. Grania let herself in shortly after, giving Maren a brief smile. Étain was already out of bed and hurrying into her smock. "Wake up, Miss Bradigan," Sister Grania said softly. "It's time you learned how things are done around here."

Maren nodded and heaved herself out of the bed. Although it was by no means comfortable, and the single worn blanket was sparse compared to her soft pillows and sheets at home, she had managed a decent sleep and was hesitant to leave its little bit of warmth. As she stepped out from under the blanket into the cold morning air, she shivered, hastening to grab her smock from where it lay draped over a chair and rapidly understanding Étain's speed in dressing. She couldn't help it; a violent shiver shook her, and Grania smiled again, not unkindly. "I trust you had a good night?"

Maren nodded politely, her teeth chattering when she tried to speak, and contented herself with nodding again. Grania waited for her to finish adjusting the smock as it fell down around her body, then followed Étain out the door. By her attitude, it was obvious that she expected Maren to trail behind them, and she did so, raking her fingers through her tangled hair and pulling her hair ribbon out of her front pocket. She worked on straightening out her hair as they made their way down the stairwell to the long hallway where she had first been brought to speak with Father Seanán and Sisters Líadan and Grania. Maren looked around with curiosity, knowing that this was to be her home for the next little while and wanting to familiarize herself with it. From all directions came long lines of other girls and women, most near her age but some as old as thirty. Their heads were all bent to look at the floor, their arms at their sides, and a look of hopelessness was etched on each of their faces. Their eyes were underscored with dark circles, and aside from a few protruding bellies in different stages of pregnancy they were all very thin, with long ropes of muscle in their arms. Maren felt pity for them. How long had these women been here? Her confidence rose as she remembered that Father Seanán had promised to come and take her home. She would not end up as one of these women, who looked completely defeated. Maren thrust her chin in the air and stalked along behind Sister Grania, determined not to be as weak as the others she was observing.

Some of the girls noticed her and whispered between themselves, but Maren ignored them even as she felt her cheeks heating. *Let them whisper*, she thought to herself. *I will not bend to these nuns like they have. I will keep my dignity.*

Maren's parents had instilled in both their children a sense of pride, both for their family and work as well as for their beliefs. Maren knew she must stand in the face of adversity, and she knew that these girls who watched her with such knowing smiles on their faces were waiting to see her fail. She refused to allow this humiliating situation to cause her pride to collapse.

They filed into Mass, and Maren felt almost at home again as she went through the familiar routine. She bent her head low and prayed that God would get her away from this situation as soon as possible, and as an afterthought, for strength to get through the day. She allowed herself a small laugh under her breath; how could these women have let themselves get so haggard and worn looking? Although there were aspects to the laundry work that Maren had to admit she was not looking forward to, she thoroughly believed that she would have no problem keeping up with the workload.

After Mass, the girls made their way down the long hallway again, into the dining hall at the very end of the building. The room was huge, and Maren's eyes bulged as she saw just how many girls and women were internees at the convent. Several rows of long tables made to hold fifty to sixty people each crowded the room, and they were lined with small chairs made of wood that the girls quickly filed into after receiving their breakfast. Two slightly smaller tables were set end to end at one side of the room, and a large woman in a cook's hat and apron was doling out ladles of something Maren couldn't quite make out into each girl's bowl.

Maren moved into place behind several other girls and grabbed a small wooden bowl from the seemingly hundreds that stood in high stacks at the beginning of the first table, snatching a bent metal spoon from the pile and looking around herself in disbelief. The thing that really stood out to her was the incredible lack of noise.

Maren had often been in rooms with big groups of people, often at friends' houses or in the foyer after church services, but never had she seen such a large collection of people milling around in such utter silence. She held her bowl out for her food without paying much attention and walked to a place at the nearest table in astonishment. The absence of conversation around the long tables was as distracting as it was unnatural.

After she had made herself as comfortable as possible in the stiff wooden chair and looked down at what was supposed to pass for breakfast, Maren thought she understood at least part of the reason why the women looked so weary. The food consisted of a small bowl of watery oat porridge and half a glass of lukewarm water to wash it down with. Maren glanced around and down the long table for sugar or milk, but saw the other girls resolutely digging in to their small meal without putting anything on it.

She saw several of the women at her table downing the stuff in two or three large bites, but the looks on their faces when they sat back from their repast were anything but satisfied. *How can they survive on this stuff?* she thought in disgust, holding her spoon above her bowl and letting the porridge spill from it in and fall with a slight plop back into the bowl. Maren made a face but forced the porridge into her mouth, nearly spitting it back out immediately as she tasted it. Most of the oats were not cooked, so the food tasted near to what Maren imagined the horses' food back home would. The cook must have set the stuff on the stove not five minutes before the girls had made their trek to the dining hall from Mass, dousing a pot full of oats with warm water and giving it a quick stir. Maren closed her eyes in distaste and followed the other girls' example, spooning up the porridge and swallowing it in three or four tasteless bites. The roughness of the oats scratched her throat on the way down, and she grabbed for her water glass, drinking it down quickly and barely repressing a shudder as it washed the revolting mess down into her growling stomach.

Her hunger barely satisfied and her taste buds repulsed, she rubbed her tummy through the rough smock and sat back for a moment to watch the other girls, but no sooner had she done so than the nun standing watch by the door shouted out a command and the girls hastened to their feet. Maren cast a look back at Sister Grania; she was standing nearby and helping a heavily pregnant girl out of her tiny chair, but she glanced up to see Maren watching her and gave the barest of smiles. Maren was unable to smile back. She was beginning to see that life in the Laundries would not be as easy as she had thought it could be.

Things got worse the moment she stepped through the door to the room she would be working in.

The laundry room looked as it had the day before, but with the girls swarming in to take up their posts behind the large washbasins, it seemed slightly more overwhelming. Maren hung back until a nun came near to grasp her arm and lead her to a spot near the east wall. "This is where you'll be today, young lady," she said shortly. "What is your name, child?"

"Maren Bradigan," Maren answered in a small voice. The nun stood watching her with her arms crossed, a disapproving look on her face, until Maren added, "Sister."

The addition seemed to mollify her, and she relaxed slightly. "I am Sister Mary. I trust Sister Grania notified you of the rules?"

Maren shook her head. "No, Sister. I'm afraid I arrived...rather late last night, and she didn't have time before lights out. She said you...she said somebody would explain it all to me today." Her hands were beginning to shake a little with nerves, and she quickly moved them behind the folds of her smock. Sister Mary did not look at all pleased. Her eyes narrowed before she spoke, and she leaned slightly toward Maren as if to intimidate her. It was not at all necessary, as Maren was already shaking in her boots.

"Very well. I will explain a few things to you, and we shall get you started and working. We don't want to waste any time, and after all, this is how you repay us for your food and lodging. I'm certain you'll not want to get behind." Maren thought of the narrow, uncomfortable bed with its thin covering and remembered the feel of the oats inching their way down her throat, and gulped to keep the bile down that suddenly threatened to choke her. Certainly it could not take much washing to repay the nuns for that!

Sister Mary continued, but her mouth had tilted in a semblance of a smile as she watched Maren work to keep her gorge from rising. She knew very well the reaction of all the girls their first day here at the Convent of the Sisters of Sacred Mercy, and she had trained herself well not to let even a flicker of human emotion respond to their fear, pain and mistrust. After all, they had condemned themselves to this punishment by disobeying the Lord's most important commandment. In her mind, as the minds of most of the other nuns in the convent, any non-virgin was considered unclean. The state of the Blessed Virgin, Mary, was the only way a woman should permit herself to be. Any girl or woman who allowed herself to be tainted by a man was inviting the devil to come into her, just like Mary Magdalen, the prostitute who had desecrated herself, soul and body, before Jesus had forgiven her and sent her on her way with the admonition to "sin no more".

Here at Sacred Mercy, working in the Laundries, was where these girls would learn the severity of their sin, and, when they had done enough penance to earn the forgiveness of the Blessed Virgin and the Lord Jesus, they would also be forgiven and sent on their way. Although Sister Mary herself had not seen many girls attain that much longed-for aspiration, she desired to help purify them with whatever means was in her power.

"You will work here, at this washbasin, for today. There are no particular assigned basins, with the exception of by punishment. You will take the linens from here—" she nodded to the large storage bin, standing beneath a laundry chute, that Maren had noticed on her quick tour the day before, "—and deposit them beside your own basin. Please take as much as you can the first time; we don't allow more than one girl to run up for retrieval at one time, and we don't want you standing with nothing to do while you wait your turn to replenish your supply."

Maren mentally noted the storage bin, with its piles of dirty laundry spilling forth, and noticed a few items with bloodstains on them. Cringing at the thought of plunging her hands into that mess, she remembered Mr. Bannon's aprons and felt tears in her eyes. Never had she dreamed that she would actually end up here, washing butcher's cloths and soiled bed linens.

Sister Mary had observed Maren's reaction to the laundry pile, but went on with her speech as if she had seen nothing. "Your water will be refilled during the day, but it is your job to fill it initially. The water pumps are over there." She gestured with her hand to a long row of pumps along one of the stone walls, where many of the girls were already hard at work filling their tubs and others waited patiently in a line for their turn. "You must have it filled as soon as possible after you begin your shift. The water is hot; be careful," she cautioned in an offhand manner. "You must take one scoop from the soap bucket before filling your tub—just one, mind you. We do not like waste here. As soon as your basin is filled, make your way back to your station and begin washing. Each piece must be completely clean before you put it aside for the drying lines. There will be several girls assigned to run the laundry out to the lines; I believe Miss Kiley is taking her turn today."

It took Maren a moment to realize who Sister Mary was referring to, but understood as Étain moved past swiftly, acknowledging Maren with a slight inclination of her head just as the nun finished her sentence. Étain swept by each washbasin, peering over the girls' shoulders and scooping up the piles of laundry that were already washed from the table beside each washing station. She sailed out the open door at the very end of the room before returning and taking her place at another washing station to continue her own laundering. It was all so smoothly and easily done that Maren felt a little overwhelmed.

As Sister Mary fell silent, obviously expecting Maren to begin her tasks, Maren lifted the heavy basin with a surprised grunt at its weight and hefted it over to stand behind the last girl in line. She was not in bad physical shape, having worked long hours before and after school on the farm with her father and brother, but she was not looking forward to having to carry the basin back to her post once it was full of water. Maren stood behind the others, moving steadily forward as the girls finished filling their tubs, her muscles straining at the weight in her arms. She watched in amazement as a pretty girl with long, scraggly brown hair loosely tied into a ponytail using a couple of loose strands of her hair, hefted her full, sudsy basin up with her thin arms to balance it on the large shelf of her pregnant belly. Maren shook her head as she watched the girl's face, which was weary but showed no signs of strain. The girl's lips moved continuously, but Maren was too far away to hear what was being said.

All at once she realized that she could hear a low murmur coming from the workstations around her. Along with the splash of water and an occasional splat of a wet garment or sheet being placed on a bare counter was the constant hum of the girls' voices. She looked over the crowded room and saw that with the exception of the girls in line, each mouth was moving incessantly. Maren turned to Sister Mary, who was watching her as she observed.

"May I ask what they are saying, Sister?" Maren said in all politeness.

"Penance," Sister Mary answered. "While you are here, you must consistently be asking the Holy Mother and God our Father for forgiveness for what you have done. You must alternate: Hail Mary, then Our Father, until your workday is finished." She finished and scrutinized Maren's face closely for her reaction.

It was immediate. Maren's mouth dropped open and the basin hit the floor with a loud clang. Not a single head turned to see what had caused the racket, though a few of the girls jumped slightly at their posts in surprise. "Forgiveness for what I have done!" she cried incredulously. "I have done nothing!" Her expression turned rapidly from surprise and shock to outrage. "Why am I even here? I don't deserve this!" She shook her head and began to stride away from the nun, but Sister Mary grasped her arm in surprisingly strong fingers and hauled her back to her place in line. When she spoke, her voice was hard steel.

"You will stay in your place and you will observe the rules of this institution, or you will find yourself severely punished," she reprimanded Maren sternly, but without malice. "The regulations are put in place for your own protection, in order to save your eternal soul from damnation. What you have done will send you there the moment you leave this earth if you do not follow our guidelines. We are here to help you, Miss Bradigan," Sister Mary finished softly, but her face did not change. She regarded Maren critically as she waited for an answer.

Maren's eyes were downcast and she shook her head weakly. "I haven't...done anything..." she whispered faintly, not intending to be overheard, but Sister Mary answered her.

"What you have done in your heart, you have done with your flesh."

Maren started. The words were so close to what her mother had said that day over breakfast that tears welled up in her eyes. She relaxed noticeably in Sister Mary's grip and stood straight up, reminding herself that earlier that day she had been completely opposed to allowing the nuns to break her. It was not going to happen on her first day.

She picked up the basin and made her way to the nearest pump, bending to take one single scoop of the soap powder from the bucket that stood beside it and place it in the bottom of the tub, before standing erect again to work the pump handle. It was stiff, and the metal cold, and her teeth chattered before she felt the warmth of the steam rising up from the water that gushed into the basin. Careful not to let the tub get too full, she worked with the rhythm of the pump and soon had a large meringue of suds built up in the basin before her. She stopped pumping and bent at the knees to heft the tub into her arms, grunting but staying steady as she made her way back to her position at the washing station. Gritting her teeth, she forced the first few words out of her mouth as she plunged her hands into the dirty laundry before her and then into the heat of the water. "Hail Mary, full of grace, the Lord is with thee. Blessed art thou among women, and blessed is the fruit of thy womb, Jesus..."

Now, as she lay across her bed in exhaustion, the words of the prayers cycled through her head incessantly. She thought she would never be able to think anything of her own will again. The many repetitions had served to drive the words into her brain, and she could suddenly see quite clearly how the many girls and women she had seen this morning and throughout the day could have such defeated looks.

Their minds were gone, pure and simple. Maren could see no other explanation than that they had been driven completely mad by the irritating reiteration of the words they were forced to utter all day long.

Twice in the afternoon Maren had observed girls forgetting to pray aloud, and they had received sound whippings on their already red and wrinkled hands from the stout ruler Sister Mary carried in her apron pocket. Even during the beatings, they had not changed their expression, but a tear ran down from the corner of one girl's eye, and Maren's heart went out to her. At supper she had been seated next to her, and discovered that the girl's name was Amy, and that she often forgot the words or stuttered during her prayers. Amy whispered this with a small laugh, as if embarrassed by her own inadequacies. "You'd think I'd know the words by now," she had murmured, and Maren had shaken her head wearily. She wanted to reassure the small, blond girl, but her head was whirling and her body was on the verge of giving out on her.

She had settled for giving her a tiny smile and whispering the name she had chosen for herself following Étain's lead. She now understood what the girl had meant the night before when she had assured Maren that after one day in the Laundries, she wouldn't want to remember who she once was. Maren Bradigan, it seemed, had ceased to exist. With the small smile still in place as she thought of her father tenderly calling her by her nickname, she had uttered softly in Amy's direction, "I'm Cassán." *Cassán,* as he had always called her, ruffling her long blond hair. *Little curly-haired one.*

The door opened and Étain came strutting in. Maren groaned and opened one eye, carefully shifting her body on the bed, as Étain directed her grin down at her still figure. "Hard day?" she asked, a laugh short on the heels of her question. "It's all right, blondie," she encouraged, stripping her smock from her wiry body and dropping down on the other bed. "Soon you'll get used to it. It's only hard for the first while." Maren muttered something into the bedclothes, and Étain leaned forward, pulling her nightgown over her head as she did so. "What was that, kid?"

Shifting slightly and groaning with the pain, Maren looked up at Étain once more and repeated her comment in a sluggish voice. "I said, how long does the first while last?"

Étain laughed. "Not too long. You'll get used to it." She herself seemed hardly ruffled by the hard work of the day; although her arms and hands were slightly reddened, she moved and talked easily. "Sometimes there's a day that's harder than others. I had one like that yesterday." She glanced over to see if Maren was still listening, then continued without knowing for certain one way or the other. "But all in all, you do get used to it." She had settled the nightdress over her shoulders and smoothed it down around her legs, peering at Maren as she lay shaking on the next bed. "Hey; you okay, kid?"

Her head wrapped in her arms and tears rolling from her eyes, Maren didn't answer, but the shaking of her body told Étain what she needed to know. She walked over to the other bed and sat down next to Maren. Putting a work-roughened hand on Maren's hair, she started to smooth it out of her tear-streaked face. "Hey, hey," she murmured. "I'm telling you the truth, baby. It really will be okay."

"I wish I could believe that," came Maren's voice from underneath the protection of her arm. Étain smiled again and continued moving her hands through the silk of Maren's hair.

"Your hair is beautiful," she said softly, lifting a handful of shining blond curls with one hand and letting the golden strands trail through her fingers. Maren sniffled and painfully sat up.

"Thank you," she sniffled. "My Da always said that, too." At the mention of her father, fresh tears broke through, and Étain shook her head. She had seen many other girls go through this for their first few days, but she herself had never experienced it. Patricia Kiley had trained herself to be hard from the beginning, and she had come to expect this of the newcomers, though she didn't quite understand it. Part of her felt like saying "snap out of it" to these girls when they bawled about Daddy or Mommy or the father of their babies, but she knew that she'd never get them to trust her or get anywhere with them if she started out that way, so she tried to mellow her attitude around them.

It seemed to be working, for Maren had leaned into her protective embrace and was soaking up the comfort of her words and her arms. Étain sighed as Maren's soft weight nestled in her lap and she rested her head on Étain's shoulder. "Don't you worry, little one," she said softly as Maren began falling into an exhausted sleep. "I'll take care of you."

Maren barely had time and energy to nod in acquiescence before she drifted off.

Chapter Seven

A week or so later, Maren had come to realize that Étain's words had been the truth. She was, in fact, becoming used to the demanding workload, and although the food was still scanty, she hardly noticed the growling of her stomach anymore. There was no question, however, of her exhaustion at the end of each day. She would tiredly climb the stairs, her red, chapped hands pressing against the wall in order to keep herself steady, and flop down on her bed barely before she fell asleep.

  The rules for hygiene were strict, but with the very little time for bathroom breaks that they were allowed—and the lack of proper amounts of drinking water—they were hard to follow. Maren barely noticed as her luxurious golden curls started to become matted and tangled, and although she tried to smooth them out at the beginning of each day, her hands and fingers ached too much to drag them through the masses of hair, and she began to resolutely tie back the snarls with her one hair ribbon without worrying about properly caring for her hair. At night, the girls would find one glass of lukewarm water beside their bed that was expected to do for teeth brushing, face washing, drinking and any other sanitation necessary. Maren began keeping her toothbrush—the one hygienic instrument she had been given in the small pile of items she started her life at the convent with—in the pocket of her shift, and when she was given permission for a bathroom break, she tried to hurriedly rinse off her toothbrush and scrub her teeth while relieving herself. She was expected back at the laundry within five minutes, so she rarely had a chance to do a good job, but she felt she was trying to stay civilized as well as in keeping with the rules about personal hygiene. Maren could not understand how the nuns expected the two hundred plus girls within the walls of the convent to keep themselves clean when they were rarely allowed access to water or sanitization of any kind, but she struggled to keep herself as uncontaminated as possible. She suspected that the nuns wouldn't notice if she didn't, however, for the smell of sweat was so prevalent in the halls of the institution, and especially in the laundry rooms, that she had fast become used to it and assumed the nuns had as well.

Étain was a great comfort to her at first, for each night when Maren would pass out across the hardness of her cot, she would half-awaken a few minutes later to find Étain helping her out of her shift and into her nightdress. She would murmur her thanks as she slid under the skimpy blanket, and Étain would sit beside her, lift Maren's head into her lap, and slide her fingers through her hair while singing or speaking soft, comforting words. Soon, however, Maren began to grow uncomfortable with the amount of closeness that Étain was trying for. She wasn't sure she liked the idea of another person—regardless of gender—stripping her down while she was half-asleep, and after the first week, she decided to stay awake long enough to undress herself. The first day she managed this, she was pulling her coarse nightgown over her head when Étain came in and looked at her quizzically.

"You don't have to do that, Cassán," she scolded as she glided forward to help straighten out the last few folds. "You must be tired. Come, let me help you down to your bed." She reached for Maren's hand, and Maren, too sleep-deprived to argue, allowed the girl to tuck her into bed and sing her a soft lullaby. She fell asleep to Étain's familiar hands again in her hair, and a slight nagging feeling at the edge of her consciousness. Shrugging it away, she pretended that the fingers stroking her hair were Faolán's, and she drifted away with a slight smile on her face.

Things went smoothly for a few days, but Maren began to find ways of avoiding any contact with Étain. As friendly and kind as the girl seemed to be, there was something about her that made Maren uncomfortable, and until she could understand it, she wanted to keep it as far from herself as possible. It was usually easy enough during the day, for she and Étain often worked in different laundry rooms, and in the evenings she forced herself to stay awake until Étain had given up on trying to put her to sleep and climbed into her own bed. Although Étain grumbled, Maren felt she was doing the right thing. What was it about the girl that made her so uneasy?

One night two weeks after Maren had started at the Laundry, she found herself choking back tears as she climbed the stairs. One of the youngest girls in the convent, barely fifteen and eight months pregnant, had collapsed at the workstation next to Maren's, her eyes rolling back in her head. Maren gasped as she saw a pool of blood beginning to form under the girl's smock, and she called out for the nun on duty to help. Sister Dáirine had rushed over, but it was too late. The girl had suffered a miscarriage, hemorrhaged massively, and died a few minutes later as two of the nuns were carrying her out. Maren wept for the girl, for her parents, and for her child who had died as well, and was completely unable to eat her supper. A few of the other girls at her table had the same problem, and the nuns were kind and did not discipline them, but the feeling of being utterly alone caught up with Maren as she ascended the stairs to her room.

Étain was already there, and she jumped up anxiously when she saw Maren's swollen face. "What happened, Cassán? Are you all right?" She put a hand on Maren's shoulder, and for once Maren did not automatically shrug it off. She reached for Étain's hand and held it tremulously.

"One of the girls... down in the laundry..." She was unable to continue, but Étain nodded sadly.

"That new one. Nessa," she stated, using the girl's real name. The girl had come to the convent, heavily pregnant, only a week earlier, and had not yet had a chance to think of a secret name for herself. "I know; I heard about it at dinner. It's all right, darling. It happens sometimes."

Maren nodded; she had heard that, but this was her first taste of it, and it was a horrific shock. "But she died right in front of me. I should have done something to help her!" Her voice trembled, and she did not bother to keep the volume down. Fear of the nuns' chastisement was the last thing on her mind at this moment. Étain automatically tensed and glanced around as though a nun would burst through the door at any second, but Maren wasn't worried, and Étain recovered swiftly.

"You couldn't have done anything, Cassán. It wasn't your fault." She moved her hands to Maren's shoulders and guided her to the bed. Sitting down behind her, she began gently rubbing Maren's tense muscles, and despite herself, Maren moaned with relief. A brief smile flitted across Étain's face, but Maren didn't notice. "Now, calm down, and let's get you ready for bed."

Maren shook her head. "I can't sleep now. I can't think of anything but her poor white little face staring up at me." She was on the verge of fresh tears.

"You can't dwell on that, Cassán. It will happen again, to someone else, perhaps even someone you know well. You must get used to it. For now, just relax, and we'll worry about it tomorrow."

Étain's fingers dug deep into her muscles, and Maren closed her eyes, finally relaxing. She let her mind drift, forgetting about her plan to avoid Étain, and thought about the days when she would get up in the morning and brush her hair with one hundred strokes before going out to see Faolán. His eyes always sparkled when they saw her, and his smile was so warm and welcoming... What she wouldn't give to see that face again. Someday, Father Seanán would come back to fetch her, and she could go back home to see Faolán, and her father, mother and brother again. What joy would be in all their eyes when they saw her again! She sighed with contentment, just as she became aware of Étain's lips gently pressing against her neck.

Maren jumped up hastily, her sore muscles screaming at her, and turned to Étain with her mouth hanging open. "What are you doing?" she hissed, her eyes wide.

Étain stretched lazily and smiled up into Maren's angry eyes. "Why do they waste so much time trying to keep us away from boys?" she questioned idly. "After all, girls are so *very* much more interesting."

Maren could not keep the shock from her face or her voice. "Étain, I don't think you understand... If I have been giving you the wrong idea...I'm sorry..." She stared at Étain, who seemed as relaxed as a cat in the sun, and realized that her hands were folded into fists and were ready to strike out if the other girl came any closer. Étain didn't seem to notice.

"I used to like boys," she continued as though Maren had not spoken. "They were all right... for a while. Then one of them tattled and I got sent here. And here is where I discovered that girls are ever so much sweeter...and ever so much softer. And," she added with a nasty twist to her mouth, "they never tell."

Pulling the blanket from the other bed to cover herself with, Maren tried to register what Étain was saying to her. The other girl must have had...*relationships*...with her previous roommates. Maren couldn't imagine anything more degrading or disgusting, and she shrunk away before saying, "Étain, I will not have anything to do with that." She was aware of how weak her voice sounded, so she stuck her chin in the air and repeated in a stronger tone, "I will *not* have anything to do with that!"

The grin that stretched across Étain's face was evidence of her confidence in the situation. Obviously, she had been through this before. "Ah, still infatuated with the little boy back home, are we? Well, what good did *that* get you, Maren Bradigan?" She stressed Maren's given name in a way that sent shivers down her spine, and she shut her eyes while she waited for the other girl to stop speaking. "I can guarantee you, Miss Bradigan, that any man you get involved with will do the same thing to you. Claim to love you, ravish you, and dump you. That's life. But not here," she added maliciously. "Here, you can have much more fun, and never get dumped."

Maren could no longer handle the tension, and her fear left her. She squared her shoulders—painfully—and looked directly into Étain's eyes. "If you come one step closer to me, Étain," she stressed, "I will run screaming down that hallway and tell the first nun I see that you made an advance on me. Let's see how you feel being dumped." Hoping against hope that the girl would take her threat seriously, she willed herself not to tremble as she waited for Étain's answer.

Étain's face grew red. Apparently, she was not used to being refused. Maren felt sick as she thought of whatever other girls had to go through what Étain had in mind, but she forced the thought from her mind and continued to wait.

The answer was not long in coming. "Fine," snapped Étain, throwing herself down on the bed and pulling the blanket over herself. "Good night." She rolled away so that she was not facing Maren's bed, and seemed to go straight to sleep.

Maren lay awake for a very long time.

The next day when the bell for Mass rang in its ominous tones, Étain leapt from the bed and threw on her clothes, stalking out of the room without looking at Maren. Maren, who had awakened instantly and looked fearfully over at the other bed, got up quickly and quietly and followed her roommate out the door and down to Mass.

When she got there, she scanned the large room but didn't see any evidence of Étain. She went through the familiar routine and headed in for breakfast, all the while giving quick glances around for Étain, but she was nowhere in sight. Feeling slightly relieved, she swallowed her lumpy oatmeal and made her way to the laundry room.

Filling her basin as usual, she moved swiftly to her post and, scooping an armful of dirty rags from the storage bin, plunged her hands into the steaming water and began washing. She began her prayers and soon became absorbed in her work, thankful not to have to deal with Étain at the moment. That, she figured, would come later.

It came not five minutes later, as the door slammed open and Maren's head snapped up from her washing, the prayer dying on her lips. Étain was standing in the open doorway, her face covered with blood and her entire body shaking. Tears streaming down her face, she pointed a trembling finger at Maren. Maren remained frozen in position, speechless.

"Her!" Étain screamed as the nun in charge ran over, her black skirts flowing behind her. "It was her! She did this to me!" Every other head in the room had lifted at this point, and the room was silent except for Étain's wails. She turned her head into the nun's bosom as the woman tried to comfort her. Maren's eyes grew.

The nun turned livid eyes to Maren and beckoned angrily for her to come. Maren rushed over and the three of them stepped out into the hallway. Maren heard the voices inside begin again as soon as the door closed, and the only rational thought she could drum up was a sneaking suspicion that the women left inside were not saying their prayers.

Close to Étain now, she could see that the other girl had a large welt next to her left eye that blood was still oozing from, and a black bruise was beginning to form around the other eye. Maren tried to keep calm, reaching out a hand to her roommate. "Étain, what hap—"

"Don't you touch me!" Étain screamed, and Maren's hand snapped back. "Don't touch me again! Stay away!" She was turning in to the nun's black chest again, squirming as far away from Maren as she could. Maren's brows furrowed in confusion, and she looked to the nun for assistance. Sister Sorcha's eyes were raging.

"Did you do this, Miss Bradigan?" she demanded icily. Before Maren could even shake her head, Étain broke in.

"She locked me in the storage room by the dining hall!" By all evidence, she was in real tears. Maren was astounded. "I couldn't even go to Mass this morning...it took me until now to get out. She hit me... she hit me!"

"Relax, Miss Kiley," Sister Sorcha ordered, still glaring at Maren. "I will take you to the infirmary and get you looked after. As for you, Miss Bradigan, you will come with me." She grabbed Maren by the arm and yanked her along as she strode down the hall, a sobbing Étain crumpled against her shoulder.

What was Étain saying? This was her revenge for Maren's refusal the night before, she was sure of it. Maren shook her head silently as the nun dragged her along, wondering what in the world would drive someone to beat herself up as much as Étain evidently had. Certainly she would not have asked anyone else to do it...or had she? The questions were too confusing to dwell on. She squared her shoulders and prepared herself for her punishment.

Maren sat on her bed a few hours later, amazed that she was allowed to be there at all. Instead of spending the day washing laundry, she had been paraded before a series of nuns, each one sterner than the last, demanding confession and penance. She had admitted to nothing, but by her silence she was apparently condemned, for she had been ordered to the chapel and had sat with a priest for the past two hours. He spoke softly of getting her to "confront" her sin, and at last she had gone along with it, knowing that nothing worse could happen if she didn't say she had beaten Étain.

How any of them could believe that she, a full four inches shorter and a good deal lighter than Étain, had been able to inflict such damage on the older girl, was beyond her, but here she sat now, her mind light and her heart joyous. Étain's "revenge" had backfired. Maren's punishment, aside from an extra hour of daily penance for the next week, was that Étain should be removed from her room and placed with a "less threatening" roommate, while she herself would be given one of the girls who were in good standing with the Sisters. "We will find someone to be a good influence on you, Miss Bradigan," Sister Grania had pronounced at last, and Maren had nodded and returned to her room for the rest of the day, to sit and reflect on her crime. She sat, but all she could reflect on was how happy she was to be getting away from Étain.

Chapter Eight

It wasn't difficult to watch Étain go. With a scowl, she picked up her few belongings and stalked out, leaving Maren with only the memory of her glare. The picture was almost burned into her brain, like the afterimage of a flash on a camera stayed to smolder on the retina. Sister Mary, the nun assigned to bringing Étain down to her new room, turned to Maren with a frown as she followed the girl. "You ought to be ashamed of yourself," she snapped, and whisked out.

Maren sighed and lay back on her worn pillow. Despite the relief she felt not to have Étain to deal with anymore, it worried her that she might end up stuck with someone even worse. She let her mind drift as she contemplated the possibilities. Would it be sweet little Amy, whom she had spent many a day working alongside, whose stutter got worse almost every day? That wouldn't be too bad; she could find herself in the position of being an older sister. The diminutive blond girl was anxious to a fault, and shy as a mouse; Maren couldn't imagine what she would ever have done to upset someone enough to send her here. Or could it be Ailbhe, the narrow-faced, tense girl who could have been Sister Líadan's cousin? Even at four months gone, and definitely showing, she still managed to act as though she owned the place – at least when the nuns were not within earshot. Maren couldn't stomach the thought of having to bow and scrape before Ailbhe even when she was not in the Laundry rooms.

Maybe they would send in Fiona, the eighteen-year-old daughter of wealthy parents, who was used to getting her own way. Although she worked hard in the Laundry, she expected to be well treated and cried every time she felt she was being overworked. Maren couldn't imagine how Fiona managed to get through such hard work as they did in the Laundry; whenever her soup was cold or there was a spot on her fork she set up such a clamor that she had ended up getting strapped for it more than once. Yet she was diligent as she scrubbed linens and aprons all day long. Ailbhe and Fiona somehow managed to alternate between being wolves snapping at each other's throats and being the best of friends, sitting close together at mealtimes and arching coolly amused eyebrows at all the pitiable lowlifes around them. She supposed it was the way they had grown up; neither wanted the other to be more important than she, but both were grateful to find someone who understood her way of life. Maren snorted to herself. *Perhaps they should make Ailbhe and Fiona the roommates*, she reflected with a chuckle.

The door started to open again, and Maren bounded up from her reclining position. Sister Grania walked in with a girl a little shorter than Maren herself, with long dark hair and hands clasped together underneath a burgeoning stomach. Her face was plain but unusual, with a small rosebud mouth and round black eyes that tilted up at the corners, even though she wasn't smiling. She volunteered a grin at Maren, transforming her whole face into an apparition of loveliness, and Maren smiled back before she could think to guard herself.

"Miss Bradigan, this is Ceara MacAodhagáin," Sister Grania announced, putting a hand on the girl's shoulder and using it to thrust her slightly forward. Ceara obeyed, taking a few small steps closer to Maren, the smile unwavering. "Ceara, this is Maren Bradigan. The two of you will be roommates."

Maren nodded at the new girl. "Hello, Ceara. It's nice to meet you."

"It's nice to meet you, too," Ceara said, resting her left hand on the berth of her belly while reaching out with her right to shake Maren's hand. After a moment Maren did the same. Sister Grania watched with an approving nod and smile.

"Ceara has been here several months already, Miss Bradigan. She has shown exemplary manners, and you will do well to learn from her. Take notes, if you must." She gave a little smirk to show that she was teasing, and laid an affectionate hand on Ceara's hair before turning to go.

"And, remember, Maren, it was I who recommended that Ceara be brought to room with you. If Líadan had had her way, you would not have that smile on your face now."

Her words alone were enough to wipe the gladness from Maren's face, but she managed another small lift of her lips as she nodded. "Yes, Sister. I thank you." Ceara turned and dropped a small curtsey as Sister Grania left, and Maren hastily copied her. The satisfied look on Grania's face as she closed the heavy door behind her assured Maren that she had done the right thing.

The instant the door closed, Ceara turned back to Maren and grabbed her by the hands. "Let's sit and talk for a few minutes before bed, shall we?" She propelled Maren to the nearest bed and sat her down on it. Maren, too surprised to do anything, watched in silence and Ceara pulled herself up beside her and methodically folded her legs under the bulk of her pregnancy. "She said your name is Maren, but what's your *real* name, here?"

Maren reflected on how many of the girls she knew here by particular names, and found herself wondering for the first time how many of them had been given those names at birth. She herself would not have told Ceara her real name if they had not been officially introduced, and she was certain that Ceara would have done the same. "My name is Cassán," she volunteered shyly. Ceara bounced back on the bed in delight.

"Oh, for your hair!" she exclaimed. Maren's eyes widened.

"Yes, it means 'little curly-haired one'. It's...my father's name for me," she finished with a faraway look in her eyes, but shook her head as the memories swarmed over her and looked back at Ceara. "How did you know what it meant?"

"I love names," Ceara said. "My mother is a linguist, and I guess I inherited some of her love for words by always wanting to know what particular names mean. My real name—Ceara—was supposedly inspired by my hair, too. It means 'fiery red'." She tugged on a lock of her lank dark brown hair and grimaced. "I guess my mother was doing some wishful thinking." She let out a laugh, but the mention of her mother had obviously pained her. Maren was thoughtful as well, thinking of her father calling out her nickname. Ceara suddenly snapped back into reality. "Did you know that *Cassán* is actually a male name?" Maren looked startled, and Ceara laughed at her expression. Her father's pet name for her was really a *boy's* name? Ceara hurried to reassure her. "It's okay; mine is male, too. I call myself Maelisa." She said the name with a certain touch of pride, and Maren grinned.

"It must have some meaning, then, if you chose it specifically for yourself," she guessed, warming up to the idea.

Ceara nodded. "Yes, it does. It's really two words, *Mael Iosa*, and it means 'servant of Jesus'. I chose it because, that's what I am," she finished, sitting forward, her expression searching.

Maren gazed back, no real emotion on her face. She could see that the girl was waiting for something, but she wasn't sure how to react. To her the meaning of the name was awful, a label of what the priest and the nuns had done to her, forcing her to bow to their idea of God. "I'm not sure if I really understand..." She held back, but at the encouraging look from Ceara, rushed on. "...Why would you call yourself that? Don't you want to escape all of this...religious stuff...after what you have seen it do to all of us?"

Ceara shook her head. "It's not 'religious stuff', Maren. I call myself a servant of Jesus because I do serve Him, in everything I say and do. I strive to live the way He would have me live. My relationship with Him isn't just being bent to His will. I serve Him because I *choose* to live my life for Him."

Eyeing Ceara's bulging belly skeptically, Maren nodded. "I don't really understand, Cear—I mean, *Maelisa*, but I'll call you that if that's what you want." She tried not to reflect on how much the meaning of the name—now that she knew it—grated on her. She did not want to be a servant to anyone, but if Ceara thought that's what she was doing, and she wanted it that way, that would be fine with her.

Ceara's eyes followed Maren's down to her rotund belly and laughed unselfconsciously. "It may not look like I've been living for Jesus, Cassán, but things are not always what they appear." She looked reflective for a moment, and watched Maren's face, but then decided not to say whatever it was she had been about to. "I'll tell you more about it as we grow to be better friends," she decided. "Now let's talk about you a little bit."

Maren gave a light laugh. "Nothing much to tell," she muttered. Making her tone deliberately lighter, she added, "I'd like to know more about this 'name' thing, though. I mean, the meanings. Do you know what other names mean as well?"

"Lots of them, I do. Why?" she responded, her eyes glittering with mischief. "Is there someone whose name you'd like defined?"

"Oh, yes," Maren announced, sitting up straight and thinking for a moment. "What about…Grania?"

Ceara beamed. "I do know that one. It means 'grain', of course, but one of the other meanings for *Grania* is 'inspiring terror'. I don't suppose that one's quite appropriate for our Grania."

Maren shook her head, her face amused. "No, not really. Of all the nuns, I find Sister Grania the least terrifying!"

"Well, how about *Líadan*? It means, 'gray lady'." They giggled together, hushing themselves before the sound carried out into the hall.

"That one is certainly right for Sister Líadan," Maren choked out. "I can't think of one better, unless it would be 'horrid old hag'."

Ceara gasped in feigned shock, but the sparkle was still in her eyes. "That's not very nice, Cassán."

Maren looked indignant. "Well, it's true!"

"Yes," Ceara had to agree, "it really is!" They collapsed onto each other again, Maren pulling the pillows off both beds to stifle their laughter. Maren looked over the old pillow at Ceara, and she realized that for the first time since she had arrived at Sacred Mercy, she was happy. Suddenly, she thrust the pillow down into her lap and reached a hand out to touch Ceara's. Ceara's giggles cut off abruptly, and she looked back at Maren, all seriousness.

"Thank you," Maren whispered. "Maelisa."

A slow smile broke across Ceara's face, and it brightened her plain features remarkably. "I'm glad I met you, too, Cassán," she answered, and reached out to put a gentle hand on Maren's. "I hope we will be good friends."

In that sudden moment of kinship, Maren felt a tumult of emotions running through her. Joy, at having found a friend at last; sadness, at the memories of home and the reality of their hopeless situation here; apprehension, wondering if Ceara would be expecting the same as Étain had. Yet, as her eyes moved down to the small hand on hers, Maren couldn't deny that it felt as though they had just started a friendship that would, given time, be very strong and real. A lump caught in her throat, and she nodded, looking back up into Ceara's tilted eyes. "I hope so, too."

Chapter Nine

The joy of finding a friend and the freedom from constantly needing to be on guard for Étain gave Maren's days of work in the laundries a new sort of flow. She enjoyed living with Ceara, and found her diminutive new roommate interesting and caring, as well as fun. By the end of the day Maren was always ready to chat, and Ceara, despite her obvious fatigue with the cumbersome load she carried, would respond warmly from her bed across the room. In these stolen evening moments, they learned a lot about each other, sharing their thoughts and worries. Maren learned that Ceara was six months pregnant, and the two friends laughed together in incredulity that the large weight Ceara was carrying still had three more months to continue growing. The two of them soon developed different hand gestures in order to silently converse with each other during the workday, and Maren found a large measure of comfort from the opportunity to glance across the dreary room, filled with its constant hum of prayers, and find Ceara looking her way as well. One of the friends would run a discreet finger down her nose to say "hi" or momentarily hold a thumb behind her ear to communicate "you can make it", and these cautious signals did wonders for their loneliness and boredom.

They had been living side by side in the tiny room, and sitting together during every meal, for almost two weeks before Maren dared to ask Ceara how she had ended up here. Regardless of how close she and Ceara had become in such a short time, it seemed such a sensitive issue that she was loath to bring it up and ruin the seemingly wonderful friendship they had created. She determined to broach the subject cautiously, slightly concerned that she would offend, but she felt certain that Ceara would not hesitate to tell her it was none of her business if she did not want to reveal her story.

Maren watched as Ceara entered the room, a towel and a worn toothbrush in her hands. She swayed slightly from side to side as the weight of her belly pulled her off balance, but her natural grace made the swinging walk appear elegant, and her smile as she saw Maren waiting for her on the thin bed made her even more beautiful. Maren couldn't help but grin back at her friend.

Ceara sat cross-legged on her own bed and placed her meager toiletries beside her on the blanket. She reached for the toothbrush and dipped it in the cracked china cup on the nightstand that held her drinking water, and began to meticulously scrub her teeth. Maren watched, running her tongue over her own gritty teeth, and then stood up on the bed to reach up to where her toothbrush sat on the tiny windowsill.

Dipping her own brush, she began to scour them as vigorously as Ceara was. She had become somewhat slack in her hygiene routine, and couldn't remember the last time she had brushed her teeth, but it certainly had been a few days for the amount of time it took her to make them feel fairly clean again. Ceara made sure to take care of her teeth every night before bed, and she scrubbed them in the morning when she woke, if she had the time before the bell for Mass tolled. Maren looked for a place to spit out the nasty substance in her mouth, but the water glass was the only thing in the room that would do, and she needed the liquid desperately. Grimacing, she closed her eyes tightly and forced herself to swallow the horrid stuff, reaching for her small water supply and eagerly downing half the glass. Ceara noticed her look and gave her a remorseful half-grin.

"What I wouldn't give for some baking soda once in a while," she commented, and Maren nodded. The taste in her mouth was still vile, although over the past while she had become slightly used to it, but at least her teeth were smooth when she ran her tongue over them once more. Sighing, she wiped the toothbrush on a lower edge of her blanket before reaching up to replace it on the ledge. She settled into her bed, bunching the dog-eared pillow into a sorry lump to try to support her neck, and pulled the negligible weight of the blanket over her muslin-clad body. Ceara stayed sitting up, though she covered her crossed legs with her blanket, and began working her fingers through her hair in order to take out some of the tangles. "And a comb would be nice, too," she added. Maren agreed with another nod.

She lay in silence for a moment, listening to Ceara's fingers as they swiped slowly and carefully through her hair, hearing Ceara grunt softly every now and then as she wrestled with a particularly nasty knot. The light had faded, so she knew that if she turned her head she would not be able to see her friend, but she could picture Ceara's face, her brow furrowed in concentration, and her long, delicate fingers working at the long, dark hair that she would have pulled over one lean shoulder. As she watched the mental picture, she focused in on the swelling of the other girl's belly, and almost before she could register what she was about to say, the words were out. "Ceara, who is the father of your baby?"

Abruptly all sound from the other bed stopped, and Maren lay silently waiting, her eyes wide and staring at the ceiling, until she heard Ceara's breath come out with a whoosh. "Well," she murmured. "It certainly took long enough for you to come out with that one. I was beginning to think you didn't ever wonder any more." That had to be untrue; Maren took so many glances at Ceara's midsection that she wondered that Ceara had not just smacked her and ordered her to look somewhere else. But no, she had learned over the course of the past month that Ceara would not say anything that she did not believe to be the exact truth. Still, for her not to have noticed Maren's curiosity was surprising.

"I do wonder," Maren said quietly. "The more I've gotten to know you...well, you just don't seem like any of the other girls that are in here. I wouldn't be surprised that you were in here if you weren't expecting—Lord knows I did nothing wrong and still managed to find myself here—but that belly just goes against everything I know about you. How could you, of all people, have done...something like that?" Closing her mouth with a snap, she refused to look in Ceara's direction, but she was grateful for the lack of light in the room. She knew that her cheeks were burning with shame for even mentioning the subject.

Ceara slid off her bed. Maren could hear the soft pads of her footsteps as she approached her, and she rubbed her cheeks furiously with the palms of her hands to take away the telltale blush. Turning toward her friend, she sat up. Ceara sat down beside her, and looked directly into her eyes. Maren could feel their intensity through the darkness, though she could barely make out more than Ceara's outline.

"His name was Dougal Corley," she began softly. "He was the son of a very prominent man in Galway, where I'm from." She cleared her throat, and her eyes became distant as she retrieved the memories. "He was very handsome...and two years older than myself. He was headed off to college in London, last I heard. He was always very...educated."

Maren waited for a brief moment as Ceara stayed lost in thought, then whispered, "Was he kind to you?"

Ceara's eyes suddenly filled with tears, and Maren heard the muslin of her sleeve rustle against her body as she hurriedly wiped them away with the back of her hand. "I can't cry now," she laughed shakily. "I've just wasted half my drinking water in washing my face." She pulled the sleeve over her fist and used it to swipe at her cheeks. "Yes, he was kind to me. I was...so in love with him...and my parents were close friends with his father. They encouraged us to start courting, and we had the understanding that there would be a marriage for us down the line."

She looked in Maren's direction again, and grasped her hand. Maren could feel the tears still on Ceara's fingers dampening her hand, but she held on just as tightly. She knew that Ceara was revealing her deepest secrets, and she wanted to be as encouraging as she could. Maren's eyes had by this time adjusted enough to the darkness that she could see that Ceara's face was nearly wild with remembered emotion and pain. "Oh, Maren, I was so looking forward to that. All I wanted was to marry Dougal, to be Mrs. Dougal Corley, and to raise his little Corley children. We would live in a big house in Galway, and we would be happy. He would trot off to his banking job in the morning – or perhaps he would become a lawyer – but he'd work and make money and think of us all day, and then, when he returned, our babies would grasp his legs and shout, 'Daddy, Daddy, Daddy!' and he would greet me with a kiss." Tears were running down her face again, and Maren gently dabbed at them with a corner of her pillow, but Ceara didn't even seem to notice. "That was all I wanted."

"But what changed it, Maelisa? What happened?" Maren searched Ceara's face with empathy. She knew what it was like to feel that for a boy, but how wonderful it must have been for Ceara! The one she wanted also wanted her, and they had officially been classified as a couple in the county. Maren fought down a ridiculous surge of jealousy, scolding herself. *I can't be jealous of her*, she reasoned; *obviously her dreams didn't come true, for look at what she's facing now.* Still, the thought of Faolán smiling at her and putting his arms around her, presenting her to all the world as his fiancé, caused a twinge of pain deep down inside. She had to force herself to focus on Ceara as the girl buried her face in her hands.

"He—he told me that he wasn't ready to wait. He told me that if I was to be his wife, I had to—to learn my—wifely duties, as he called them. I didn't really know what he meant. I hadn't—had a lot of education on that sort of thing. My mother always said that we would have some things to discuss on my wedding day, and she made it seem so mysterious and wonderful and scary and everything all rolled in to one." Her eyes glazed over with painful memory and Maren leaned in to listen to her voice as it suddenly softened.

"We went out to dinner one night," Ceara whispered, her quiet voice muffled even more by the tears she was choking back. "It was beautiful...candles, soft music, everything...and then we walked back to his house. His parents were away that night, but I didn't know that. I would never have gone in with him if I had known!" Her voice became adamant and she looked to Maren with imploring eyes. She grasped her friend's hands between her own. "You must believe me, Cassán, I wouldn't have!" Maren nodded silently and waited for Ceara to continue.

Ceara watched her wildly for a moment, her mind obviously raging with guilt and shame, until she had satisfied herself that Maren believed her. Then, relaxing slightly, but the tension still evident in the square set of her shoulders, she went on. "He brought me a glass of wine from his parents' liquor cabinet. I took it, just to hold, but I really didn't want to drink any. It just seemed...so elegant, like everything else about that evening had been. I wanted to feel like an adult." She sniffed and rubbed her nose with the back of her hand. "It did feel good to be there with him, in my beautiful new dress, with my hair up...I really felt like I was grown-up and we were a husband and wife winding down after a hard day. It was...exciting."

Maren gave Ceara an encouraging smile as she looked up as if for affirmation. "I understand," she murmured, uncertain if she needed to speak but wanting to assure Ceara that she was there for her. Ceara seemed not to hear as she returned to her story.

"Dougal drank the wine—quite a lot, really. I didn't worry; I had seen him drink socially with his parents and I never knew him to lose control. He seemed to be able to hold his liquor quite well, and for a little while he was just like his old self. He laughed and told me funny jokes, and we snuggled on the sofa a bit. Then he started to get too close."

She swallowed. "He kissed me, but much harder and...fiercer...than he had ever kissed me before. He had always been so gentle, but..." Ceara put a trembling hand to her lips as though they were still bruised from Dougal's affections, and tears welled up in her eyes again. "When he started to touch me—differently—in a way that felt wrong, I suggested that we find his parents and have a card game or something. Then he laughed and told me that they were out, for the weekend. I should have just gotten up and left, but I—I was so stupid!" She burst into tears and leaned forward to lay her forehead on the pillow that she held in her lap.

Maren, her own eyes beginning to fill with tears as she understood what Ceara was saying, leaned over her protectively and rubbed her back. Ceara cried for several minutes, and then abruptly sat up, wiping her cheeks with her knuckles and smiling weakly at Maren. "He had his way with me, Cassán," she stated emotionlessly.

"I don't know if I could have done anything about it, but I didn't, and that's how I got pregnant. It was only that once, and Dougal was all smiles afterward. He said that now, we were really prepared to get married. I felt so dirty...I didn't even want to look at him...but he seemed to feel it was something wonderful that we had shared together." Her short laugh was stilted enough to almost be called a bark. "And when I found out that the baby was on the way, I went to him, assuming that we would marry sooner than planned, but he...he left me...and then he went to my priest and told him that he—" Ceara's tears started up again, and her voice caught on her words. She swallowed several times, holding tightly to Maren's hand, and continued. "He told him that he couldn't marry me because I was...because I was—*soiled*. He told my priest that I was a whore, that he had long suspected that I had been with many other men, and now that he had found that I was with child, his suspicions were confirmed." Squeezing her eyes shut tight against the hurt, she finished her story in one breath. "They waited for me to start to show, and as soon as I did, the priest came to get me and whisked me away from the shame of my family and Dougal's...and that's how I got here."

"Your family..." Maren whispered. "Did they know?"

She nodded. "They knew about the baby, and they were completely disgraced. I don't know if Father Marcus ever told them he was taking me away, but I don't think they would have stopped him if they did know. I was their good little girl, and I had shamed them." She managed another feeble smile and wiped away the last of her tears, splashing some of her drinking water on her face. The tiny beads of moisture glistened on her skin in the dim light. "If you ask them, it was all my fault."

"You don't really believe that, do you, Maelisa?" Maren almost hissed. "You did nothing wrong!"

Ceara moved heavily off Maren's bed and stood between the two as she gazed down at Maren's angry face. She had calmed down as suddenly as she had gotten worked up, but she looked anything but defeated. Instead, her tear-streaked face radiated peace and acceptance. "No, Maren, I know I didn't really do anything wrong. I was just a little too trusting, I suppose. But it doesn't matter, anyway, because I am here now, and this is where I am going to deliver the only grandchild my parents may ever have, and I am content with that. I really am."

Maren shook her head fiercely, the matted golden curls crackling with static electricity in the blackness in the room. "I don't believe that. You've lost everything!" Realizing that what she had said may have been hurtful to Ceara, she clapped both hands to her mouth in consternation. She wanted to apologize, but she kept her mouth firmly closed lest her tongue run away with her again.

Ceara merely shook her head. "It may look that way, but I haven't. My best friend in the world is here with me, always, and He comforts me often, as He is comforting me right now. I have many sad memories," she continued, settling into the bed and lifting the blanket over her small frame, "but the Lord was with me then, and He is with me now. I just wish you could know His peace, too, Cassán," she stated regretfully, and turning her back to Maren, fell asleep.

Even as exhausted as she had been before the exchange, Maren lay there in the silent dark for many long moments, frustration warring with confusion inside her. Ceara had been through so much, and yet *she* was the one lying awake! Ceara's soft breathing only served to irritate her more. *It's not fair for her to be so peaceful,* Maren raged in her mind. *Why can't she just react to things normally and scream and yell and be bitter? Why?* Deep down inside, however, she yearned for the peace that allowed Ceara to drift into a serene, contented sleep just minutes after telling of the worst thing that had yet happened to her. Maybe, just maybe, she would ask Ceara a bit more about this best friend of hers.

Chapter Ten

Maren pulled back the coverlet of the bed as soon as the bell for Mass rang, but a sudden excruciating pain in her belly doubled her over before she could stand up. Ceara looked at her with sympathy as she stripped off her nightdress and reached for her shift.

"What is it, Cassán?" she asked quietly, pulling her matted hair back off her face and tying it around itself into a crude knot. "Did you eat something bad?"

"Everything here is bad," Maren groaned, "but no, it's my time of the month." She let out another loud moan and hugged her arms around her stomach. "It's not usually so bad, though. I wonder why it hurts so much?"

Ceara moved over to rub Maren's back gently. "Soon it won't come at all. Most of the girls here have already stopped flowing; it's the scarcity of the food and the hard work that stops it from coming. Most of the nuns are happy when they see that you've gotten it – it means that you haven't snuck out and gotten yourself pregnant. This is probably the first cycle you've had here, isn't it?" Maren nodded, her eyes clenched shut to ward off the pain, and Ceara gave an answering nod. "Usually they're especially happy to see that in a new girl, for generally that's the only chance you would have had to get with child. Not many of the girls who manage to sneak out would be stupid enough to come back and let themselves get caught in a pregnancy. Don't worry; climb back in bed and I'll alert Sister Grania that you're not well. That's most likely the only way you'll get out of work around here, if your pain is bad. They also don't like the idea of the girls with 'the curse' doing the laundry, anyway; it might soil the garments—figuratively, I suppose—with their 'uncleanliness'." She turned and opened the large, heavy door, smiling at

Maren as she slipped out. "Just get some rest while you're able." The door closed with a loud creak behind her.

Maren reached over to snatch Ceara's pillow from her bed and lay back on the meager cushioning with a sigh. Perhaps it was the sudden lack of good healthy food that was causing the fire in her belly. She normally had no problems with her menstruation, and didn't understand why it would change now, unless it was the stress and strangeness of her new situation. Another pain racked her body and she groaned.

The night before, when she had discovered her menses, she had no choice but to strip the case off the pillow and fold it neatly into a small pad to place inside her drawers. The pillowcase had absorbed most of the blood, but Maren had been uncomfortable all night with the bulkiness between her legs and the horrible smell of the filthy pillow she had been given. Now she wondered if there was a supply of menstrual pads here in the convent, for if there weren't, she didn't know what she would have to do. Ceara hadn't seemed worried, though, and that was a comfort. Then again, Ceara never seemed all that worried about *anything*, even though she was alone in this horrific place, forced to work like a slave, and carrying the heavy physical burden of her child as well. She always trusted that God would get her through.

Maren sighed. God. She didn't think she would ever understand Him. How could Ceara have such faith in a God who demanded so much from His servants? Maren and Ceara had never done anything wrong in their lives, or certainly not anything that would justify being sent to this place. Maren had been a devoted Catholic, going to Mass weekly and occasionally more often, saying her prayers before bed each night, and doing unto others as she would have them do to her. Certainly Ceara must have done so as well, for with her faith she would doubtless do nothing that was wrong in God's eyes.

But here Maren frowned: Ceara's reason for striving to do what was right in God's sight was not because she feared His punishment; rather, it was because she desired to be *like* Him. She loved Him so much that it had become second nature for her to do what He would approve of. Maren had always worried about how God saw her; she knew that she was a sinner by nature and made it her duty to keep that nature far away from her actions, in case God would punish her. She was not searching for God's appreciation, but rather made every effort at perfection in order to keep God's wrath away from her.

And look where it had gotten her. Fear of God's punishment and anger had sent her to Father Seanán, to confess her very minor sin of finding Faolán attractive—if, in fact, that was to be considered a sin at all—and he, acting on God's behalf, had condemned her here to the convent to wash away her sins along with the blood and soil on every garment she scrubbed. How could she see God as a God of love when He had brought His servants to this point? How could anyone with *any* love in their heart condemn a child of their own to this kind of suffering?

Her Bible lessons came back to her, memories tumbling over one another, and she snorted derisively as she realized that God had sent Jesus—His own *Son*—to the earth to suffer a fate far worse than the one she and Ceara were enduring now. He could not possess any love at *all* if He would allow His own Son to die painfully and horribly, nailed to a cross in humiliating display to all passersby. And the Church taught that this was God's divine mission! His mission, to kill His Son? No, Ceara's worship and adoration of this God was pointless and misguided. Maren was sure that she would disown her own mother if she had treated her in this manner...now she decided that she must definitely distance herself from this God who called Himself her Father.

The door creaked open as Maren reached this conclusion. She looked up, suddenly remembering the pain in her belly as Sister Grania strode in with a grim expression. She laid a few cloths and a belt down on the table by Ceara's bed and stepped forward to stand by Maren's bedside. "Are you not feeling well, Miss Bradigan?" she questioned softly. Maren shook her head.

"It's my time of the month, Sister. It's not usually so bad...I don't know why I'm feeling like this." She searched Sister Grania's eyes for sympathy and understanding, but the usually kind nun's eyes were determinedly cold. Maren shrank away from the unusual sight of Sister Grania's glare.

Grania sighed, unconsciously patting her long black skirts as she glanced around the room, sniffing with distaste. "Well, I can certainly tell you are telling the truth. It smells terrible in here." Maren hung her head, shamed, as the nun continued. "When did your menses start?"

"Last night, Sister," Maren mumbled, embarrassed. "I didn't have anything to use for it."

Grania gestured to the table. "There are cloths and a belt there you may use for the duration, as well a few changes of underclothes. Put the soiled ones in this bag"—she produced a folded trash bag from her apron pocket—"and bring them down with you to the laundry when you return for your penance. Now, how long does your cycle usually last?"

Maren quickly calculated, trying to remember. At home she usually didn't pay much attention, just dealt with the problem and went on with things. "Maybe three or four days, Sister."

Grania sighed. "This is horribly inconvenient, Miss Bradigan. You are the fifth girl to start her menstruation in the last two days. They are all claiming to be too ill to work." She shook her head in frustration. "Sister Líadan is not pleased."

Maren made the effort to sit up and grimaced with the dull ache that intensified as she tightened her stomach muscles. "I can...try to work, Sister, if you would prefer I—"

Grania cut her off. "Just rest, girl. Take as much time as you can, for I can't promise you that tomorrow you will be allowed to stay in your room." She looked as though she wanted to say something, but abruptly tightened her mouth and moved again to the door. "Just rest," she encouraged again, with a small, tight smile as she closed the door behind her.

Maren climbed out of the bed carefully and let out a slow exhalation of relief. She would have tried to work if Sister Grania had asked her to, but she was grateful for the rest and hoped she would be able to use the time to make up some of the strength and sleep she had lost over the past few weeks. Quickly changing out of her soiled underwear and depositing it, along with the stained pillowcase, into the garbage bag Sister Grania had provided, she washed herself as well as possible by dipping one of the clean cloths into her water glass and using it as a washcloth. She put on another folded cloth and attached it to the belt, hooking it around her waist and pulling on a fresh pair of underwear from the pile. Feeling much cleaner and better, she climbed back into the bed, tying a loose knot in the garbage bag and tossing it into a far corner. With a brief thought about how Ceara was faring, she allowed herself to drift off to sleep.

After what seemed only moments of peace, the door opened with a loud screech as the door was forced across the uneven concrete floor, waking Maren instantly. She sat up quickly, gasping both in pain and surprise.

Sister Líadan stepped in and reached both arms out to grasp Maren by the frayed collar of her nightshift. "Young lady," she seethed, "you are not fooling me with this act! Do you think I don't know that already five other girls have complained that they have started their menses?" Maren, still tired but completely startled out of her sleep, opened her mouth to answer, but the angry nun cut her off. "You think this is all a joke, don't you? You wanted an excuse to stay away from Mass and from your penance, and you heard that the other girls got the curse and were allowed to stay in, so you faked it in order to stay in bed! Didn't you, you lazy girl? *Didn't you?!*"

The tendons in her neck and fists stood out clearly in her fury and her face was suffused with anger as she hauled Maren bodily out of the bed and threw her down on the floor. Maren struggled to her feet, gasping for air the moment Líadan let go of her collar. "We shall see who is telling the truth here," Líadan snapped. "Now you come with me!"

She took a firm hold of Maren's left ear and, ignoring the stifled yelp of pain, dragged her through the door and down the hallway to the stairwell. Maren struggled to keep up, her feet racing along the floor as she followed Líadan's swirling black skirts, and pressed her fists into her belly to ease the pain she felt there. Unfortunately, the act put her slightly off balance, and she stumbled as they reached the stairs, knocking one knee on the stone floor and nearly pulling the nun down the staircase with her. Líadan scowled in frustration and swiftly dealt her a stunning blow to the head, knocking Maren against the wall but continuing to drag her down the stairs by her ear, which was by now screaming in pain. Maren's eyes fogged and she fainted, dropping to her knees again and barely feeling the cold stone floor as it sent shock waves racing up from her kneecaps to her brain. She lay motionless on the landing for a moment, and Líadan, frustrated, let go of Maren's ear to put both hands to her hips. "Get up, girl," she commanded, giving Maren a careless kick in the backside.

Maren roused enough to feel another pain coursing through her from Líadan's blow, and she made a great effort to focus her eyes as she made her way back to her feet. She grasped the wall to haul herself up, its cool stone bricks reminding her of the first time she had explored the outer walls of the convent laundry outside Somhairle. *It seems so very long ago,* she thought in a fog. *Oh, Da, if only you could come and rescue me now!*

She managed to stay on her feet and follow an impatient Sister Líadan down the rest of the stairs, but her mind was whirling and her head hurt tremendously. "Da," she whispered under her breath, a sob catching in her throat as she pictured her father's loving face. "Da, I need you..."

"Quiet!" Líadan snapped. "You should be calling out to the Lord for help. It is He you have offended, and from Him you should be begging mercy." She placed both hands on Maren's shoulders again and shoved her into a small room down the corridor.

Five girls scrambled to their feet as they entered. Maren recognized only two of them enough to recall their names: Anya, a tall, beautiful girl who had arrived at the convent only a few days after Maren, and whose head had been shaved in order to reduce her loveliness; and Deirdre, a fiery redhead whose temper matched her hair. She had only been here for a week. Though she held her head high, Maren could see that she had been crying, and there were dark hollows under her eyes that hadn't been there when she had arrived. It gave Maren pause to wonder how much she herself had changed since she had come to the convent.

Líadan threw her over to join the other girls, who reached out with supportive arms to brace her as she fell against them. Deirdre looped her arm through Maren's, giving her a reassuring look. Maren smiled back gratefully, her focus wavering as she strived to stay on her feet. Deirdre supported her easily, standing slightly in front of her so that Líadan would not see how much help she was giving her.

Líadan folded her arms across her bony chest and gave them all an icy glare. "Now, *ladies*," she enunciated slowly, "you all know why you are here. I must say, you have hatched a *very* clever scheme, but it is unfortunate that you all happened upon it at once. Having to miss your laundry duty because of your little visitor is clever, indeed. But I do not believe for one instant that you are *all* suffering the same affliction." She began pacing, looking to the six frightened girls very much like a lion circling its prey. "I intend to find out just which of you are telling the truth. Pull down your knickers."

Maren and Deirdre exchanged startled looks, and the other four girls gasped in protest. "But, Sister—" Anya exclaimed in her soft, melodious voice, "you can't possibly expect us to—"

"Silence!" roared Líadan, her hand flying out to cuff Anya behind the ear. "How dare you speak unless spoken to? I told you; I am intent on routing out you lazy children and finding out just who is telling the truth here! *Now pull down those knickers!*"

The six girls stared at the floor in humiliation. They knew that Líadan had them trapped. Any one of them who agreed to pull down their underwear would suffer the mortification of revealing something incredibly private to both the nun and the other girls, but any girl who refused to show her the evidence of her menstruation would be deemed a liar and sent to work extra hard in the laundries as punishment. Maren closed her eyes. How, oh how, could this be her life?

One of the youngest girls, her legs and hands trembling and shame coloring her cheeks, reached up underneath her shift and began to drag her panties down her legs. Maren shook her head in disbelief, and a tear escaped from her eye on behalf of the young girl as she and the others turned their heads to carefully avoid looking at her. Líadan awarded her no such respect, smirking and nodding as the young girl exposed the confirmation that she was in fact menstruating. "Thank you, Miss Beckett," she said smoothly. "You may go back to your room now."

Shaking with mortification, the little girl drew her underwear back into place and made her way from the room, her eyes downcast. Maren dared a glance in her direction and saw a long streak of bright blood on the inside of her knee as she walked out. Closing her eyes in sympathy, she shook her head.

"And who will be next?" Sister Líadan inquired of the remaining five girls. One by one, they stepped forward, shamed and disgraced, to disclose their bleeding. Each time, the other girls kept their eyes respectfully averted, and each girl was dismissed in turn. Sister Líadan looked disappointed that they had all been telling the truth, but she turned an expectant face to the two who were left, Maren and Deirdre. "Well, girls, who will it be? Miss Farrell?"

Deirdre cast her a sharp glance, then muttered under her breath, "Never."

Maren was ready to step forward, but anger flashed bright in Líadan's eyes at Deirdre's refusal. "Well, then, Miss Farrell, I'm sure you will not mind going to have a little *talk* with Father Conall later this afternoon. You can confess to him your sin of *lying* then."

Deirdre's face paled, and she stepped forward with a fist raised, seemingly ready to plow it into Sister Líadan's face. Maren had no idea why she became so angry; being sent to a priest for confession certainly was not the worst punishment around here. She watched in worry as Deirdre advanced on Líadan, who was smiling coldly. For a moment she hesitated, and then the redheaded girl let her fist drop and glared into Líadan's placid face. "*Go n-ithe an cat thu' is go n-ithe an diabhal an cat*," she whispered threateningly. Maren's eyes widened. *May the cat eat you, and may the cat be eaten by the devil.* She could not believe that Deirdre would dare to utter such a disrespectful, mocking curse to the nun's face.

Líadan was shocked enough that her mouth actually dropped open enough for her chin to nearly hit her chest. For a moment she stood gawking at Deirdre, and had the moment not been so shocking, Maren would have been tempted to laugh. The two faced each other silently, Deirdre shaking slightly in her anger, and Líadan's face slowly recovered its color. Red began to creep up from her neckline to her forehead, until she looked as though she were about to explode. Without warning, she reached out to grab Deirdre by the throat with both hands.

Maren rushed forward as Deirdre fell to the floor, knocked off balance by Líadan's sudden forceful yank. Líadan pulled the girl close to her face and hissed at her. "If you ever, *ever* say such a thing to me again, you will dearly regret it, I promise you." Deirdre's face began to suffuse with blood, and her eyes bulged out, but she made not a sound. Maren was unsure if she should try to help, and stood shifting her weight from one foot to the other, her hands out in supplication as she yearned to reach forward to help Deirdre. She glanced out the open door; no one was walking by. Her mind raced; would Líadan actually manage to kill Deirdre right here, with Maren unable to help? If she did try to help, what punishment could she expect later? She moaned, completely at a loss.

Deirdre suddenly slumped under Líadan's grip, and Maren knew that she had lost consciousness. Surely Líadan would let her go now.

The nun's eyes were glazed over with fury, but she slowly released her grip from Deirdre's neck, and the girl dropped the rest of the way to the floor and lay in a heap in front of Líadan. The nun straightened up and shifted her gaze from the fallen girl to Maren, who stood uncertainly, wringing her hands. "Knickers down," she muttered, and Maren hurried to comply. She yanked her underclothes down and lifted her nightdress just enough to show the bulky cloth and belt, but Líadan stopped her before she could fumble with the hook enough to pull the belt off. "Go on back to your room, Miss Bradigan," she said, sounding suddenly weary. "Rest while you can."

Maren didn't wait another minute, but hurriedly pulled herself back together and exited the room, giving one last glance back at Deirdre. She ran down the hall and looked once more at the door. Sister Líadan was dragging Deirdre's limp body out by her hands when Maren rounded the corner to the stairway and lost sight of them.

Chapter Eleven

Having returned to her room immediately, Maren climbed back into her bed and fell into a deep, exhausted sleep. For the next three days she languished in the knowledge that she could sleep through the bell for Mass, dragging herself down the steps for breakfast before heading back to sleep again. Far from feeling refreshed, however, she felt troubled and restless. What had happened to Deirdre? Had she, also, been sent back to her room, or had she suffered the threatened punishment even above and beyond Líadan's malicious beating? Maren had never met the Father Conall that Líadan had mentioned, but could not fathom why Deirdre's being sent to him would constitute a harsh penalty.

      Before coming to the convent, where the girls were often sent to one of the varying priests who made their way through to take confessions, the only priest Maren had contact with had been Father Seanán, who had always been kind and understanding, if a bit gruff. Maren felt that she understood his reasoning for sending her here, and had found it in her heart to forgive him for his misunderstanding of the situation. Maren could not imagine that Father Seanán was even half aware of the disgraceful living conditions to which he had sentenced her; she could never again trust another priest if she felt he realized the extent of what he had done, and done it anyway. Regardless of her new, rebellious animosity toward the Catholic Church itself, Maren had recognized that not every person in service to the Church was mean-spirited. Sister Grania, though at times quick to temper, always softened her occasional harsh tones with a smile of recognizance, and would often place her warm hands upon the girls affectionately. The fact that these two, at least, truly believed that what they were doing was God's will mellowed Maren's anger toward her situation.

After her three days of laziness were up, Maren returned to work, scanning the crowds at Mass for a sign of Deirdre before heading in to breakfast. She was nowhere in sight, and Maren sighed as she went through the motions of eating, unable to keep herself from grimacing at the taste even after these long weeks in the convent.

Once in the laundry room, Maren automatically headed for her post, smiling briefly as Ceara gave a tentative wave from where she stood waiting to fill her washtub. She gently touched the tips of her fingers to her mouth, communicating in their silent language: *You okay?* Maren glanced around and nodded tightly, holding her right pinky in the air and slashing it quickly and subtly through the air. *Thanks.* It was good to know that Ceara was thinking about her and concerned for her welfare. She grasped the rusty iron handles of her tub and hefted it onto her hip, joining the line at the faucets.

The room, quiet but for the regular timbre of dripping water, slowly filled with a warm murmur as the girls began their prayers. The gentle slapping of water against metal and a hundred worn cloth garments swishing against themselves joined the chorus, and Maren easily fell into the rhythm she had become so used to. The girls kept their eyes down and stayed focused on their work, but slowly Maren became aware of someone's eyes on her. She lifted her head slightly and glanced to her left to see Deirdre watching her from the next row over, where she was industriously scrubbing. The other girl quickly looked away as Maren's eyes met hers.

Maren looked around the large room to make sure the nun on duty was not looking her way and surreptitiously examined Deirdre's face. Her eyes were swollen from crying, and patches of red on her cheeks marked where her blood vessels had broken from Líadan's harsh throttling a few days before. She had a large pile of laundry before her, and Maren was surprised to see dark red blood dried into a stain on the hem of a dress that Deirdre pulled from the mass. It was an internee's smock, very close to the one Maren herself now wore.

Deirdre averted her eyes from the garment and hastily pushed it under the water of her washbasin, choking back a sob and hastening on with the words of her prayers. Maren wondered whose dress it was, and where the blood had come from. Her eyes filled with tears at the melancholy look on Deirdre's face; the formerly strong and forthright girl had been broken into submission. *Why, God?* she questioned the One who had condemned her to this place. *Why have you allowed this to happen to us? Were we not good enough for you?*

No one is good enough, whispered a voice in her ear. She jerked her head upright and threw a glance around the room, searching for the source of the voice. A few of the girls stole confused looks at her as she stared at them, wondering which one of them had spoken, then returned their eyes to their work. None of these girls could have murmured the words; the voice she had heard had been decidedly masculine. Maren stood stock still, her back ramrod straight, and stared at a crack in the wall, her ears straining furiously for any sound of the voice repeating itself.

"God?" she chanced to whisper tentatively, softly enough so that the girls on either side of her didn't even turn their heads. Her hands had stopped their movement in the fast-cooling water, and her arms, covered with suds, trembled slightly. Something inside her pleaded for the voice to speak to her again, for God to make Himself known to her. The sound of the dripping pipes and the water rushing through them faded away, and the murmurs of the girls' prayers diminished until all Maren could hear was a slight hum. She stood transfixed for long moments, waiting for the voice, but it didn't come again.

Snapping out of her self-induced trance, she shook her head. *God wouldn't speak to me anyway,* she reprimanded herself, annoyed that she had been so hopeful. *I'm the wrong kind of girl, remember? Just like all of us here are. God has forsaken us and left us here to die. The only thing I'll hear from His voice is His laughter when I leave here for hell.* She straightened her arms and plunged her red hands back into the water, heaving a deep sigh before starting her prayer from the beginning.

"Our Father, who art in Heaven, hallowed be Thy name..." The hollow words drowned out her thoughts, and she worked relentlessly until it was time for dinner.

That evening, sleep did not come easily to Maren. In the half-light, as she lay staring at the cracking ceiling, Maren could hear Ceara talking in the softest whisper she could manage. Careful not to create any sounds that might interrupt her friend, Maren listened silently, trying to catch Ceara's words.

They were words of love, of hope and pain, and from her prone position under the thin blanket Maren heard the slight sweeping sound of Ceara's palm lightly brushing her swollen belly through the rough muslin of her nightgown. "Little baby..." she heard Ceara say. "I long to see you...to hold you in my arms...will it ever really happen?"

A tear fell onto the worn pillow beneath her cheek as Maren listened. What would it be like, she wondered, to carry a child inside oneself, never to know if its face would ever be seen? In her loneliness, she knew Ceara's pain, and longed for someone to talk to about it. Even though Ceara might never hold her child in her arms, at least she had this time with it. At least she had someone to talk to. Maren tried to hold back her sobs, but a slight sound escaped her as she made the effort to keep silent. Ceara heard her and turned toward the other bed, though she could not see its occupant.

"Cassán?" she whispered. "Is everything all right? Are you in pain?"

Maren couldn't speak, but the tenderness in Ceara's voice struck her with such a pang of longing for her mother's arms that she began to cry anew, releasing the sobs into the scratchy fabric of the uncovered pillow. Pulling the material of her blanket over her head, she let the tears wrack her body, still careful to keep quiet lest she attract the attention of the nuns. She heard Ceara slide off her bed, a soft thump as her feet hit the floor, and then a cool hand was on her face. "If you need to talk, I'm here," Ceara soothed quietly. Maren managed to get herself under control, and then turned to face the other girl. Ceara's features were barely visible, but Maren could see the gentle curve of a smile on her face.

"How can you stand it?" she managed, wiping the remaining tears off her cheek. "How can you still smile after what they're doing to you? Haven't you suffered enough? Now they might take away the only thing you've got left."

Ceara's smile faded slightly, but was replaced with a look of intensity as she leaned closer. "You listen to me, Cassán, my dear friend," she said urgently. "They have our bodies in their hands, but they will never have our souls. It is true that these fragile moments in the dark may be my last with this child, but do not ever think that I am all alone once my baby is taken from my body. My Lord has promised me that He will never leave me, nor forsake me, and that is the truth I am clinging to. *That is where I draw the strength to stand it when they work me so hard I bleed and worry that the child will slip from me at any moment. My body is ruined with the life I am living now, but my spirit is intact. They can never break me, for the God I serve is an infinite number of times stronger than the god in whose name they torture us. My soul is in His hands, and He has proven it to me time and time again in this prison.*" Her face was strained with the effort and force of her words, and Maren felt a timid sort of hope flare inside her heart as her friend continued. "He gave me the strength to love the baby inside me, regardless of how it was conceived. He has sustained me through the pregnancy in this place. And just when I thought I would die with the loneliness of it, He sent you here, and I found a friend."

Maren smiled distractedly at the kind words, but her thoughts were troubled. "I don't know, Maelisa; I find it so hard to believe in a God who would allow those who serve Him with all their hearts to be put in such a place. It just doesn't seem right. Neither of us did anything wrong, but He's punishing us anyway!" She placed a hand over her eyes and shook her head. "God is not fair. We don't deserve to be in this horrible place."

Ceara measured her words carefully before speaking. "We can't ever know what is in God's plan for us, Cassán, but we can know and believe that God *is* fair. The people who abuse others in God's name may have the power here on earth, but they will face judgment, just as you and I will. No one will escape the justness of His judgment. They will suffer for what they have done." Her voice held a note of sadness, and Maren sat up straight, glaring in Ceara's direction.

"You feel sorry for them! I can't believe that you would have pity for those—those—" Disgusted, she threw her hands up. "Maelisa, these people are evil. You can't mean to say that you feel *bad* over the fact that they will face judgment, can you? *We're* the good ones. *They're* the ones who will burn in hell." Suddenly the memory of the voice from earlier in the day swept through her mind: *No one is good enough.* She pushed the remembrance aside and focused on Ceara, who looked miserable. "I just don't understand how you can have pity on them when they are so full of sin."

Ceara reached forward and placed her hand over Maren's. "We are full of sin, too, Cassán. We're no better than they are."

"How can you say that?" Maren questioned angrily. "You didn't do anything wrong to get you here, just like I had nothing to confess when I took the Sacrament of Reconciliation. We're innocent, and yet we suffer."

"The Bible says that all mankind are sinners, and that for our sin we face eternity in hell. You ask me how I can have pity on them when they are so full of sin; well, it's easy for me. I just look at them and I see myself. I am a sinner, too, and yet Jesus took pity on me and loved me, and died so that I will not face that penalty for being human. He died for you, too, Maren, but you have to accept it." Her eyes were pleading.

Maren threw off her words. "I don't accept it, Maelisa. I'm not a sinner. I've done nothing wrong in my life. I was raised to be a good Catholic, and I followed the rules and took the sacraments and went to confession even when I had nothing to confess. I am *innocent*, and I don't belong here."

Filled with anger and confusion, she turned her back to Ceara. Tears flowed from her eyes. She wanted nothing more than to listen to what Ceara had to say, and yet something was holding her back from hearing the words. The resentment flew up from nowhere at Ceara's soft words. Maren couldn't understand what they meant, but they were a threat to the way she had always believed, and she couldn't face hearing any more. Ceara stood beside her bed for a few long moments as Maren waited in tense silence for her to give up, then padded slowly back to her bed. Maren waited until Ceara's breathing deepened before daring to whisper to her friend.

"Maelisa," she hissed softly, hoping that Ceara was asleep. "I think...I think God spoke to me today." She held her breath, fearing she had said too much, but there was no response from the other bed. Letting the air out of her lungs, she continued, emboldened by the thought that Ceara could not hear her. She simply needed to be able to talk about it, but she was terrified that if Ceara was awake, she would start in on another sermon. "He said to me, *No one is good enough*. I couldn't figure out what that meant." Maren stopped, thinking it over, imagining what Ceara would say to her if she were awake. "I guess it meant that no one is good enough to go to heaven. I guess you have to be pretty perfect to get there. But, it didn't feel like He was finished talking. It felt like...like there was something more to it."

Frustrated by her inability to sort out her thoughts, she found herself speaking slightly louder. "I waited and waited for Him to finish what He was saying, but...He didn't say anything more. I...I just wanted to hear the rest of the sentence...but I guess I never will." She squeezed her eyes shut tight against the confusion of her brain. "There's something there, though; I know there's something else He wanted to say." Maren sighed and leaned into her pillow, determined to put the predicament out of her brain. Forcing herself to think of other things, she settled in for sleep, counting sheep to help herself relax.

She had just begun to drift off when a small but clear voice came from the other bed. "I know the end of the sentence, Cassán," Ceara whispered. "He was saying to you: no one is good enough...*but I Am*."

Maren felt a slight pang in her heart at the words, but kept her eyes tightly closed.

Chapter Twelve

Maren dumped the sticky glop of oat porridge into her bowl and hurried over to the table where she had seen Deirdre seat herself. She had been worrying about the girl for weeks, and now determined to take the opportunity to attempt a whispered exchange. Deirdre sat silently, mechanically moving the spoon from her bowl to her mouth as Maren pulled out the chair next to her and sat down, placing the wooden bowl on the table with a small clunk. Deirdre jumped slightly at the sound and then slowly turned her big round eyes to Maren.

Wasting no time, Maren rushed into conversation. "Have you been all right, Deirdre?" she inquired, her eyes warily searching for any approaching nuns as she took a swallow of the lumpy oats. Deirdre nodded quickly.

"I've been fine, thank you," she muttered hastily into her bowl, not looking at Maren. She continued to eat in that strange, methodical way as Maren continued on.

"I've been worried about you, since last I saw you." Maren hesitated, feeling terrible asking Deirdre about such bad memories, but was concerned at the once vivacious girl's lack of life. Something horrible had happened to her, Maren felt sure, and she wanted to help console her if she could. "Did...did Líadan hurt you badly?" A flush crept out of Deirdre's collar and made its way up to suffuse the broken blood vessels in her cheeks.

"No, she didn't," Deirdre stated emotionlessly. "Thank you," she said again, standing and picking up her bowl as if to leave. Maren reached up to grasp her sleeve, and then noticed the dark stain on the hem of the back of Deirdre's shift. She couldn't hold back the gasp that flew from her mouth.

"Deirdre! What happened?"

Deirdre glanced back at her dress and immediately flung herself back into her seat. Reaching behind her, she pulled at the discolored fabric, rubbing her palms on it desperately. "I thought I got it all out," she said in a voice filled with alarm, her frightened eyes darting up at Maren's. "I thought I got it all out!" She continued scrubbing at the stain in an absolute panic. Yanking on the sleeve she still held, Maren managed to pull the upset girl down back into her chair before a nun came hurrying over to mete out discipline.

"It's okay, Deirdre," she reassured the girl, though she was fast becoming nearly as upset as Deirdre was. "Just tell me what happened. I saw you washing that bloodstain a while ago, but I didn't know it was your shift." She forced Deirdre to look into her eyes. "What happened to you?" She was determined that she would get the truth out of this girl, if only to help her confront her pain and bring back the strength and vigor Maren had noted in her that day in Líadan's office. "Please, Deirdre! I only want to help you, like you tried to help me."

Deirdre began to cry, hunching over the dark red edging of the dress she still clasped between her fingers. Leaning over, Maren reached down to touch the other girl's hair in a comforting manner. "They took me to Father Conall," Deirdre sobbed, leaning into Maren's arms. "They took me to Father Conall again..."

"Does he beat you?" Maren questioned, speaking quickly as she saw a black-clad figure across the room heading their way. The small scene in the corner of the room had received attention from the girls at the nearby tables, and the nun had noticed the slight commotion as a murmur of concern made its way through the room before the girls could silence themselves. Soon she would be upon them and take Deirdre, who was obviously the one causing the trouble, away. Perhaps both girls would receive a punishment. "Tell me, Deirdre! Does he beat you when they send you to him?"

The other girl was a trembling, sobbing mess in her arms. Deirdre shook her head violently, her matted red curls the only part of her visible in Maren's lap. "Noooo...." came her long, hoarse cry before Deirdre managed to get hold of her emotions. The slight hum of worried noise in the room became louder as the nun worked her way closer, edging her long black skirts around tables and chairs.

Deirdre, her head turned in Maren's lap, saw her coming and raised herself at once. She gripped Maren's arms and looked up at her, her eyes red and wet. "Don't let them send you to him, Cassán," she wept urgently. "He's the devil...he forced me to lay with him..." At Maren's sharp intake of breath, Deirdre's head fell back into her lap and she broke into fresh sobs. "It was my first time...I never had..." Her voice, muffled by Maren's smock, was full of anguish. "He used to make me do other things, before," she added suddenly, turning to one side to look up at Maren again with pain-filled eyes. "But I never thought he would... He's the one who got me sent here. He...he said I was a whore, but I never...I had never..."

"Come on, girl; up with you," came the nun's harsh voice, and Sister Daírine reached down to grab hold of Deirdre's hair in firm, strong fingers. Deirdre's head snapped back, and she came up from Maren's lap with a fierce howl. Maren, stunned at Deirdre's revelation, had the strength to do nothing but lean back in her chair in disbelief as Sister Daírine pulled and tugged a violently struggling Deirdre from the room. Every head in the dining hall turned as the two figures jerked their way out the door.

Maren suddenly became aware of a hand on her shoulder, and turned to see Ceara's solemn face, and that of little Amy MacCeallach, looking in concern over Ceara's shoulder. From the look on her face, Maren could tell that Ceara had heard everything.

"Come on," Ceara urged her friend, gently helping Maren to her feet. "Let's get to our work." She allowed herself to be kindly led from the room, but as the three girls turned to make their way down to the cavernous room at the end of the building, Deirdre's haunting cries followed her.

Maren made her way through the filling line in a daze, her thoughts focused only on Deirdre. How horrible it must have been for her, to have someone treat her like that! And by a priest, who was supposed to be God's messenger on earth. Maren couldn't fathom what it must have been like for the other girl. The image of the large, dark stain on the hem of Deirdre's smock confronted her even when her eyes were open.

"What will happen to her now?" she had hissed at Ceara as they entered the laundry room. A sudden wave of worry hit her as she realized that she might be responsible for Deirdre suffering an even worse punishment.

"You can't worry about her now," Ceara admonished, but her voice was weary and her tone dismal. "Let's just do our work and try to forget about it. We can't do anything about it now, Cassán," she added as Maren started to argue. "It's in the Lord's hands." She put a comforting hand on Maren's shoulder and they took their places in the room, Maren braced by the reassuring presence of Ceara on one side and sweet little Amy on the other.

At the beginning of each day, the wash water would be so hot that Maren's arms were instantly scalded, but after a mere two hours of work, it would be filthy and freezing cold. Maren usually looked forward to the hour after starting, when the water would be a pleasant warmth, but it never lasted long as the piles of dirty laundry were washed clean, taking the heat with them as they were laid aside to be brought to the drying lines.

She knew that soon it would be time for the wash water to be changed, bringing a welcome relief from the cold, but to plunge one's nearly frozen hands into water that had just come off a stove at its boiling point was to start the vicious cycle all over again. The nuns cared not how the girls' hands and arms looked after a long day of toiling; the important thing was that the laundry got completely clean. The girls were often reminded of how important it was to do their job well. After all, they were cautioned, if it weren't for the income that the laundry brought in, the girls wouldn't have a place to live. The thought of living outside the walls of the Laundries was a pleasant one for most of the girls and women who lived there, but what kept them dutifully washing clothes in the horrible temperature of the water was what the nuns in charge would do to them if they neglected their duties. Many of the women had been there for years, and what they had seen happen to those who did not do their job properly forced them to keep their hands in the water no matter what its temperature.

Maren's teeth chattered as she plunged her hands into the icy cold water, dragging the soiled garments across the washboard and trying not to shriek from the shock of it. Between clenched teeth she muttered her Hail Marys, trying desperately to keep from stuttering as her jaw inadvertently shook. She didn't dare look to either side, but she could hear Amy and Ceara reciting their prayers as well, their voices tired and stilted as they forced the words out from between chattering teeth. Every once in a while little Amy would get stuck on a word, and Maren would close her eyes and pray earnestly that the prayer would continue.

"Hail Muh-muh-muh—" came now from her left. *Please, let her finish it,* Maren pleaded silently—to whom, she knew not. She tried not to look up, but she could feel the presence of the nun who sat watching with squinted eyes, her back square against the tall wooden chair that had been placed at the end of the room. Although Maren was grateful that Amy had stayed close to her in order to lend her support on this difficult day, she knew how risky it was for the girl. Amy's placement at the wash basin at the far end of the long row had put her a little too close to the nun for comfort; her stuttering appeared now not only as a reaction to the extreme cold in the long room, but also in nervous response to the gray-faced, hard-edged woman whose ears picked up every mistake.

Maren, her breath catching in her throat from concern, knew exactly how worried Amy was. Her time in the Laundry had taught her that Sister Líadan was a harsh woman, and did not shirk from the dubious responsibility of punishing any girl who did not say her prayers correctly during the workday. Maren's breathing resumed in relief as Amy managed to make it through the first several words of the prayer, but a few moments later she was having difficulties again. "...Full of gruh-gruh-gruh..." Sister Líadan's black-draped head turned slightly in the direction of the three girls as they stood side-by-side. Noticing her slight movement, Amy took a deep breath and began again: "The Lord is wuh-wuh-wuh..." She gulped and her eyes darted toward Ceara as Sister Líadan slowly pushed herself up out of the chair and took a small step toward her. "The Luh-luh-luh..."

"My dear Miss MacCeallach," Sister Líadan began, her voice soft but hardened with a deadly edge. "May I make the assumption that you are *trying* to say your Hail Marys correctly?"

Amy shook slightly but nodded without looking up. "Yes, Sister. I—"

"—And may I also assume that you have a reason for such blatant annihilation of your prayer?"

Maren dared to sneak a look toward the smaller girl. Amy's cheeks were drawn of all color, her large blue eyes seeming huge in the whiteness of her face. She continued washing the laundry before her with determination, seeing the bluish tinge to Amy's hands, which worked automatically in the dirty water in front of her. The prayers tumbled from Maren's mouth with no thought, but she only had eyes for the scene before her. Amy's lips trembled as she tried to give the nun a reason for her stuttering. "Sister, I didn't mean to—"

Líadan cut her off once again, her voice rising in anger. "Of *course* you did not mean to make such a blasphemy of those holy words. You would *never* want to insult the Holy Mother in such a fashion, making a mockery of your petition to her. That is *not* what you were intending, was it, Miss MacCeallach?" Amy shook her head ferociously, then nearly stumbled as sudden dizziness almost caused her to pitch to one side. She put one small, reddened hand to her forehead and used the other to right herself with the washtub in front of her. For an instant, her thoughts were not on Sister Líadan, and she swayed slightly as she clutched onto the tub.

To Maren it seemed almost as though the people in front of her moved in slow motion, yet it all happened at once. Amy's knuckles on the sides of the tub were as white as her oval face as she struggled to maintain her footing. Her imbalance caused the tub to tip, just enough for some of the cold water it held to slosh over the side and deposit itself on Líadan's gray skirts. Líadan jumped back with a shriek, causing most of the heads around the room to swivel in her direction, although some of the more seasoned women did not look up from their washing. Amy was on the floor in an instant, cowering before the furious nun. Her pale face touched the floor, her hunched shoulders obscured by the long, greasy blond waves of her unwashed hair.

"Forgive me, Sister! I di-di-didn't muh-muh-muh—"

Líadan rose up ferociously, her right hand coming up to smack Amy with stinging vigour on her white cheek. Ceara reacted immediately. "No, Sister! Don't!" Before Maren's shocked eyes, Ceara grabbed for Sister Líadan's arm and pulled her away from Amy's cringing form. Líadan didn't move at first, her glittering eyes focusing on Ceara's face in complete disbelief. Regaining her composure after a long moment, she very deliberately pulled her forearm out of Ceara's grip and glared down on her trembling body. Maren noted with surprise that Ceara was trembling with anger, rather than fear. However, her hands instinctively went to her belly in order to protect the life within her, fluttering back to her sides after a brief moment.

"Is there a problem, Miss MacAodhagáin?" Sister Líadan asked icily, her gray eyes snapping at Ceara. "Do you *disapprove* of the manner in which I am about to discipline Miss MacCeallach?" The look on her face dared Ceara to say anything but apologetic words, humbling herself before the angry woman. Ceara refused to be intimidated.

"I do, Sister. She did nothing wrong." Ceara's back was straight as she faced the sister, her face calm and her hands at her sides. Maren could see the rage in her eyes, though, and wondered what in the world had snapped inside Ceara to set it free. Perhaps the scene in the dining hall had affected Ceara more than she had let on, and the new danger to Amy was the straw that broke the camel's back for Ceara.

Líadan nodded slowly, a dangerous look in her eyes. "And what gives you the right to make that judgment?"

Ceara's eyes flashed fire. "What gives *you* that right?" she demanded. "We are not animals, Líadan." The nun's eyebrows rose in annoyed surprise at the use of her name without the formal "Sister", but she folded her arms and listened to Ceara even as her words got stronger and angrier. "You cannot treat us like we are pigs in a stable, mindless and stupid and only following your orders because you dump some slops in front of us once or twice a day. How can you live with yourself?"

Maren couldn't believe what she was hearing. Ceara usually endured the daily torture and grind better than any of the other girls, never giving in to anger and always quietly admonishing them to keep things in perspective. Now she was confronting the nun with the worst reputation among the internees at Sacred Mercy. "*Maelisa!*" Maren hissed, hoping that Ceara would come to her senses and shut her mouth. Ceara ignored her, giving no sign that she had even heard, and continued to boldly face the nun.

Sister Líadan heard, and gave Maren a cold glance. "Better heed your friend, *Maelisa*," she said icily, stressing the secret name with distaste. Her countenance grew more scarlet with every word. "We wouldn't want anything to happen to your baby, now, would we? You'd better not let yourself get too worked up."

Ceara's mouth tightened and the tips of her ears reddened, but she stood straighter and faced Líadan bravely. "I will be fine," she murmured tightly.

"You think so?" Líadan snapped. "I don't know, Miss MacAodhagáin. I don't know if that little body of yours could take much more punishment." She let her eyes trail down the length of Ceara's small frame to the burgeoning silhouette of her belly and gave a small, sarcastic smile. "Although I imagine any punishment *I* could give you might not have much effect. From the looks of you, it seems as though you may have a taste for doing damage to your own body."

Maren gasped as Ceara's arm shot out toward the nun's face almost before she could form a thought. Sister Líadan reached out and caught Ceara's fist a fraction before it would have connected with the side of her head, bringing it down in a vicious twist that made Ceara cry out in surprise and pain. Her voice was as tight with anger as was her face. "Don't ever make the mistake of talking back to your superiors, missy," she whispered harshly as she pulled Ceara's arm down behind her back and held it against the waist of her dress. Maren's eyes watered as she watched her friend bravely endure what must certainly have been a dreadful pain; Ceara's eyes squinted and her mouth tightened as she tried to keep from crying out.

Sister Líadan's free hand was snaking down the gray front of her dress into a hidden pocket, and Maren's eyes traveled down unwillingly to see what she was bringing forth. Her breath caught as she saw the broken-off stump of an old-fashioned long-stemmed hairbrush emerge from the folds of the skirt. The bristles had been snapped off to create a weapon of the handle that remained. Jagged pieces of wood stood out from where Líadan was gripping it, and slivers flew through the air as she swiftly brought it around to connect with Ceara's shoulder with a sharp cracking sound.

Ceara screamed in pain and tried to jerk away, but the angry nun hit her again and again on her right side with the end of the brush handle as her other hand pinned the girl in place. Maren's eyes filled with tears, but her feet felt frozen to the floor as the beating continued. Ceara was crying bitterly now, and while Maren longed to rush forward and snatch the brush handle away from Líadan, to protect her poor friend from the vicious onslaught, the scene had taken on an unreal feeling for her. After the overwhelming revelation from Deirdre that morning, the shock of seeing her best friend being beaten right before her eyes was too much to take in.

She closed her eyes tightly and willed herself away from the horrifying reality of the moment. For an instant she was back in her own little room in the farmhouse, sitting in front of the little mirror where she usually fixed her hair, and humming to herself as she tied her long curls back with a silky ribbon. *This is where I belong,* she thought to herself. *No one can harm me here.* She tried to fade into the picture of home, feeling the brush sliding through her hair and sighing at the wonder of being able to reach the ends without getting tangled in the knots that covered her head. She allowed a small smile to play along her lips, and unconsciously reached up to touch the smoothness of her hair. Faolán would be just outside, she knew, and she wanted to look her best for him. *Nothing is wrong here. This is where I want to stay.*

A sudden shriek brought her back to the present. Ceara had managed to pull away from Sister Líadan and was running down the length of the washbasins, searching for escape. Líadan, tight-lipped with anger and determination, strode after her with long gliding movements, bringing the brush handle down on whatever part of Ceara's body she could reach. Ceara tried to run faster, lurching the bulk of her heavy belly past all the women who stood watching openmouthed, but she could never quite get out of Líadan's reach. The nun whacked her once on the head before she could scramble away, following her incessantly around the room, hitting Ceara again in the shoulder, then on the side of her face. Maren's mind raced disbelievingly as she observed the scene before her; she could not remember having seen Ceara lose her dignity, to respond to the nuns' cruelty with tears.

At this moment, she felt as though she were observing the impossible; Ceara's eyes were streaming with tears as she struggled to stay out of Líadan's way, the skin around her left eye already turning purplish-black. Maren knew she should do something to help her friend, but in her confusion she stayed put, realizing somewhere inside the turbulence of her mind that all she could do was make the nun angrier and cause more hurt to Ceara, or to herself. She simply stood as the other girls did, watching and crying on the inside, her heart breaking as she observed Ceara's agony, and wishing above all else that she could escape this horrible place and bring Ceara with her.

Ceara finally collapsed in an exhausted, shivering heap near the opposite end of the room from where Maren stood. She lay face down, unmoving, her dark hair lying in bloody, matted tangles around her face. With Ceara finally in one spot, the nun continued her assault, beating every inch of Ceara's body that faced her. She stood with her feet planted squarely on either side of the unconscious girl, bringing her weapon down harder and harder on whatever was presented to her. Several small trickles of blood ran out from under Ceara's hair, and a few spots of dark red began to grow on the gray dress she wore. Maren stood in shock, unsure if Ceara was even alive. The only movement she could see was the slight jerking of her body when the brush handle hit a nerve. Sister Liadan's swift movements in her attack obscured Maren's vision enough to make it impossible to see if Ceara was even breathing.

Finally Liadan straightened up, her chest heaving. For a breathless moment her eyes centered on the still heap that was Ceara, and then she looked slowly around the room as if seeing it for the first time. Every hand immediately plunged back into the basins, and every eye focused on what laundry was before them. Several girls began their Hail Marys again, and Liadan's eyes narrowed. She straightened rigidly and gave the room a stare that encompassed all the girls within.

"She is not dead," she stated calmly. Maren sighed with relief, but she was filled with a deep underlying disgust that the announcement was even necessary. She was sure that if Liadan's beating had ended Ceara's life, the woman would state the fact of her death just as emotionlessly. "She will be all right. But let that be a lesson to all of you—you are here to do God's work. In this institution, anyone who disobeys or counteracts the Lord's will must answer to His wrath. And sometimes—" She gave Ceara's motionless form another look, shaking her head ruefully. "Sometimes, His wrath is overwhelming. I do not want to have to execute the Lord's judgment on any other one of you. So, heed His command, do your work diligently and properly, and remember your place."

With one last commanding glare accompanying her ominous words, she stepped delicately over Ceara's body and crossed the room to sit down once again in the stiff ladder-back chair.

Chapter Thirteen

The last few days had been difficult for both the girls. Ceara lay on the thin pallet day and night, often unattended by the nuns. Sister Grania stopped in occasionally to check on Ceara's physical state, sometimes cooing soft songs at her as she stroked her hair and rebandaged her wounds, but no other nun darkened her door unless it was to bring a tray of food too tough for her bruised jaw to chew.

Ceara hadn't eaten since her beating three days earlier, and before Maren's eyes she seemed to be wasting away. Even the large roundness of her belly seemed to have shrunk, until Ceara looked as though she had months left instead of a mere week or two. Maren spent long days in agony as she worked and prayed, her thoughts on the still form of her friend back in the room they shared. The instant she was released from her duties in the laundry room, she would hurry down the hall and up the three flights of concrete stairs to their room to see how Ceara had fared in her absence. Usually she would find Ceara asleep, the blanket pulled up to her chin, the meager light in the room accentuating the dark shadows under the pale girl's eyes. Forgetting her own exhaustion, Maren would sit with her friend until she awakened, and then they would spend a few minutes in soft conversation until Ceara dropped off again.

At first Maren had worried about how much Ceara seemed to sleep, but then reflected that the extra rest was probably just what she needed. Apart from the lack of appetite Ceara suffered from, it was apparent that Líadan's beating had been a blessing in disguise for her. She was getting the sleep she had been deprived of for the past few months, when she had needed it the most, and if she had been able to eat Maren wouldn't have fretted about her in the least.

Her wounds were healing nicely, and would soon be completely unnoticeable apart from a large cut underneath the front length of her dark hair, which the nuns had not thought was necessary to be stitched. It broke open often, as she occasionally tossed her head on the pillow, and her long hair would be pinned beneath her shoulder and pulled hard on the roots of her hair and her scalp, tearing the barely healed skin. If Maren found it bleeding again down the side of Ceara's head and soaking the rough pillow, she would clean it up as best she could with her meager supplies, sometimes tearing a small strip from the bottom of her nightgown and using it to tie a semblance of a tourniquet tightly around the wound. It looked as though it was healing, but Maren found herself despairing as Ceara lost more blood every day.

If only she would eat, she thought to herself, but Ceara was barely conscious long enough to give Maren more than a sweet, tired smile and words of thankfulness for her help. Whenever she stayed awake for longer than that, she said she had no appetite. "I would rather just talk a little bit," she would say softly, her eyes begging Maren to tell her something hopeful. Maren told her of how her day had passed, trying to find humor in the tediousness of life in the Laundries. She knew that whatever she said was appreciated by the girl on the narrow bed, and she herself found hope in Ceara's unfailing trust in God and His ability to help her get through the pain and the sorrow of her life.

The fourth day after Líadan's beating, after a long, hard day of work and a meager ration of supper, Maren found herself climbing the stairs with less vigor than usual. Sister Líadan had instructed her to inform Ceara that she would be allowed only one more day of bed rest before she was ordered back to work. Maren's heart had fallen at the news, but she nodded mutely and made her way back up to the girls' room. *How can she go back to work?* she fretted. *If only she would eat. Maybe she could bring some of her strength back in time to start working again if she stayed awake longer and filled herself with good food.* She didn't try to think of where Ceara would get such wholesome food; she knew the trays the sisters left twice a day were not nutritious enough to nurture Ceara back to health in such a short time. She just knew that she needed to do something to help her friend.

When she walked into the room, the door scraping across the rough concrete floor and shutting with a quiet click behind her, she could see the outline of Ceara's shape lying beneath two blankets, her own and the one from Maren's bed. She smiled to herself. So Grania had been there to see to her, and left a tray of food as well. She moved on careful feet over to where the tray sat on a small wooden bedside table and looked over the food with distaste. The food was all right for some of the stronger girls, but Maren couldn't believe that anyone who had been through what Ceara was going through would be helped by it in the least. Maren sighed in frustration, placed her hands on her hips and shook her head disgustedly.

Ceara shifted on the small bed and turned toward the slight sound. She smiled as she looked up at Maren's indignant figure. "What is it?" she whispered, one hand stretching up to push her bangs out of her eyes. She winced in pain as the dried blood on her hair pulled away from her skin, but continued looking up at Maren as she stood staring down at the pitiful display of food.

"Won't you at least try eating some of this, Maelisa?" she asked quietly, gesturing slightly toward the tray. Ceara's gaze moved down and her smile faltered.

"It—doesn't look very good, does it, Cassán?"

Maren gave a small, regretful smile. "No, Maelisa, I suppose it doesn't, but it would be better than nothing. You should at least try to see if you could manage to get it down." She contemplated her options, then spoke hesitantly. "Is…is there anything you feel you could eat?"

It was plain to see that Ceara was too tired to fully comprehend the meaning behind her question. She rolled her head slowly back to her friend and answered thoughtfully. "I would…really like some…soup." She gave a weak grin and licked her dry lips. "Mother used to make me a wonderful soup when I was sick…all vegetables and potatoes, with big chunks of chicken…I loved it." Her smile grew stronger as the memories drifted across her mind. "I always felt better when I had some of that soup, no matter how sick I was."

Maren gave her friend an answering grin. "I'll see what I can do, Maelisa." She took another look at the tray before heading back to the door. Ceara stopped her before she could open it.

"Cassán—what are you going to do?" Her weak voice was tinged with worry, and she reached out a trembling hand as if to prevent her from leaving. Maren tried to reassure her with a careless wave of her hand.

"Don't worry about me. I'm just going to see if I can find you some of that soup you need so badly." It was on the tip of her tongue to tell Ceara that she would be required back at work in the laundry in one short day's time, but she held back. It would not do Ceara any good to spend the next day worrying about how she was going to get her strength back. *No, I'll do that worrying for her*, Maren determined. She forced another casual expression to cover up the concern on her features. "Maybe Sister Grania is about. I'll tell her that you can't eat this food; she might help me find something a little easier on the palate. Not to mention that sore jaw of yours," she added with a twinkle in her eye. Ceara nodded, but the troubled look did not leave her face. Maren gave her a thumbs-up and opened the heavy wooden door, pulling it quietly shut behind her.

Once in the hallway, she gave a great sigh, partly of relief and partly of determination. Ceara could read her too easily, she knew, and she hadn't wanted to worry her any more than she already was. The poor girl had enough to deal with at the moment. The only thing Maren needed to concern herself with now was to find some way to get the proper sustenance into Ceara's wasting body.

She crept down the silent hallway, holding her breath without even realizing she was doing so. When she reached the landing of the steep stairwell, she glanced around to make sure all the doors in the hall were closed, then pressed herself tightly against the wall and made her way slowly down the first flight of stairs. There was no worry about the concrete creaking beneath her feet the way wooden boards would have, but she remained cautious and stealthy, bracing her arms and back against the wall and ready to press herself into the plaster and hide in an alcove if she heard a sound.

She had two more runs of stairs to get down, and the danger of encountering a nun was great here in the narrow stairwell. If she did happen to meet one of the sisters, she would find herself in a great deal of trouble. None of the girls were allowed out of their rooms past nine o'clock at night, when the rooms were all dark and everyone was expected to go straight to sleep. Most of the girls did fall into an exhausted slumber as soon as they went back to their rooms, so Maren was not worried that someone who would run to find a nun might hear her, but she knew that the women who ran the institution often stayed up later than the internees did. Of course, they were not as completely fatigued as the girls who worked hard all day, so they wouldn't find it necessary to sleep as soon as their young charges did. Maren kept her breathing quiet and her fingers crossed that she might have the luck not to be caught heading toward the forbidden section of the convent, where the kitchen was located.

Maren herself had never seen the kitchen, but she knew the direction the cook headed after serving up the many bowls of porridge every morning as the girls lined up at the long dining hall tables. It couldn't be very far from the dining hall, she reasoned, else the cook would grumble far more than she did about the distance the porridge had to travel once it left the cook pot. She had reached the bottom landing of the last run of stairs now, and she crept hesitantly to the door and peeked around it.

The hall was clear. She let out a loud, fluttering breath before she realized she had been holding it, and stood there for a moment—relieved, but still tensed for conflict. Giving a quick glance to either side of her, she dashed across the empty corridor and headed for the dining hall. Slipping inside the heavy double doors, she pulled herself into a corner, looking momentarily at the long rows of tables, now swept clean of the clutter they had held earlier in the day. To her left she heard the clink of the supper dishes being cleaned up, and shrank back against the stone until she could decipher where the sound was coming from.

Recently washed plates and saucers sat stacked in a neat heap at the end of a table situated near to her hiding spot, and her fleeting look revealed a small swinging door situated behind a wall hanging. The tapestry was drawn back enough to allow the kitchen workers free access with their piles of chipped china plates, and as Maren leaned slightly further forward, she could see a sliver of the light from the kitchen. The old cook moved surprisingly smoothly and quietly for someone with her bulk, muttering to herself as she thrust pudgy hands beneath the freshly billowing suds in the sink. The familiar, homey sound of dishes being washed and stacked to dry reminded Maren suddenly and violently of her mother, so much so that she pressed her palms to her mouth in order to keep back the unexpected sob that rose in her throat.

She moved slowly toward the door, keeping watch for one of the young novices who might come to retrieve the last load of dishes from the table, and found herself a hiding place among the folds of the wall hanging. For a moment she crouched in the privacy of the scratchy needlepoint, waiting for a chance to sneak into the kitchen without being noticed. She could still hear the old cook rattling around, wiping down the countertops and cooking implements with long, smooth swiping motions, but soon the noises quieted and she heard the swish of the elderly woman's skirts as she made her way out of the kitchen. With a small click a door on the other side of the kitchen closed, and Maren dared to peek out from behind the tapestry.

The way seemed clear. She looked around hurriedly and darted into the large, clean-smelling room, keeping her feet quiet and her skirts pulled tight around her legs in order not to knock anything over that might attract unwanted attention.

The kitchen sparkled with its recent cleaning, but the lemony scent that filled the air didn't do much to cover the smell of food. Her stomach growled as she caught the aroma of a heavy beef stock, and her twitching nose soon drew her eyes to a spot across the room. A large cast-iron stock pot stood simmering on the counter where it had recently been removed from the stove, a long wooden spoon standing in it. Her stomach felt ready to fold in on itself, she was so hungry, but she forced her mind and her belly to quiet as she concentrated on her reason for being here. *Maelisa needs to eat, not me,* she cautioned herself. *Don't let your desires get the best of you now, when you're so close.* She glanced once more around the large room before tiptoeing across to the pot.

It was more than half empty, but there still remained a portion large enough for several people. The soup seemed to be exactly what Ceara needed. Substantial chunks of potatoes and carrots floated in a thick broth, almost the consistency of gravy, and she could detect the faint tang of onions. Maren reached for the spoon and drew it through the soup, watching eagerly as large pieces of beef and onion swirled up from where they had rested on the pot's bottom. Her mouth watered. This was certainly not the kind of food she and the other internees were given for their meals; it must be for the nuns. Shaking her head in amazement that they had left some—she could have devoured the whole pot alone, the way she felt now—she cast her eyes around for some sort of container to spoon the soup into.

A stack of clean china bowls stood on a nearby counter. Maren hurried over to grab the deepest one she could find, and ran back cautiously, her head constantly moving back and forth and her eyes always watchful. No one was in sight.

She dipped the spoon into the soup and swirled it around the pot again, unable to resist watching the heavier chunks of meat and vegetables moving up once more through the deep brown stock. With a sigh of desire, she pulled up a large spoonful and emptied it carefully into the deep china bowl. The steam from the soup caressed her nostrils, causing another subterranean growl to erupt from her belly. Pressing a hand to the front of her smock, she muttered a short "Stop that!" before continuing to pour the soup into the dish.

When the bowl was nearly full, but with space enough left not to spill as she walked up the stairs, she replaced the spoon in the pot and left the soup with a regretful sigh.

She had made three steps across the shiny, scuffed floor when a loud voice suddenly spoke behind her.

"So, Miss Bradigan, you have taken to stealing from us now."

Maren nearly fell in her shock, just barely managing to keep the bowl from emptying onto the tiles. A drop of hot soup landed on her left hand, and she let go of the rim quickly to lick the brown gravy off her thumb, steadying the full bowl with her other hand. The taste of the beef stock nearly caused her to moan, it was so delicious, but she forced herself to stop thinking about it and turned around slowly.

She almost groaned as her eyes fell on the tall, thin nun, who stood with her long arms crossed and a frown on her narrow face. Of all people, it would have to be Sister Líadan who caught her here in the kitchen. She could not say a word, only stood speechlessly and waited. Maren was sure that her face had drained of color, and by the satisfied look that crossed Líadan's face, she must have been right.

"Did you not get enough dinner for yourself today, Miss Bradigan, or do I dare make a guess that you are robbing from us in order to feed your young friend upstairs?" Maren flushed and opened her mouth, but Líadan cut her off. "—I see. Well, now. It's not really a surprise, I suppose." With a sigh she uncrossed her arms and leaned casually on the counter, the seemingly relaxed pose very much at odds with the dangerous gleam in her eyes. "I really don't know what to do with you, young woman. Here we take you in—when we really couldn't afford it, you know—and offer to help you out of your...shall we say...*dangerous* situation at home, and how do you repay us? By stealing from us and going against strict orders!" She shook her head. Her silent reproving look was chilling; Maren never knew how the woman would react. Sometimes she wished that Líadan would simply start yelling, but the cool calm was often much more worrisome. Maren knew that she was in deep trouble.

Líadan strode over to where Maren stood frozen and reached out with both hands to remove the steaming bowl from her trembling fingers. Maren was too frightened to even give the soup a wistful glance as Líadan placed it on the counter and folded a hand around one of Maren's arms to pull her away from the kitchen in a death grip. Maren had to run to keep up with the woman's long strides, and found herself all but pulled across the kitchen. The fat old cook wandered in, giving Maren a surprised look as they strode by, and then dashed across to the soup pot to set any disturbance to rights.

They reached the other side of the kitchen, and with the hand that was not keeping Maren's arm in a firm grip, Líadan yanked open a drawer and withdrew something from it. Maren couldn't see what it was, for in an instant Líadan had thrown her down on the floor and pushed her into a prone position on her stomach, yanking out the string Maren used to pull back her curls. Maren flinched but said nothing, sure that any words would only make Líadan angrier. The old cook watched warily as she cleaned up the bowl with Ceara's precious soup in it, dumping it down the sink and washing it, chunks and all, down the large drain. She was careful not to interfere but stared at the two of them, a worried light in her eye as she looked at Líadan.

The nun pulled both Maren's hands behind her back and tied them with the string, taking no care with Maren's arms, the muscles already aching from all the washing she had done that day. Maren's eyes closed in pain, but she refused to allow herself to cry out. Her mind raced, worrying only that Líadan would blame Ceara for Maren's misconduct and hurt the other girl even more. The consideration that Líadan might beat her as badly as she had hurt Ceara flickered briefly through her thoughts, but she dismissed it quickly and squeezed her eyes shut tight. As long as Líadan centered her punishment on Maren's crime, it would be okay. Her only worry was that Ceara would be hurt worse than she already had been, so as long as she could keep Sister Líadan's anger focused on her, any punishment would be tolerable. Maren just couldn't stand the thought of anything else happening to Ceara.

She shrieked in sudden pain as Líadan grabbed a handful of her thick, fair hair and dragged it back over her shoulders into a semblance of a ponytail. Maren's eyes watered as Líadan's strong fingers pulled at the roots, and her scalp prickled at the sudden tension. What was she going to do?

Then Maren felt the sensation of something sawing across her hair, close to her neck. She could still feel the length of her hair resting in the middle of her back, but it felt looser, and she gasped as she realized that Líadan was cutting her hair off nearly to her chin. Twisting to see what the woman was using, she ignored the soreness on her scalp until Líadan gave her hair an extra yank in reprimand. She cried out in pain and turned around again, putting her face to the floor and wishing she could bury it in her hands. In that brief moment, she had seen Sister Líadan's instrument of punishment: a long-handled bread knife. It sawed back and forth across her hair until the tension let go, first on the left where the knife had finished sawing through its thickness, and then slowly across to the right side of her head. The reassuring weight of her hair on her back was gone in an instant, and her head snapped forward as the last few hairs were cut through and the pull of Líadan's fingers on her head released.

She stayed with her face to the floor, trying not to cry and not looking up at the woman next to her. Her hair. Her beautiful, long hair, the reason her father called her "Cassán" and her crowning glory since she was four, was gone. Líadan smirked.

"Sit up," she commanded. Squeezing her eyes shut tight, Maren tried with difficulty to do as she was told. Her hands were still bound behind her back, and she used them as leverage as she rolled onto her side and forced herself into a half-sitting pose. She nearly cried again as she realized she had half-expected to feel her hair settling around her shoulders as she moved back into a vertical position. "Open your eyes, girl."

Maren shook her head. "Please..." she whimpered, realizing it was the first thing she had said since Sister Líadan had caught her in the kitchen. "I can't."

"Open them!"

Dreading the sight of her hair in Líadan's hands, she did as she was told. Líadan stood with a triumphant look on her face, but Maren's hair was nowhere in sight. Ignoring the throbbing skin on her head, she glanced around quickly but did not see any evidence of what had just happened. The bread knife was either in the sink or back in the drawer, for it was closed. The cook must have gone, for she didn't see her anywhere either. Sister Líadan allowed her a moment to look around before speaking again.

"And now, Miss Bradigan, you will return to your room. You will tell your little friend that you were unsuccessful in your theft, and if anyone asks what happened to your hair, you will remind her of the price of disobedience. I did not think you were as strong-willed as Miss MacAodhagáin, but you have proven me wrong. Just remember, though...the next time you are in defiance of the rules, you no longer have any hair to be cut. We will have to think of a different punishment, and I don't think you can quite handle that for a while."

She reached into an apron pocket that Maren had not noticed was bulging, and pulled out a handful of long, blond curls. Maren's throat caught as Líadan tossed the hair at her chest, and tears rolled down her cheeks as it settled into a glowing heap on her lap. Líadan ripped the string from her wrists in a painful movement. "Toss that into the fire on your way back upstairs, and stay for a moment to watch it burn. Reflect on the punishment for stealing, and remember that in Hell it's not just your hair that burns." She gave Maren one last, inflexible look before striding out of the kitchen and down the hall. As Maren listened to her hard-soled shoes clicking down the stone corridor, she wondered vaguely why she hadn't heard them before Líadan had surprised her in the kitchen.

Pushing herself painfully to her feet, she gathered the mass of hair in her hands and stumbled out through the doorway and past the tapestry she had concealed herself behind. The hair in her hands was soft though unwashed, and Maren found herself crying into it as she made her way back down the hall to the large common room where the nuns often gathered in the evening. Every night for as long as she could remember before coming to the Laundries, she had sat before the mirror in her room and brushed her waist-length hair with drawn-out, firm strokes. She couldn't recall a time when she hadn't seen a reflection with long, curly hair, and it was all she could do to keep herself from reaching up to touch the shortness of her hair at the nape of her neck. Her back seemed vulnerable, unprotected, and she hunched her shoulders until she could feel the ragged strands touching the collar of her dress. The cool air no longer whispered against her neck, but she still felt naked.

Dazed, she wandered into the room, passing the nuns without a look or a comment. Several jumped up to chastise her, but Líadan's entrance one moment behind hers gave them pause, and her tight-lipped nod settled them back into their chairs. Maren walked to the large stone fireplace that dominated the room, stood for a brief moment, and then deliberately tossed the lengths of golden hair into the fire. She could not watch them, however, and stood with her back to the roomful of nuns and her eyes tightly closed, knowing that Sister Líadan could not know they were not open. Tears ran down her cheeks, and almost against her will, one of her hands snaked up to touch the few straggly hairs that barely touched her neck. She heard an echo of her father's voice as she burst into renewed sobs: *"My Cassán...my little curly-haired one...you will break many a man's heart with that hair of yours."*

She stood with her face buried in her hands for a long time as the nuns observed, many with blank looks, but Sister Líadan stood erect and watched her with a satisfied expression on her face before striding back out into the hallway.

Chapter Fourteen

Maren dragged herself back up the stone stairs to the room she had shared with Ceara these past months, her steps interrupted by occasional bursts of weeping. She leaned against the hard stone wall and sobbed with her palms bracing her face, her heart crying out desperately for her mother and father. *Why am I here?* she thought angrily once again. *How could any God allow this to happen to His people, the people He claims to love? We serve Him, day after day, doing **everything** just to please Him, and where does it get us? Death and pain, that's all.* Her hands dropped to her sides resignedly and she stared off into space, the short wisps of hair around her face clinging to her wet cheeks. *Death and pain.*

For a long moment she rested against the wall, gazing blankly, dreading having to face Ceara. *I failed her,* she told herself. *All she wanted was something to eat, and I had the power to do that for her. If only I hadn't let myself smell it! I allowed myself to get distracted. That's the only reason Líadan caught me. I'm stupid, stupid, stupid!* The image of Ceara, her eyes glowing as she spotted the full bowl of soup in Maren's hands, danced in front of her eyes, teasing her. Tears welled up in her eyes. *I'm so stupid.*

Resolutely, she plodded back up the stairs, wiping the hot tears from her cheeks and making her way to their room.

Ceara looked up with a glowing smile as Maren pushed open the heavy door. Feeling almost naked, Maren hid behind the door and held it open with one hand as she entered, pushing her remaining hair behind her head in a mock ponytail that she held with both hands as soon as she had made her way into the room. She used her hips to push the door closed and stayed in the shadows as much as possible, unwilling to let Ceara see what Líadan had done to her hair. "Thank you for going, Cassán," Ceara said gratefully, and gestured to the small table tray that lay across her lap. "Sister Líadan said that I should be very thankful to have a friend who is so concerned about me, and she's right." Her eyes sparkled, and she looked better than she had in days.

Maren looked down at the tray and gasped, her hands falling from behind her head in disbelief. A large crockery bowl was precariously balanced on the tray's surface, and Ceara clutched a round soup spoon in her hand. She looked immensely satisfied as she lifted the big bowl to her lips and drained the last few drops of soup. "Ahhh..." she sighed happily as she set the bowl back down, and looked back at Maren with a contented smile that rapidly changed to a look of shock as she noticed the scraggly blond strands framing Maren's face. "Cassán! What...what happened to your hair?" Her mouth had dropped open in surprise, and Maren felt tears gather in the corners of her eyes once again. Speechless, she moved forward and lay down on her bed, turning her face away from Ceara so that she wouldn't have to see her friend's alarm.

"Líadan...brought you soup?" she managed, her voice breaking. Ceara shifted on the bed, and Maren heard a soft clunk as she placed the tray on the floor. Then she was there beside her, a soft hand on Maren's back, moving slowly up to touch her hair. "Don't," Maren warned abruptly in a thick voice. "Please, don't touch it." She had to close her eyes tightly at the thought of having to explain to Ceara what had happened.

"She brought me a huge bowl of soup and a wonderful, thick slice of white bread with butter," Ceara answered softly, distress in her voice. "She told me to thank you...for your sacrifice for me." She started to cry and laid her forehead against Maren's back. "I thought she meant...to thank you for having the courage to ask her for food for me. I never dreamed..." She faltered and was silent for a moment. Maren could feel the other girl's tears on her back, warm and wet. It was a strange sort of comfort to her. When Ceara spoke again, she put a hand on Maren's shoulder in order to bring her down onto her back. "Cassán." Maren resisted her touch momentarily, but then allowed Ceara to pull her shoulder down onto the bed so that she lay flat, staring at her friend's teary face with unblinking eyes. "Please tell me what happened."

"You know what happened," Maren responded flatly. "She's killing us all, Maelisa. All I wanted to do was help, but she couldn't let me do that. She had to humiliate me and belittle me as much as possible." She refused to cry, and instead forced herself to think of Anya, the beautiful girl whose head had been shaved because she was a temptation to men. "Anya never cried," she stated decisively, "so I won't either." She was rewarded with a smile from Ceara.

Reaching forward hesitantly, Ceara ran her fingers through the uneven ends of Maren's hair. "I don't think this would be so bad if we trimmed it up a little," she declared. "Your hair is curly enough that if we just evened out the ends, it would bounce right back into shape." She studied Maren's hair critically, tilting her head slightly and narrowing her eyes. "It actually looks kind of cute!"

Maren allowed herself a short laugh as Ceara straightened up and moved slowly to the old wooden dresser that stood across the room. It was never used, since each girl was only provided with one shift to wear during the day and a nightdress for sleeping, but when she had first moved in Ceara had taken the time to look through the drawers anyway, searching for something of value. She headed immediately for the bottom drawer and triumphantly held up a pair of dull-looking, rusty scissors. "Aha!" she proclaimed, coming back to Maren's side. She helped Maren to a sitting position.

"Now, wait a second, Maelisa. I think this hair has seen enough cutting today," she objected, trying to avoid the scissors. Ceara waved her protesting hand away and stood behind her.

"Now whatever you do, don't move!" She grinned at Maren, who put down her hands, and delicately trimmed the longer ends of her hair. "There! Easy as pie, and no harm done. You can use your hair ribbon to pull the front back a bit, and you'll be the envy of all the girls down there." Maren smiled at Ceara's exuberance and watched as she waddled back across the room to replace the scissors in the bottom drawer of the dresser. Reaching up to delicately touch her hair, Maren felt the urge to cry well up inside her once again, but she stifled it as Ceara's expectant, encouraging face came toward her.

She reached up to give Ceara a hug, feeling gratefulness flow through her for the love and caring that she exuded. "Thank you, Maelisa," she whispered, squeezing her friend tightly. "You're the best friend in the world."

Ceara hugged her back, saying softly, "Thank *you*, Cassán."

There were no questions from any of the girls who saw her hair the next day, and Maren soon forgot all about it in the routine of the day. To these girls, it was not news to see someone who had been changed in appearance by the nuns, and it was not considered important. Survival was the only important thing in the Laundries.

Maren quietly thanked God for Ceara's understanding and help on the day Líadan had cut her hair. Her thoughtfulness and love helped Maren to realize that her hair was not important in the scheme of things, and that it would, eventually, grow back and be even more lustrous than ever. After a few days of work, Maren realized that the shorter hair was actually an asset while she worked in the laundry room; it no longer fell in the dirty wash water and soaked her shift when she tossed it back, and as the days grew cooler, the short cap of curls hugged her head and kept her warmer than she had been when the weight of her hair had pulled it down.

Deirdre had not been seen nor heard from since the episode in the dining hall, and so Maren's ears perked up three weeks after the incident when she heard Deirdre's name being mentioned at the next table at dinner. She leaned back surreptitiously and whispered, "What's this about Deirdre?"

The small brunette sitting in the chair behind hers hissed back timidly, "She's been caught out. Pregnant. The nuns figure she must have been sneaking out somehow." The message delivered, the little girl quickly leaned forward over her plate.

Rage filled Maren, and her cheeks turned red. She reached back to tug at the little girl's sleeve. "But don't they know about Father Conall?"

The girl barely turned, but said out of the side of her mouth, "Everyone knows about Father Conall. That doesn't mean they'll admit it. Deirdre will catch all the blame and he will go on doing what he's always done."

Another girl from Maren's table added softly, "There's more than one girl in this place that's delivered one of his babies."

Tears pricked at Maren's lids. *Poor Deirdre*, she thought painfully. *Poor, poor Deirdre.* She stood up slowly, her mind reeling, as the girls hushed their chatter and moved out of the room.

As she left the dining room to go up to bed, something in the corner of the hallway caught her eyes. Squinting, Maren tried to see what it was, and then stooped down as she recognized it, grinning in delight at the unexpected treasure. Ceara would be thrilled. Maren stole a quick glance behind her to make sure no one was around and then snatched it up, tucking her newfound possession into her sleeve and continuing on to the stone steps.

That evening, Maren watched Ceara's rounded silhouette as the girl walked awkwardly around the dark, tiny room. Her belly bumped gently against the side of the bed as she leaned over it to reach her nightgown, which was tucked, folded neatly into quarters, beneath her flat pillow. She was feeling well again and had been keeping up with her tasks in the laundries as well as was possible in her advanced state of pregnancy. Maren felt strangely proud as she watched Ceara prepare for bed. Her long dark hair fell in a messy tangle across the dingy gray blanket, and Maren remembered the treasure she had found in the hall that evening.

"Maelisa, come over here," Maren said suddenly, her voice low. Ceara looked at her friend curiously and edged slowly over as she slipped her shapeless shift over her head and tossed it on her bed.

"What is it?" she asked in the same quiet whisper, her arms stretched high as the muslin nightgown dropped over her head and fell in a drape to cover the bulge of her breasts and stomach. Shaking her head to loosen the tangles, she grimaced as she sat on the edge of Maren's narrow bed. "I wish this hair would stay in shape. It used to be quite nice, really." Ceara gave a small, endearing smile, the wistfulness evident both in her tone and on her face. Maren snorted.

"Just be glad you still have your hair." She ruffled her own short blond curls with a grimace of her own, and Ceara's face changed instantly.

"Oh, Cassán, I'm so sorry. I didn't mean—"

Maren waved her hand in the air. "I know you didn't. It's all right." She smiled encouragingly at her friend so that Ceara would see she was honestly not hurt by the thoughtless comment. "But that's why I wanted you to come over. Look here; see what I have." Ceara's eyes dropped to Maren's other hand, where she was holding a small, sharp-looking wooden comb. Her eyes widened in delight.

"Where did you get that?" she hissed in as sharp an exclamation as was possible under their noise restrictions. Maren grinned with the delight of giving Ceara such pleasure and shuffled over on the tiny cot so that she could sit behind her friend, who leaned back in anticipation. Ceara gave a sigh of pure happiness and closed her eyes as the other girl gently pulled the shining teeth of the comb through a small section of the dark, matted hair.

"I found it, do you believe it?" she reported excitedly. "I was on my way back up here from dinner and it was just lying there in a corner. It was half covered with dust, of course, but I knew what it was right away. Does it feel all right?" She glanced over Ceara's shoulder anxiously, but Ceara merely shook her head.

"Don't stop. It feels wonderful." She gave a heavy sigh and Maren returned to the task of unraveling the knots from the masses of hair before her. It was slow, tedious work, but as she continually picked at the knots with the sharp comb she could see progress section by section, and within fifteen minutes one side of Ceara's hair lay flat, smooth and shiny against her shoulder. Maren thrilled with the sensation of guiding the comb in a long, endless glide from root to tip, and with one last satisfying pull through Ceara's newly untangled hair, she moved on to the rest of the tangled mess.

She worked in silence until Ceara complained about her back and moved off the edge of the bed, leaning against the end of it so that Maren was combing her hair right on the surface of the bed. The silence broken, Maren asked a hesitant question that had been on her mind for some time, and that she had been thinking about anew after what she had heard about Deirdre earlier that evening.

"Maelisa...have you ever thought about running away from here?" She glanced around the room in sudden paranoia that a nun would emerge from a dark corner and point a condemning finger. When none appeared, she turned back to her work and waited for Ceara's answer.

Ceara opened her eyes and rolled them back, tilting her head against the bed to look at her friend. "Of course I've thought about it," she replied in a tone that questioned the sanity of anyone to whom the thought *hadn't* occurred. "Who hasn't? But what would be the point? I'd never be able to do it, even if I *did* decide to try it." Dropping her head back with a sigh, she folded her fingers across her belly and felt the movements of the child within. "I haven't the faintest idea of a plan." She glanced down the length of her thin arms and then toward the long, slender legs that stretched out from underneath the simple nightdress she wore. "I'm too weak, as well, and the child takes the last of my energy, so it's useless even if I could think of some wonderful way to do it." With a long-drawn-out sigh she finished, "I suppose I'm resigned to it now."

"But what about the child?" Maren rushed in with urgency. "They'll take it from you once it's born, won't they? How could you stand that?" Suddenly afraid that she had said too much, and not wanting to hurt Ceara, she hastened to quiet her tongue. Ceara was silent for a moment, and Maren wanted to ask if she was all right, but hesitated to speak lest she say the wrong thing again.

"They...they will take the child away from me. It's not worth anything to them, just the bastard son or daughter of another wanton young girl who got herself caught out. They'll take it as soon as it's born. They always do, you know, so there's no bonding." Maren snorted, and Ceara looked back again with a slight smile. "I know; they say that as if we're not *already* bonded together." She caressed her child's form absently through her nightgown, and Maren could only guess at the tumultuousness of her thoughts.

When she spoke again, her voice held a hint of anger, and Maren's fingers on the comb stilled in surprise. Aside from the confrontation with Sister Líadan, Ceara had very rarely shown any maliciousness in the time they had been together at Sacred Mercy. "They put the children in the orphanage right next door, you know. Maxime's babe was taken straight from her and put right to the care of other women. Maxime never even knew if it was a boy or a girl, and all she saw as they carried it away was one little pink bloody hand stretching up from the swaddling." Ceara raised her left palm to the sky unconsciously as she recalled Maxime's story, and a tear welled in her eye. "She swore she knew it was a daughter, though; every time she heard a baby cry from the other building her breasts would fill with milk, and she would be sure it was her own. As time went on and she would see the sisters bringing out the little ones—you know, the crawlers—she would point to this one little girl and say to me, 'That's her. That's my Kathleen. Isn't she beautiful?' Then she would say, 'Doesn't she have the most perfect little hands? Can you see her hands?' She based her recognition on the little one's open hand; she said she would never forget how her baby's tiny fingers were shaped."

With a sigh she stared down at her own small hands, now resting again on the berth of her stomach. "The thing was, she always pointed out a different little girl to me. I don't think it was the same one twice, even."

Maren kept silent for a long moment. Her heart welled with sorrow for the girl named Maxime, and for the child she had never had a chance to know. Was that what would happen to Deirdre, now that she was pregnant, or to Ceara? The thought of her dear friend spending her every waking hour hoping for a glimpse of her baby's shadow broke her heart, and she felt she had to speak.

"But that's what I mean, Maelisa. How can you stand that? How can you not hope against every hope in the world that you and your child will not have to go through that horror? You should be out there in the world, with your family, being able to care for your baby and love it the way it should be loved! You deserve to have that chance to be loved that way yourself, to meet someone special, to grow old with him, to raise your children together—"

"I *know* I should have that chance, Cassán! Do you think anyone feels that more than I do right now?" She had whirled around and now grasped Maren's hands between her own. The sharp points of the comb dug deep into her right palm, but she didn't seem to notice. "Here I am, maybe a day away from birthing this child, and I know I will never get to see its face. Its father will never know of it, or of what becomes of me, and perhaps he won't even care. Don't you think that hurts me? Of course it does! I'm just as human as the rest of you are! I want nothing more than to get out of this place, to meet the man of my dreams, to marry and to be loved and safe for the rest of my days, but I know that's not to be. It's not what I am here to do."

"Then what *are* you here to do?" Maren broke in angrily. "To waste away in this...this prison? To give birth to a baby only to have it stolen from you? To suffer and die a little more each day until you finally collapse in a heap and they throw you in a mass grave with all the other girls who are here to do the same horrid thing? I can't accept that, Maelisa. I just can't accept that that might be all you're good for."

Ceara sat on the cold stone floor and looked up into her friend's ferocity with a calm that emanated from her entire body. During Maren's tirade she had relaxed into the same composure that Maren was used to seeing, and her face was framed with silk as her untangled hair flowed in soft, shiny chestnut waves down to the small of her back. Maren felt some of her own fear and anger draining away as she stared into those peaceful eyes. She realized that she had her fists clenched and was holding her whole body so tensely that she was shaking, and she forcefully relaxed her tense arms as Ceara spoke. "I think I know what I'm here for, Cassán," she whispered with a tiny smile, "but I have a feeling it might take you your whole life to figure out what it is."

With only a slight pass of her hand over the swell of the baby giving away the continuing emotion of her thoughts, she stood up and made her way back to her bed, her legs shaking slightly. Maren watched her lie down and cover herself with the sparse blanketing, quietly turning over so that Maren couldn't see her face. It was a sign that the conversation was over as far as Ceara was concerned, and Maren lay down on her pillow, determined to hide away her troubled thoughts as easily as she slid the small tortoiseshell comb underneath her sagging mattress. *The rest of my life...*she thought. *I really hope I don't spend the rest of my life thinking about this conversation.* With a concerted effort, she quieted her mind and tried to will herself to sleep.

Chapter Fifteen

The girls fell back into the rhythm of the Laundries, and Ceara seemed to be doing very well even as her pregnancy progressed. Even so, Maren found herself keeping a watchful eye on her friend as she worked in her washbasin.

There was no clock on the wall of the large stone room, but after these many weeks she had caught on to the rhythm of the place, and she knew as she washed yet another large apron and set it aside to await the drying lines that the day was nearly done.

Her mouth moving automatically with the words that she no longer needed to try to remember, she chanced a glance over to the next row of washtubs. Ceara was saying her prayers, and her hands worked rhythmically in the water before her, but her face held a peculiar look. She looked tense, her teeth tightly clenched together and her forehead wrinkling in what seemed to be pain.

Maren frowned, her brows drawing together, but as she watched discreetly, the moment passed and Ceara's face smoothed back into its normal peaceful lines. Relieved, but still slightly concerned, Maren looked back to her washing, but continued to steal cautious, quick looks in Ceara's direction. Occasionally she would catch Ceara in the midst of one of those odd, pain-filled looks, but they would always smooth out again within a matter of seconds. Ceara looked up once and saw Maren's apprehensive face, and she forced a smile. Quickly scanning the room to see that the nun was on the other side, where she couldn't see her hand movements, she gave a slight nod and held up two fingers, then drew a small circle on her chest. *It's okay. I can handle it.*

Maren grinned. Their hand signals had extended to perhaps two dozen separate signs, each meaning one single word or a complete thought. It wasn't often that they dared to use them right in front of the nuns, but in certain circumstances they had found it incredibly helpful. It was good to know that Ceara was aware of her concern and was confident enough that she could get through whatever was paining her. Maren knew that they would talk later.

When they were finally dismissed from the room and allowed to file slowly out and down the long maze of stone hallways to the dining room, Maren managed to maneuver herself into line behind Ceara, who was walking very slowly and using one hand to support the weight of her belly. "Are you okay?" she whispered quietly.

Ceara nodded and started to reply, but Sister Dáirine's voice came sharply from the tail end of the line. "Quiet! There is to be no talking in the line!" The girls bent their head submissively and continued walking to the dining hall.

When they were seated and eating their small meal of corn, broiled potatoes and a slice of bread, Maren managed to ask Ceara again how she was doing. The tense looks were coming more often now, she noticed, and Ceara seemed to be uncomfortable as she sat in the small wooden chair. "I'm all right," Ceara answered timidly, her eyebrows pulling together in sudden pain. "We'll talk more later." She rolled her eyes to encompass everyone in the room, and pointedly rested a hand on her belly.

Maren's eyes widened. The baby was coming! It was all she could do to keep herself from jumping up and escorting Ceara down the hall to a nurse. But no: Ceara had been explicit with her sign when she rolled her eyes: *Not in front of them.* She finished her meal hastily but in silence, keeping a wary eye on her friend. It did her no good to be done her meal before the others; they were dismissed all at once a few minutes later regardless of whether they were all finished or not. Maren scooted out of her seat and ran around the table to help Ceara out of her chair, ignoring the disapproving looks from a few of the nuns. They left the dining room and headed up the stairs to their room.

Ceara climbed the stairs slowly, stopping every once in a while to catch her breath. Maren waited patiently behind her, one hand on the narrow railing and the other out in front of her, nearly touching Ceara's back, to help steady her if she fell back. Ceara tried very hard not to show the hurt she was feeling, but her laboured breathing and an occasional pain-filled gasp betrayed her. The other girls, on their way up to their rooms, moved to the left side of them and gave the two girls curious glances, but Maren paid them no mind. She knew they were all too anxious to get to their own rooms to really pay any attention to what was going on.

It took them a good ten minutes past the time the halls were clear of the other residents to climb the three flights of stairs and make their way to their room. As soon as Ceara was in the room, Maren closed the door and rushed over to help her lie down on the bed.

"What does it feel like? Is it hurting?" she asked in a low voice. Ceara nodded briefly, and her face was tensing again in that look Maren had seen so many times in the past hour. Maren put a hesitant hand on Ceara's belly and drew it back immediately in shock. The smock was pulled tight across the tightly stretched skin of Ceara's distended abdomen, and her belly was rock hard. Maren was amazed. "Oh, Maelisa," she whispered worriedly, "I don't think I should be the one to help you with this. I'm the youngest! I've never seen a baby born."

Ceara was panting, but she held up her hand in a signal for Maren to wait. As soon as the contraction was finished, the muscles in her abdomen noticeably relaxing, she pulled herself up on her elbows and directed a fierce glare toward Maren. She was still winded, but between gasps of air she managed to get the words out. "I do not...want them...coming in here," she breathed heavily, "and taking away...my baby...before I have a chance to...spend...some time with it. Maren—" The use of Maren's given name hit home, and she sat down on the edge of the bed to pay careful attention. "—you must be brave. We can do it...together...with God's help." Maren nodded and gave her friend a watery smile, which was returned gratefully.

"What do I do, Maelisa? Do you know what happens next?"

Ceara nodded. It was an obvious effort for her to speak, but she tried as hard as she could. "I know a little." She reached for the blanket and tried to tuck it around herself, but Maren hurriedly took it and finished the job for her friend. "Right now...there's not really anything...we can do...but wait." Maren bobbed her head anxiously in assent. "The baby...will come...but my body is just...trying to help...get it...Owww..." She trailed off into a long moan and curled onto her side, doubling over the hardness of her stomach. Maren came forward and stroked Ceara's hair, which was beginning to dampen with sweat.

"I'll stay as long as it takes, Ceara," she murmured.

The next two hours passed slowly, and the light diminished quickly until all that Maren could see was half of Ceara's face and body in the thin line of light that floated in through the window from the moonlight outside. Ceara was in obvious agony, but despite the rivers of perspiration that ran down her face and soaked her bedclothes, she maintained an even temperament. She refused to cry out with the pain lest a nun hear and come to take the baby away, but a few times she bit her lip so hard that it bled. Maren continued to murmur comforting words as the contractions grew closer and closer together, but she began to feel hopeless after a time when it seemed like Ceara was just enduring one long contraction. She used her precious drinking water to wipe the sweat and blood from Ceara's face, stripping her pillowcase from the thin, dirty pillow and wetting a corner in the drinking glass. Tears leaked from Ceara's eyes, but she whispered under her breath, "Jesus...help me, Lord...I know You are here with me..."

Maren, leaning close to hear her friend's words, was surprised that at a time like this she was still focused on her God, but she drew comfort from the thought that Jesus could be in the room soothing Ceara in her labour. A few minutes later, when Ceara buried her face in the pillow to keep from crying out and her hands gripped Maren's so tightly that her fingernails left deep gouges in her palms, Maren's concern was so deep that she almost didn't realize it when she said, "Jesus, help me, too." Her eyes widened and she looked down at Ceara quickly, almost embarrassed to have her friend hear her, but then stopped and stared into the darkness of the room.

A sudden peace came over her. *I am here.* The words seemed to drift into her head and out again as quickly as they had come, but there was no mistaking their message. Had she dreamed it? She tried to push the thought away, but realized that as soon as she tried to distance herself from the voice that had whispered to her, she felt cold and alone. "I need you, Jesus," she heard herself whisper. "Help Ceara to deliver this baby safely. Help me to be here for her in whatever way I can." She let go of Ceara's hands and sank down to her knees beside the bed. "I can feel you, Jesus," she choked out, her eyes brimming with tears. "You're here." That peaceful calm enveloped her again, almost like a feather brushing across her heart, and she put her face in her hands and sobbed.

After a moment, she felt a light touch on her hair and looked up to see Ceara smiling at her, her face still pinched with pain, but her eyes full of love and happiness. She smiled back and sat back up on the edge of the bed. "We can do this, Maelisa," she asserted in a strong voice. "We can do it together." There was no mistaking the fact that she was including one more in the word "together". Ceara nodded and squeezed her hand tightly.

Suddenly Ceara made a grunting sound. "Oh, Cassán, it's coming!" she gasped in surprise. "I can feel it!"

Maren hastened to her feet and stripped the blanket off her bed, folding in into quarters and laying it aside for the baby. She helped Ceara into a half-sitting position, placing Ceara's pillow and the one from her own bed behind the labouring girl's back. When Ceara fell back on the nearly flat pillows, however, Maren muttered in disgust at the lack of proper supplies and rolled up the blanket that she had just neatly folded. Stuffing it behind Ceara's back so that she could recline but still be nearly sitting up, she moved down to help Ceara out of her underclothes and to pull her smock up around her waist. At first she was embarrassed to look, but when she dared to sneak a peek between Ceara's spread legs, she gasped. "Oh, Maelisa! I can see its head!" The amazement of the moment filled her, and she stood gaping at the sight. "It has dark hair!"

Ceara didn't answer, but Maren could hear her making that grunting sound again. The baby's head moved further out for a brief moment, and then disappeared almost entirely as Ceara let out a loud breath and relaxed, sinking back into the sparse cushioning behind her and letting her head fall back tiredly. "You have to...catch it..." she panted. "Help...the baby...out." Maren nodded.

"I will, Maelisa. I'll help. Is it still coming out?"

Ceara nodded. "I can feel it...I'm going to push again...Here it comes...Mmmpphhh!" She managed to turn her cry of pain into a muffled sound by turning her head to the side and grabbing a piece of blanket between her teeth. Maren returned her concentration to the baby's head, which was slowly emerging. She moved her hands forward, but there wasn't enough of the baby's head out yet to get a hold of. As Ceara relaxed, the dark head slid back inside, but there was more of it still showing than there had been. Still, Maren let out a small hiss of frustration.

"I can't grab it, Maelisa. It's not coming out."

Ceara opened one eye. "It will...keep watching...here it comes again..." She trailed off and pushed, the veins in her neck bulging with the effort and her face turning a deep red. Maren watched as the baby's head slowly emerged, rotating slowly, showing puffy eyes and a delicate nose. She gasped with delight.

"I can see its eyes! Oh, Maelisa, it's so perfect!" She reached forward to guide the little head, placing her fingers delicately on either side of its face. It was soft and warm and wet, and her eyes misted over with wonder.

Ceara didn't answer, and in a moment she sat up as straight as she could and began to push again. With Maren's help, the little head came out completely, its mouth closed and its complexion mottled. "It's out! Just a little more, Maelisa!" She held the tiny head reverently. "You're so perfect," she whispered to the little creation as Ceara geared up for another push, and with a great whoosh and a loud grunt from Ceara, the little body slid from its mother and rested on the bed in Maren's hands. She stared down at the baby, awestruck. The little head was in her left hand and its little backside in her right, and the cord that still joined it to Ceara was attached to its navel and wrapped loosely around its neck. "It's a girl, Maelisa," she whispered, glancing over to Ceara. She was lying on her back, her eyes closed, but when she heard Maren's pronouncement a weak smile crossed her face and she moved into a better position to see Maren's face.

"Clear her mouth," she said sluggishly. Maren gently laid the baby on the bed and opened its mouth with one hand, hesitantly sticking a finger in and wiping out some mucus. Then she reached for the blanket that had been on Ceara's bed and was now lying on the floor beside her, and gently wrapped the tiny body in it. The baby moved slightly in her hands but didn't draw breath. Maren frowned. "Why isn't she moving, Maelisa?"

Ceara opened her eyes and managed to pull herself into a sitting position. "I—don't know..." she said in confusion. "Why is that cord around her neck?"

Maren looked at the cord, which pulsed weakly. "We're supposed to cut the cord, right, Maelisa? I've heard that before." Her wonder over the baby had quickly turned to fear when she realized that the child wasn't breathing. Standing up, she picked up the little bundle and placed it in Ceara's arms. The cord stretched slightly but managed to reach. Maren hastily pulled both shoelaces from her worn shoes and reached over to tie a knot around the cord, close to the child's belly button, and another an inch further along. Then she looked around for something to cut it with. "What should I use, Maelisa?"

Ceara looked up from her baby and glanced around the dark room. "The scissors! Remember, Cassán, those little scissors in the bottom drawer of the dresser over there; the ones I used to trim your hair. Get them." She glanced back down at her baby, whose face was beginning to turn a deeper shade of red. "Hurry, Cassán," she urged, the first touch of real anxiety evident in her voice. Maren groped her way across the room and managed to find the wardrobe, pulling open the bottom drawer and sliding her hands across the bottom until they touched something metal. She pulled the scissors out and stepped quickly and quietly across to the bed.

"Here," she offered, moving toward the baby. Her face had become slightly purplish, and she shifted sluggishly in her mother's arms. A tiny sound came from her mouth, like a kitten, but the sound was cut off. Maren had no time to listen; she grasped the cord and cut it just beside the knot. The cord snapped back toward the baby's face, and Ceara used her free arm to grab the free end.

"We need to get it off her neck," she managed to say, though her throat was suddenly frozen in fear. The baby had stopped moving completely, and her face was a deep blue. The cord was still pulsing as the blood flowed through it from Ceara, and the two loose loops around the baby's neck were tightening.

Ceara began to panic, and her fingers didn't seem to work. "Quickly, Cassán!" she ordered frantically. Maren hurriedly unwound the cord from the baby's neck, and they could see the red marks on her skin where the cord had been wrapped tightly around her throat. The blood returned to the baby's face slowly, but her skin was still blotchy, and she didn't open her mouth or breathe. Ceara put two fingers to the little chest, then leaned over as far as she was able to place her ear on the baby's ribcage. Tears filled her eyes, and she gathered the little girl close to her chest, crying helplessly. "She's gone, Cassán," she wept. "My baby's gone."

Maren sank to the floor and buried her face in her skirts, weeping hysterically. *No, God, no! How could you do this to Ceara? All that work...all that pain...I thought you were here to help us!* She could hear Ceara crying softly, but behind the desire to let out all her anger and grief was the vague awareness that a nun may be able to hear it and come in to take the child away from them. Ceara longed to hold her baby for as long as she could, and Maren refused to let a nun see her friend in so vulnerable a state. So, they sat together and cried as quietly as they could for endless short minutes.

Eventually, the muffled sounds coming from Ceara subsided, and Maren raised her head to peer at her friend. She was leaning against the pillows and blanket, cradling the swaddled child in her arms. Tearstains streaked her cheeks, but she was smiling. She glanced up at Maren and beckoned. "Come…come and look at her, Cassán." Maren shook her head and folded her arms, but at Ceara's nod and encouraging look, she stood and moved hesitantly forward.

The baby was nestled in her mother's arms, and looked for all the world to be a living, breathing child merely resting contentedly. Ceara was looking down on her face fondly. "Isn't she beautiful?" she asked softly.

Maren's tears started to spill from her eyes again as she reluctantly nodded. The baby *was* beautiful. Ceara opened the blanket and looked over the tiny, perfect body.

Although the baby was still covered with blood, Ceara had managed to clean her face with the blanket so that her skin glowed white in the moonlight. Her little lips were pursed as though for nursing, and her hands were folded into tiny fists that lay motionless beside her little chest. Her legs and arms were perfectly formed, and as Maren watched, Ceara counted her fingers and toes. "Amazing," she said quietly. "God is so amazing."

Maren cast a sharp look at her friend. "What does God have to do with this?" she snapped angrily, and a small smile flitted across Ceara's face.

"Look at her, Maren. How can you not say that God is amazing when you see what He has created? Down to her toes, she's perfect, and He made her."

Maren ground her teeth to keep from screaming out that He had also taken her away, but she saw the peace in Ceara's eyes, and behind her anger, the reluctance to hurt her friend kept her mouth shut. "She *was* perfect," she couldn't refrain from saying, hurt and bitterness filling her voice. Ceara caught the past tense, but didn't react with tears or anger. She merely wrapped the baby up again and gazed at her face.

"Yes, she was," she agreed. She kissed the pale face and looked tenderly down on her daughter. "Her name is Treasa," she announced quietly, looking toward Maren for approval. Maren sat down beside her and kept her hands tightly folded in her lap. However much she ached to hold the baby, she would not ask, and she would not cry again.

"Does that name have some special significance?" she inquired cautiously, knowing Ceara's fascination with names and their meanings.

Ceara looked directly into her eyes, and Maren nearly drew back at the intensity in them. "Strength," she said. "Her name means *strength*." Still looking deep into Maren's eyes, she lifted the baby from the bed and placed her gently in Maren's arms. Maren managed to tear her eyes from Ceara's gaze, and finally chanced a look down at the baby. As Maren looked down on the tiny creature, her eyes filled with tears and she began to sob again quietly. Ceara lay back against the pillows, feeling strangely contented despite the enormous physical and emotional pain she was feeling, and began praying aloud. Maren tried not to listen, but she heard every word.

"Thank You, Lord, that You gave Treasa to me to hold for these few special minutes. Thank You that You designed her just for me, and that she will never have to live as a slave to this horrible system. She will never be anyone's but mine now. And thank You, too, Lord, for Maren. Give her the strength that she needs, the strength that is Yours. She called out to You, Father, and we both heard it. I know she is not far from accepting you, Jesus, but please help her through this terrible time. Don't let it bring her further away from You."

Maren cuddled Treasa, carefully wiping the tears from the dead baby's face as they fell on her skin, and glanced up to see Ceara's eyes also wet as she continued her prayer. "I know that it will take us a long time for both of us to get over her, Lord, but please be with us. Remind us every time we think of her name that we draw our strength from you. Be

Maren's strength now, Lord," she finished, and settled back against her pillow as she closed her eyes, exhausted.

Maren shut her eyes and drew the tiny body closer to her.

Chapter Sixteen

In the deep sleep Maren had crashed into while lying curled around Treasa, she felt as though hours had passed when something awakened her. She blinked sleepily, unsure of where she was and what this tiny bundle was doing in her arms. "Cassán," she heard Ceara whisper. "Cassán, wake up."

Maren looked down at the baby and drew back slightly, pulling the blanket closely around Treasa's face. She was starting to get cold and stiff, and her little face was tinged with blue around its edges. Maren glanced back to the other bed at Ceara, a tear rolling from the corner of her eye. "Oh, Maelisa, it really did happen," she whispered dejectedly, sitting up and gently laying the baby down on the bed. "I was hoping it had been a dream."

Ceara shook her head in sorrow. "It happened," she replied, and suddenly grunted and bent over double. "And I don't know what's going on, but it feels like it's happening again." She placed her hand on her belly, feeling it harden beneath her palm. Maren stared for a moment and came over, leaving the blanket-wrapped bundle on her bed. She put her hand beside Ceara's and her eyes widened. Her abdominal muscles were as hard and tense as they had been in the middle of her labor.

"Oh, Maelisa!" she gasped in hopeful awe. "Do you—do you think there's another baby in there?"

Ceara shook her head. "It couldn't be—there's no room in there for another one." She relaxed against the bed for a moment, but then sat up again quickly as her abdomen tightened again. "But something is definitely happening." She could feel the urge to bear down, and told Maren so. "You'd better get that blanket again."

Maren looked toward the other bed, where Treasa lay unmoving and silent in the rough wrapping. She was loath to pull the blanket off her and leave her exposed, but reluctantly she did as Ceara asked, gently unrolling the blanket from the still little body and placing her, naked, up against Maren's pillow. She looked so little and alone on the narrow bed, and Maren felt as though she were leaving her own child out in the cold. She had to remind herself that Treasa was feeling no pain.

Ceara glanced at the tiny figure and tears welled up in her eyes again. "My baby," she said softly. "I will miss you."

"Is it hard for you, Maelisa?" Maren asked cautiously, suddenly feeling foolish at asking such an obvious question. She folded the blanket again and tucked it beneath Ceara's bottom as she tried to explain what she meant. "Not having her in there anymore, I mean?"

Ceara nodded. "She moved so much," she replied. "I could always feel her and know that she was happy and comfortable in her little home, and every time I felt alone or scared I just talked to her and knew that she loved me, in her own way, and that we knew each other better than anyone else could. She was always real to me, even before I saw her." She smiled weakly and ran a hand across her belly. "It suddenly feels very lonely in there." Then she gasped and leaned forward again. "Something is coming out, Cassán!" she cried.

Maren quickly moved between Ceara's legs and saw what she had been talking about, and drew back in disgust. The afterbirth fell with a plop onto the coarse blanket, and Maren backed up a few steps. "Maelisa," she said slowly, "something horrible just came out of you."

Ceara tried to look down at the blanket, but failed to see what Maren was talking about, and fell back on her pillow with a sigh. "Go find a nun," she said resignedly. "Tell her what happened, and ask her to come and help."

"Are you sure?" Maren asked. "But they'll take Treasa away!" She looked miserably at the little body on the other bed. Ceara smiled gently through her tears.

"What would we do with her here?" she questioned reasonably, though she hurt tremendously inside. She held out her arms. "Let me hold her one more time before they take her away for good."

Maren stood observing her friend for a brief moment before walking over to retrieve the little bundle from the bed. Treasa was by this time very cold and stiff, and Maren hesitated. She wanted Ceara to remember her child as warm and soft, not unmovable and hard as a plastic doll. "Are you sure, Maelisa?" she asked softly. "She's... not..." She struggled with the words, unable to believe the situation. She had never dreamed that the birth of Ceara's baby would end like this.

Ceara sat looking at her, waiting, so she heaved a breath and leaned over to place the baby in her arms. Ceara looked startled at the way Treasa felt in her arms, and suddenly began crying desperately. She pressed her face into Treasa's little belly and wept.

Maren watched in helpless sorrow, and then left to find a nun.

Sister Dáirine, in her nightgown and with her light-colored hair in a long braid down her back, was hurrying down the hall that led to the dining room when Maren appeared in front of her at the base of the stairwell. The nun, surprised to see the young girl still in her shift from the night before, halted immediately. "What are you doing here, Miss Bradigan?" she demanded, looking at the large clock on the wall. It was a little after three in the morning.

Maren wrung her hands miserably. "It's Ceara—Miss MacAodhagáin, Sister," she whispered. "She's—she's had her baby."

Dáirine's eyes widened, but she nodded and placed the water glass she had been going to refill on a small shelf on the wall. "Take me to her." She followed Maren, who fairly ran up the three flights of stairs to their room.

Ceara was sitting with Treasa pressed close to her breast, her eyes closed and her mouth moving silently. She didn't move when Maren entered with Sister Dáirine, who took one glance around the room and quickly assessed the situation. She sighed inwardly and shook her head. "Miss MacAodhagáin," she murmured softly. "Are you all right?"

Ceara's eyes popped open and she smiled weakly at the nun. "I think so, Sister," she answered, "but something just came out of me, and we're not sure what it is." She gestured with a tilt of her head to the mess on the blanket. She had moved her legs and covered herself modestly, and Sister Dáirine nodded.

"That's your placenta, child. It's perfectly normal to pass it after delivery." She hesitated, but then asked cautiously, "The baby?"

"She's dead," Maren answered for Ceara, her voice ringing hollow and desolate in the small room. Ceara nodded, tears forming in her eyes again. Sister Dáirine sighed.

"I'll take it, then," she replied, holding her arms out for the baby. "I'll send up a clean blanket and a bag for this mess, but I don't think you'll be able to see a doctor tonight. You're going to have to wait until tomorrow."

The girls both nodded, feeling numb as they watched Sister Dáirine wrap up the baby in Ceara's blanket, pulling its corners up around her, tying them together and lifting it by the knot. She carried the package heedlessly, as though she were taking out the garbage, and it served as a painful reminder to both girls of what Ceara had truly lost this night. No one would have guessed that the inert package the nun held carelessly in one hand carried a child.

Maren felt like beating on the woman as she moved toward the door, the weight of the baby causing the blanket to sway back and forth slightly. How dare she be so calm and cruel? Didn't she realize how much they were both hurting? Didn't she *care*? She would now carry the one tiny beacon of hope Ceara had had in her life out that door, and they would be left to carry on their lives as if there had never been a tiny, soft baby named Treasa MacAodhagáin. The door closed and she sank to the floor, cursing God in her mind. *How could you, God?* she demanded. *How could you let it be this way? I will never forgive you. Never!*

For the next few days she did her work in angry silence, refusing to say the Our Father. She kept her mouth tightly shut unless a nun glanced her way, in which case she would quickly start a Hail Mary. *Mary* was a mother, she thought. *She would never cause Ceara to lose her baby. She knew what it felt like. How dare you, God? How **dare** you think you could do this to my best friend? She'll hate you, too, when she realizes that you stole her baby from her. I don't care what she says about you; you will never be my God!*

After Sister Dáirine had left that early morning, she had sent another nun up with a trash bag and blanket, with some cloths and a menstrual belt folded inside. Still sleepy, hair mussed and dressed in her white cotton nightgown, she had dropped the items on the table with barely a nod, giving Ceara a slightly mocking glance as she left. Maren had been left to clean up the bloody sheets and placenta herself, having no choice but to simply fold the soiled blanket around the thing and dumping the whole mess into the bag.

Ceara lay in silence, washing herself when Maren encouraged her, and then sitting up obligingly so that Maren could help her into the menstrual belt. She retrieved Ceara's underclothes from the corner where they had been thrown during her labor, but they hung loosely on her after having lost the weight of the baby. Ceara didn't complain, however, merely folding the waistband over on itself and twisting it, securing it under the elastic of the belt. They finished up in utter quiet, putting the bag of dirty cloths outside the door to bring down the next morning, and gave each other a sad hug before retreating to sleep. Maren thought she would lie awake for a long time, but exhaustion crept over her and she drifted off to sleep in a matter of minutes.

She had been awakened by the bell for Mass only an hour later, and dragged herself out of the bed to pull off her nightdress, realizing as she did so that she had never changed out of her shift the night before. Ceara lay sound asleep, her lips parted and her breathing deep and even. She made a tiny movement when the bell tolled but did not awaken. Maren tiptoed around her and opened and closed the door as quietly as possible, though she figured that if the other girl didn't even awaken with that massive bell going off just outside the window, nothing would be sufficient to wake her this morning. She met Sister Grania in the hall amidst the milling girls on their way to Mass and explained the situation.

Sister Grania listened with her lips pressed tightly together and a worried look, but she nodded and moved quickly away, motioning for another nun to take her place in charge of the lineup. Maren watched her walk hastily up the stairs and turned back, satisfied that Ceara would be well taken care of, and grateful that the nun on duty this morning had been Grania and not Sister Líadan.

Chapter Seventeen

The days following Treasa's short life were a blur to Maren. She moved from task to task without seeing what she was doing, working through the day with only cold, bitter hatred keeping her moving. She kept her mouth tightly shut as the other girls dutifully went through the recitations at Mass, glaring up at Christ on the Cross with her lips pinched together and her brow furrowed in anger. She scrubbed clothes and linens ferociously, her hands and arms aching as she pushed herself harder and harder.

It was easy to forget the warmth and love she had felt during Treasa's birth, when she had been sure that God was with them in that tiny, dank room. *Everyone prays to God in times of trouble,* she reasoned. *I was so worried about Maelisa that I was grasping at whatever straw came to mind.* Now she felt no remnant of the presence of God that she thought she had experienced in those few endless moments of Ceara's labor. The only things she saw were Ceara's and Treasa's faces, and the only thing she felt was rage.

The other girls watched Maren with interest, whispering among themselves whenever the nuns were looking the other way. Maren tried to ignore the looks and kept her head high, refusing to meet the eyes of anyone as she walked along. *Let them serve you, you false god,* she thought to herself. *I will never bow, not now. I thought I was getting closer to understanding Ceara's God, but I know now that you are nothing but a bitter, hateful entity bent only on destroying us even as we worship you.*

She was quiet with the nuns, but they took her defiant glaring as impudence and did not miss an opportunity to reprimand or punish her for it. Maren barely noticed. *I don't care,* she thought during a beating from Sister Líadan. *I just don't care anymore.* When the beating was through, Maren righted herself and stood staring into space without a hint of pain.

She did not feel the sting in her backside from the belt buckle Líadan had used to discipline her until she had walked back up to her room and collapsed on the bed, fighting tears.

Here in the room she shared with Ceara was the only sanctuary she had, the only place where she could feel again. Whenever she looked at the two narrow beds, she thought of Ceara braving her way through labor and Treasa's tiny body lying still on the pillow. The blankets brought the image of Sister Dáirine yanking its corners up around the dead baby and carrying it through the door, Treasa's slight weight shifting the rough material gently from side to side. The next day, Sister Grania had brought in a tiny piece of paper for Ceara to sign, listing Treasa's weight and length and the date and time she had been born. Maren had watched from the other bed and squinted to read the printing on the paper, but she couldn't see what it said.

She asked Ceara about it as soon as the nun had left, and Ceara's eyes were wet as she answered. "Her weight was 2700 grams and she was 50 centimeters long. In the place where the paper asked for her name, they filled in 'Illegitimate Child MacAodhagáin'." Maren had shaken her head and stalked out with anger. She could feel Ceara's sad eyes on her back, but she refused to acknowledge them.

Now she lay on her bed and cried, grateful to be alone and not to have to explain herself to anyone. She had been here in this torture chamber for months, and experienced and witnessed suffering such as she had never believed possible. How long had it been since the last bit of hope had been stripped from her? She didn't know. Treasa's birth and death seemed all at once a recent happening and an ancient memory. She felt as though she had been sleepwalking, and suddenly awoken to realize that she was alone, and the dream of Treasa would never be a reality. For the first time she allowed herself to come out of the fog and mourn the life she used to know and the tiny ray of hope she had held for the life she was now living.

She cried as hard as she could, hoping to have it all out and over with before Ceara returned from her first day back at work in the laundry, her mind filled with tumultuous thoughts about home. Would she ever see the faces of those she loved again?

Fresh sobs burst from her as she pictured the farm as she saw it every morning from her upstairs bedroom window, her father and Rian waving up at her with huge smiles on their faces. The excitement of Ceara's labor and the pain of losing Treasa had kept her mind off her incredible longing to be home, but now Maren clasped her hands to her face as she once more heard her father and brother bantering back and forth. *"She thinks of nothing else but making herself pretty, Da. If only she'd been a boy." "Don't think there's a one of us who **really** thinks that...Get to work!"* Maren grinned into her hands as she remembered the way her father would whack Rian's shoulder with his sweat-soaked hat when he was feeling affectionate. Rian had always complained, but she knew he had basked in his father's affections, as she had.

At home, she had known the security of her parents' love, and had never really thought to consider herself fortunate. Now that everything she loved had been taken away from her, she found herself suddenly realizing how privileged she had been, and how little she had appreciated it. "I took it all for granted, Da," she whispered into her wet, tear-salted hands. "I never knew how good I had it." Maren moaned into her palms, mourning for the life she had not realized could ever be stolen from her.

A gentle hand was placed on her back and Maren started, frantically wiping the tears from her eyes with the back of her hands. The blanket was musty and stale, but she used it to dry her hands and then turned slightly to look up at Ceara.

She had not recovered well from her ordeal of the week before. Her face was haggard and tired, and the dark circles under her eyes were much more prominent than they had been before Treasa was born. Slight worry lines had formed on her forehead and around her mouth, and her breathing was ragged after the exertion of climbing the stairs. Still, her eyes radiated peace, and the small hand she rested on Maren's back was a comfort to her. "Are you all right?"

"Me? I'm fine," Maren managed, clearing her throat slightly and sitting up. "How about you? You don't look well at all." She reached forward to brush a stray lock of lank hair from Ceara's forehead, noticing as she did that small bruises and slight red patches had formed by her temples. Her heart thudded at the thought that the sisters would beat Ceara so soon after her delivery. "Maelisa! Did you get punished?" She moved closer to examine the marks.

Ceara shook her head. "I broke some blood vessels in my face during my labor. It's because I was straining so much. I didn't notice them either until Amy pointed them out. Don't worry; I'm fine." Her voice was strained, however, and she punctuated her words with a rasping cough.

Maren recognized that she had been so wrapped up in her grief that she had not even noticed Ceara's obvious ailments. She reached out to hug her friend. "Maelisa, I'm so sorry." The tears began again as she felt how fragile Ceara was beneath her smock, but Ceara held her tightly.

"It's all right, Cassán. It's all for the best." She helped Maren lie down on the bed and lay down beside her, close enough that their noses almost touched. "There," she said with a grin. "We can share a bed now. We couldn't do this before."

Maren shook her head through her tears. "Don't joke about it, Maelisa. I can't stand it. Maybe that's how you cope, but not me."

"No, I've noticed," Ceara responded quietly. "You cope by turning away from the only One who can offer you peace." She tried to look into Maren's eyes, but Maren refused to meet her gaze, turning away to look intently up at the cracks in the ceiling.

"Don't tell me that. I'm not interested in hearing your sermon. God can't help me. No one can! I'm the only one who can get myself out of this situation. And somehow I will, you'll see. I'll get both of us out of this horrible place."

Ceara was quiet as Maren stared upwards, and then asked softly, "How?"

Maren's brave, angry exterior cracked and she allowed the tears to fall uncontrolled again. "I don't know!!" she cried. "I have no idea. I'm weak. I'm stuck here forever and I'll never see my family again. I'll never see Mother"—she gulped—"or Da, or Rian...and..." She squeezed her eyes shut tight as a familiar face flooded her memory. "...and I'll never see Faolán. I'll never see any one of those people that I love because I made the mistake of telling someone how I felt. I can't allow myself to share myself again...I'll only get hurt."

Great sobs burst from her as she lay on her back and looked up at the ceiling. Ceara stayed beside her silently and kept her hand on Maren's shoulder until her cries had lessened somewhat, and then she began to sing softly as Maren lay with her arm across her eyes. "*Lord Jesus, my King...my sins purged away; In thy loving embrace...I endureth each day.*"

With disgust, Maren turned her head. *Just what I need now, a song about the Jesus who was betrayed by His own Father. How comforting.* Ceara continued in a soft voice, though, and Maren found herself relaxing as she listened.

"*O Jesus, my Lord...I serve Thee to find; Your promise of rest...And quiet of mind.*" Her voice swelled with emotion as she sang, and as Maren turned to look at Ceara she found that her eyes were closed as she immersed herself fully in the song. Something tugged at her memory, and as Ceara continued to sing, Maren found that she was humming along, forming a harmony that blended beautifully with the singing.

She closed her eyes and listened as their voices rose sweet and strong in the dank room. "*Lord Jesus, Thy Son...Nailed high on a tree...Through darkness and shame; Make Him known to me.*" Maren found herself remembering her knees pressing into the dirt, her hands sliding down across rough stone to rest on her skirt. She felt the wetness of the dewy ground melting into her skirt as their voices mingled in the stale air, and felt the caress of a morning breeze against her face.

Her eyes popped open and her mouth dropped as the song died on her lips and she lurched up into a sitting position. She remembered!

"Maelisa!" she shrieked.

Ceara had stopped singing as soon as Maren had risen from the bed and now slowly sat up as well, propped up on her elbows. "What is it?" she asked in wonder.

"That song...that song that you were singing just now...do you sing it often?" Her eyes were wild, and Ceara began to feel slightly worried about her friend.

"I sing it sometimes. Usually just when I'm alone. Why?"

"Because I *know* it, Maelisa! I've heard you singing it before, I know I have. Only it wasn't in here!" She jumped up from the bed and paced around the room, her coarse smock swishing against her legs as she moved hurriedly around the room. "I was on deliveries with my father and we stopped outside the convent laundry just outside of Somhairle. I was poking around the walls trying to see something...and I heard you, singing that song! I *know* it was you...I will never forget that voice. I sat down by the wall and closed my eyes and hummed along with you, just like I did now." She stopped her panicked movement briefly and closed her eyes, remembering that crisp morning and the wonder she had felt in that moment. "It was like...it was like our souls were joining together right there."

Ceara had raised herself up completely and she looked at Maren in disbelief. "I remember that day," she replied softly. "I heard you singing on the other side of my wall. I couldn't believe it; I thought that God had sent an angel to comfort me. And it was *you*?"

Maren rushed over to hold her friend's hands. Ceara couldn't understand her sudden frantic excitement. "Maelisa," Maren demanded, "were you ever in any other convent or is this the only one? Tell me! It's important!"

Ceara shook her head. "Only this one, Cassán." Maren threw her hands up in exultation and gave Ceara a huge hug, causing the smaller girl to struggle to keep her balance. Ceara looked absolutely bewildered as Maren rushed around the room once again. "Why is that so wonderful, Cassán?"

"Don't you get it, Maelisa? They drove me around for hours on the way here, *hours!* There was black paper over the windows, too, so I couldn't see out. And now I know why they did that; it was to confuse me! If I thought we were so far from home, I'd never dream of trying to escape. We're in Dublin, Maelisa, and Somhairle is only moments away from here! My *father* is only moments away from here! He could be here tomorrow morning, outside those walls, delivering milk to the farmers down the road. We have to get a message to him! He could come and get us out of here!" She fairly danced in her jubilation, joy written on her features for the first time in months. "To think that I've been so close to him all this time!"

Ceara smiled at Maren's enthusiasm. "But Maren, how do you plan on doing that? These walls are so thick and tall. You wouldn't dream of trying to get to the other side."

"I wouldn't if I didn't know my father was there. But Maelisa, you must tell me: where were you when you were singing that morning? Were you in the dining hall? Were you at Mass? Where?"

Ceara held up a hand, laughing slightly. "Hold on! I was in my room. I was feeling sick that morning, so they let me stay in to rest."

"Then you must show me which room you were in before you came here to room with me. Don't you see? If I could hear you singing, then that means that whichever room you were in must have bordered directly on the outside wall! And it *also* means that the wall there is thinner than it is elsewhere, because I could hear nothing through the other parts of the outside wall. We have to go check and see if there is a way to get through!"

She was breathing heavily in her eagerness, and her eyes pleaded with Ceara to help. Ceara thought a moment before slowly standing and reaching out for Maren's hands.

"We will do it. I will show you where the room is, but we cannot go now. Étain and Fiona will be there, and it would be impossible to find anything with them there. We cannot let them in on the scheme." Maren shook her head earnestly as her heart raced. She didn't want Étain to know anything about what she was planning. "We will plan a time for tomorrow, when everyone will be working and we can sneak away for a few moments." Ceara was glancing around the room even before she had finished her sentence, and then moved quickly to the dresser's bottom drawer, opening it and drawing forth the sharp scissors they had used to cut Maren's hair and Treasa's umbilical cord. Maren tried to force away the flood of memories that swept across her as she looked at the shears that Ceara held out to her. "Here. You take these and hide them deep in your pocket. We'll see if we can get through the wall with those. I'll pretend to be sick during Mass and sneak down the hall to wait for you behind the first set of stairs. When you are standing in line to fill your basin, do something to make it necessary for you to go back to our room."

Maren nodded, thinking quickly. "I'll...spill the tub on myself! Then I'll tell the Sister that I need to go change."

Ceara agreed. "That should work. Then come quickly down to the stairs and I will take you to the room. We won't be able to stay long, though," she warned, and Maren bobbed her head again in concurrence. The thrill of plotting suddenly gave way to an incredible fear, and she grabbed Ceara in her arms for another tight hug.

"Oh Maelisa! I'm so scared and excited all at once."

"I know. But we have God on our side. If He wants it to work, it will. Now go to sleep." She bent her neck slightly and they touched their foreheads together affectionately, and Ceara moved to her own bed. Maren climbed under her blanket and lay awake in anticipation for another hour before finally drifting off to sleep.

Chapter Eighteen

As the bell for Mass rang loudly outside their window, Maren woke immediately and clambered out of the bed, tossing the scant blanket aside in excitement. She had slept deeply despite her tossing and turning earlier in the night, and was wide awake and ready to follow through with Ceara's daring plan. She moved to Ceara's bedside even as she was throwing her smock over her head.

"Maelisa!" she whispered urgently at the still form on the narrow cot. "Come on! We've got to wake up and get on with it!" Ceara shifted slightly and moaned. Maren's brow furrowed as she shook her friend's shoulder. "Come on!"

Ceara's eyes were glazed as she rolled slowly over and gazed up at Maren. "What...what is it?" she asked in a very strange voice. Maren took a step back in surprise.

"It's time to get up. The bell for Mass just rang and we want to get on with the Plan, remember?" Maren couldn't hide her concern as Ceara sat up, the strange look still in her eyes. She rubbed them sleepily with her fists and managed to stand up, and groped for her smock before Maren reached for it and helped her out of her nightgown. "What's wrong?"

Ceara shook her head. "I don't know...I feel very strange..." She tottered around the room slowly, pulling the coarse shift down around her knees and straightening it out with her hands awkwardly. Maren watched and worried as she shook her head, blinking rapidly in an effort to clear her vision. "But the Plan...yes, I remember. Let me just think a moment..." She reached for her water glass and drank thirstily, emptying it in one long gulp as Maren stared at her with wide eyes. Never had she seen Ceara drink all her rationed water so quickly. She stepped forward and grasped Ceara's shaking hands in her own.

"Maelisa..." She spoke quietly. "Are you going to be all right?" She held her friend's hands firmly and tried to look into her eyes, but Ceara's pupils were dilated and she had trouble focusing on her. Nevertheless, Ceara nodded.

"I will be fine. Let's just get this day underway!" She smiled weakly and gave Maren's fingers a slight squeeze before turning toward the door. Maren grabbed the scissors from the table where she had placed them the night before and carefully slipped them into her apron pocket, resisting the urge to kiss them for luck.

They made their way down the stairs and joined the teeming mass of girls moving steadily toward the chapel hall for Mass. Ceara leaned heavily on Maren for support, and though Maren was concerned about her, she couldn't help thinking in the back of her mind that Ceara's strange affliction would certainly help her to convince the nuns that she was ill and needed to leave Mass to lie down. The first part of their plan would succeed; of that she was certain. Her heart raced at the thought of what else would need to be accomplished during this day.

They took their seats and bowed their heads reverently as Father Conall began the Mass, reaching across the lit candles that stood on the richly covered altar cloth and taking up a large loaf of bread. As always, the girls watched raptly from the hard wooden pews, some with their mouths hanging open at the sight of the precious loaf of bread. Maren saw Amy, sitting a few benches away, use her sleeve to wipe some saliva that was beginning to move stealthily down her chin from her hanging mouth.

She shook her head at the frustration that began welling up inside her; not one of these girls had been allowed to eat anything substantial in the past few months, and some not in years, yet they were forced to sit there watching the priest wave soft, fresh bread in front of their faces. Every one was waiting for the moment when they would share in the Sacrament of the Eucharist and would be allowed a tiny morsel of that bread. Not a single girl there cared about the intentions behind the

Sacrament; it had long since lost any meaning for them aside from that one moment when they received one small taste of home.

    Father Conall lifted the bread high above his head and Maren forced her attention back to him as he spoke, squeezing his eyes shut with supposed reverence. "Blessed are You, Lord, God of all creation. Through Your goodness we have this bread to offer, which earth has given and human hands have made. It will become for us the bread of life." Maren kept her head up and her eyes straight ahead, focusing all her hatred and rage at this man who stood draped in glorious vestments, proclaiming his undying love and devotion to God while she knew he was more devoted to defiling innocent young girls. She thought of Deirdre and her hands curled into fists at her sides. She assured herself once again that if this were truly a man of God, then He was certainly not a God that she wanted anything to do with.

    But she stole a sideways glance at Ceara, whose face was lifted to heaven and her eyes tightly shut. Although there was an unhealthy, worrisome cast to her face, she was moving her lips silently, praying in the way that Maren had often seen her do. She seemed enraptured with the moment and clearly was everything that this man leading the Mass was not; Ceara knew her God and was truly dedicated to Him. Maren felt torn. Did Ceara follow the same God that Father Conall preached about, or was He different? Was there a choice to be made that was different from the one she had already made? Maren had decided that she would not follow a God whose most loyal citizens tortured and raped young girls, but was the God of the Catholic Church that she had grown up with truly the same God that Ceara bowed her head to?

    Father Conall put the bread back down on the altar and poured a small amount of water from a tiny glass into a chalice full of wine, praying under his breath: "By the mystery of this water and wine may we come to share in the divinity of Christ, who humbled Himself to share in our humanity." He lifted the chalice high and proclaimed loudly, "Blessed are you, Lord, God of all creation. Through Your goodness we have this wine to offer, fruit of the vine and work of human hands. It will become our spiritual drink." Replacing the gleaming goblet on the altar, he gestured to the congregation of ragged girls. "Pray, brethren, that our sacrifice may be acceptable to God, the Almighty Father."

Automatically, still eyeing the bread, the girls responded, "May the Lord accept the sacrifice at your hands for the praise and glory of His name, for our good, and the good of all His church."

The Mass continued, and Maren kept a wary eye on Ceara as her friend seemed to wilt more and more in her seat. As Father Conall lifted the bread up into the air once again and blessed it, telling the story of the Last Supper and pronouncing the words that were to turn the bread into the actual body of Jesus Christ, Ceara wavered in her pew and suddenly pitched forward onto the floor. Maren gasped and moved forward to help her friend, calling out for a nun just as she grasped Ceara's shoulders and turned her over onto her back. "Maelisa! Are you all right?" She glanced up to see Sister Sorcha moving rapidly down the aisle to where the commotion was taking place.

Ceara gave her a wink and then let her head loll to the side. Relieved that Ceara's fainting attack was still part of the Plan, Maren allowed Sister Sorcha to move in and gently lift Ceara's head into her lap. "Miss MacAodhagáin!" She slapped Ceara's face, causing Maren to wince, but Ceara didn't react. Sister Sorcha looked up at the girls nearby, who had gathered around. "Back to your seats, girls! The Sacrament of the Eucharist is about to take place!"

Indeed, Father Conall had not paused once in his recitation of the Liturgy, so most of the girls moved back to their places, remembering the tiny morsel of bread they would receive and unwilling to miss out on it. Sorcha glanced at Maren and hissed, "Help me bring her out into the hall." As Maren reached for Ceara's legs, the other girl coughed and opened her eyes. She let her hands drop.

"Maelisa! Are you all right?" she whispered urgently again. In a daze, Ceara looked from her friend to the nun, who was watching her in expectation.

"I feel...funny..." She put her hand to her head and tried to stand, Sister Sorcha supporting her around the waist and Maren hurriedly moving to her other side. They walked as quietly and quickly as they could down the aisle and into the hallway outside the chapel. Ceara gained strength as they walked, but swayed slightly when they released her. "I...I think I need to go lie down..." She put a hand to her pale cheek and closed her eyes.

Sorcha nodded. "I should say so. You are obviously not yet recovered from the birth. I shall tell Sister Líadan to excuse you for the remainder of the morning, and we shall come to check on you later. Rest up and make sure you drink lots of water. We need you back in the laundry room as soon as possible." She patted Ceara squarely on the shoulder and looked her up and down, then turned to Maren, apparently satisfied that Ceara could make it up the three flights of stairs on her own. "Come, Miss Bradigan. We must return to Mass and get on with our day." She strode briskly back into the chapel and Maren followed, turning at the door to give Ceara a wink and a thumbs-up. Ceara was pale but smiled back, turning and disappearing around the corner of the stairwell. Maren knew she would wait there under the stone of the stairs until she was able to leave the laundry and join her friend there.

She found her place on the pew just in time to have the plate of bread passed to her. Gratefully she took a piece of the soft, fresh bread and found herself breathing a prayer of thanks to God for the timing, stopping in surprise when she realized what she was doing.

The Plan was being carried out as smoothly as could be. Maren hurried through her breakfast and practically raced to be at the front of the line of girls ready to file to the laundry room, anxious not to leave Ceara in her weakened state for any longer than was absolutely necessary. She kept her fingers lightly on her apron as she stood with the other girls, feeling the outline of the scissors through the rough material, and shut her eyes tightly as she whispered another quick prayer. "God, if You're there and You care, let this work."

Did God even care about the little things? Maren felt sure that the god that Father Conall and the nuns here at the convent laundry didn't—he didn't even seem to care about the *big* things—but in her heart, she prayed that Ceara's God did. Despite all her anger toward God for letting Treasa die, for allowing Deirdre to be raped and have to bring another bastard child into the convent to be raised without ever having a father or knowing its mother, she knew deep inside herself that now was the time to trust, and Ceara's God was the only God she could ever come close to having even a tiny hope in. She closed her eyes again. "Please...show me that You're there. Let this work."

They filed out of the room and down the long corridor to the laundry room, taking large piles of laundry from the large bin and bringing their washbasins over to the long line of water pumps to be filled. Maren itched for the line to go faster, and finally she was there. She placed her basin beneath the spout and threw a scoopful of soap powder into the bottom of the tub before beginning to pump. The muscles in her arms had hardened and grown wiry from the months of hard labor, and she filled her tub in a fraction of the time it used to take her. Grasping the handles and moving out of the way of the other girls, Maren took her place and began to scrub. She fairly bounced with anticipation, but knew that she must wait for the water to cool down before she spilled her basin, lest she burn herself.

Suddenly there was a sharp screech of fear to her left. Maren turned to see what the disturbance was and saw a girl stumbling toward her, backing quickly away from whatever had frightened her. Before Maren had time to react, the girl had slammed into her station full force, knocking the tub over and emptying its contents onto Maren's smock. Maren jumped back and let out a yell of surprise, feeling the water soaking through her clothes.

The girl turned as the nun on duty rushed over. "I'm so sorry!" she apologized frantically, running her fingers through her long golden hair nervously. "I thought I saw a mouse! I just reacted...I didn't mean to run into you!"

Maren couldn't seem to focus. "It's...it's all right—" she managed, shaking her dripping sleeves and trying to figure out what had just happened. Sister Mary surveyed the mess with a disdainful look on her face and her arms folded across her chest, her glare focused on the unfortunate girl who had tripped.

"Well, I see we have gotten the morning off to a great start. Clean up the mess now and then get back to your duties." The young girl nodded hurriedly and bent down to retrieve the basin and the soaked laundry, and Sister Mary turned to Maren, who stood sodden and confused. "Miss Bradigan, you may fetch a clean smock and apron from the drying lines and return to your room to change. Then see the nurse in the infirmary about your burns." She turned and strode away as Maren nodded speechlessly.

The girl with the golden hair watched the nun go from her crouched position on the floor and then stood, giving Maren a wink. "Now there's no question about your excuse," she whispered with a glowing smile as she turned to go. "Now go carry out your Plan." She began to walk away as Maren tried to understand how this girl knew about the Plan, but as she moved past the rows of workers a sudden realization took her mind off the girl's strange knowledge.

The water, fresh from the pump connected to the vast tanks of boiling water that were kept hot by raging fires in another part of the convent, had not been hot as it splashed across Maren's smock, but only lukewarm.

She gasped and turned to look for the girl, feeling strangely sure that she would have an explanation, but she was gone, the mess by Maren's station cleaned up and the stone floor dry. Maren scanned the room but could not find even a glimpse of shiny blonde hair; indeed, everywhere she looked there were tangles and dull heads. She realized with a start that although all the faces in the room were familiar, she had never before seen the girl who had bumped into her washtub. Her mind began to race, but she quickly reminded herself that here was her opportunity. Before she got too distracted from the Plan, she quickly put aside all her questions and ran out the door, her hand in her wet pocket and closing around the scissors as she made her way down the hall to where Ceara waited.

Chapter Nineteen

Ceara was asleep when Maren reached their agreed-upon meeting place below the stairwell. Maren crouched down next to her and shook her shoulder gently. "Maelisa! Wake up; I'm here. We can go down to the room now," she whispered urgently. Ceara's eyes opened and took a moment to focus, but when she realized that Maren was with her she smiled.

"You made it," she smiled, sitting up groggily and looking Maren over. A frown crossed her face. "How did you get out of there? Didn't you spill your washbasin on yourself like you said you would?"

"I was going to, but I didn't have to after all!" Maren replied in hushed excitement. "Some girl I've never seen before bumped into me and spilled all my water right down me, from my head to my toes! It was great; she got in trouble and had to clean it up while I was automatically dismissed."

Ceara searched Maren's eyes, still confused, but saw nothing but excitement. "But Cassán..." she said, faltering, "you're not even wet."

Maren looked down at her smock and became aware with a start that she was completely dry; in fact, she distinctly remembered feeling the smock clinging to her as she walked out of the laundry room, but realized now that she hadn't felt its wetness after that. She turned to Ceara, pale-faced, but Ceara was glowing. "Maelisa," she asked under her breath, sure that Ceara already knew what she was going to ask, "do you believe in angels?"

Ceara grinned widely and linked arms with her friend. "Cassán, I have been praying since yesterday that God would provide a way for us to get you out of here, and I know for a fact that He works in mysterious ways. I *do* believe in angels, Cassán. And maybe you've just met one." Her smile brightened her pale face as she yanked Maren forward. "Come on; let's find that thin wall and do our part; He's already done His."

Maren was filled with awe as they walked stealthily down the corridor to the room that Étain and Fiona now shared. She remembered her prayer as she stood in the line earlier that morning, and a small voice whispered in her head, *Your prayers do matter to me, little one.* She halted for an instant, biting back tears, then shook her head to clear it and followed Ceara's determined stride. She would think about it all later; right now they had work to do.

They managed to get to the room without running into any nuns, and Ceara smiled. "Heavenly protection," she whispered, pointing up. "He wants you out as badly as we do." Maren smiled as Ceara started opening the heavy door, then joined her friend to push their way into the room. It smelled musty, and the sunlight streaming through the small, high window on one wall illuminated millions of dust particles floating in its beam. Maren wrinkled her nose.

"Does *our* room smell like this?" she asked in a whisper. Ceara chuckled softly and moved over to the bed.

"Here's where I slept," she said. "And when I was sick that day, I sat up on the bed like this—" She pulled herself up onto the mattress and sat with her back to the wall, resting her head against the stone as though it were a headboard and gazing up at the window on the adjoining wall. "—and I just sang quietly."

Maren was excited. "That stone looks exactly like it does from the outside! I was right; this wall must just be a part of the boundary wall they built around this place. They used the wall as part of the building!" She moved around the room animatedly. "Look! These other three walls are made of a different stone, not so big and solid!" She ran her hands over one of the massive stones that held the great wall together, feeling the pits and dips underneath her hand, and closed her eyes, remembering what it had felt like on that crisp morning. Perhaps her father was out there at this very moment, on the other side of the wall, making a delivery to the farm across the road. "Oh, Da..." she murmured as she caressed the wall. "I'm here. Come and get me..."

Ceara had been examining the stonework above the bed. "Look here, Cassán!" she called in a low, animated voice. "The mortar around the one edge of this stone here is nearly gone! It looks like someone's been picking at it for quite a while." She grinned again and brushed a few pieces of the dry, dusty cement out of the crack as Maren joined her on the small bed. "That must be why we could hear each other; the mortar just needs a few more pieces chinked out and then we'd be through!"

Maren put her ear to the wall and listened: nothing. Then she shivered. "I can feel the cold air seeping through right here. You must have frozen sleeping here!"

Ceara nodded. "It was cold when I first got here. I thought it was always that way until suddenly it got warm, and I realized that it was spring. That was the only way I could tell what time of year it was." They sat staring at each other in an anticipatory stupor, and then Ceara nudged her friend urgently. "Come on! Break out those scissors and let's see what progress we can make on the mortar!"

Maren smiled gleefully back and produced the scissors from her apron pocket. She reached up and began to chip away at the mortar, which tumbled out from its loose nesting place beside the large stone and fell on the bed. Ceara busied herself with brushing the mortar off onto the floor and then under the bed as Maren worked at the small hole that was quickly becoming an opening, their ticket to the outside world.

With a small exclamation of triumph, Maren broke through. The cold wind wafted in through a hole about an inch long and about half as wide. Maren's cheeks were red from the breeze. "Feel it, Maelisa! We made it through!"

Ceara clapped her hands together, sending a gray cloud of cement dust into the air, and coughed as she clambered back up on the bed and pressed her eye to the hole. A tear coursed down her cheek as she choked out, "It's snowing, Maren; I can see it! It's winter already!" She wiped her cheek with her palm, leaving a grimy smudge, but was unable to move for a moment as she treasured her first glimpse of the outside world in over eight months. Maren sat happily as she watched her friend cherish the moment.

"We're going to make it, Maelisa; I just *know* we're going to get out of here!"

Ceara smiled and moved away from the wall. Her eyes were wet. "So, what's next in the Plan, Cassán?" she asked quietly. "How are we going to get through? There's no way we could get even this one stone completely out, let alone enough for you to climb through."

Maren ignored that Ceara didn't mention herself escaping, and thought hard. Finally, it came to her. "Well, if we had some paper, maybe I could write a note and stick it through there. I guess there's a small chance that he would get it, isn't there? Or maybe someone else would find it and bring it to him!" She sat back against the stone, disgusted with herself. "But of course I don't have any paper. Why didn't I think about this before? Now we're going to have to try to sneak out again!"

Ceara's fatigued eyes were twinkling. She reached into her apron pocket and drew forth a large piece of stiff, heavy paper, folded into quarters, and a newly sharpened pencil. "I had some time on my hands while you were away at breakfast and in the laundry," she revealed slyly. "I thought this might come in handy."

Maren snatched the paper from Ceara's hands with a gasp and a squeeze for her friend. "Where did you get this from?" she practically shrieked, opening the precious paper in delight, noting that one edge was ragged as though it had been torn from a book.

"Well, after everyone left Mass there was no one left in the chapel, not even Father Conall or the Sisters. I just let myself in and walked up to that big Bible on the podium at the front of the chapel." She pretended to be chagrined as Maren gaped at her in astonishment, but the gleam in her eye was hard to disguise.

"You tore this out of *Father Conall's Bible?*" Maren yelped, nearly dropping the paper as she realized where it had come from. Ceara nodded matter-of-factly.

"There were lots of blank pages at the back, where he wrote down his favorite Bible verses. He had only filled a few of them, so I just ripped this page out, grabbed a pencil from the drawer in the podium, and took off out of there as quickly as I could."

Maren was amazed. "Maelisa, can you imagine what he could have done to you if he had found you?"

There it was again, that peaceful look in her eyes. "It doesn't matter anymore, Cassán. What matters is that we let your father know—*somehow*—that you're in here, and then he can come to get you out. That's all I was thinking about." She looked slightly withdrawn as Ceara's hand moved automatically to her empty belly, and she winced as she felt the pain of losing Treasa all over again. "There's no one else for me to look after now. I wanted to help you any way I could."

Maren reached for her friend and the two girls held each other closely, feeling bound together in their affection for one another. "Thank you," Maren finally said, drawing back and smiling into Ceara's eyes.

"Let's get this letter written now and get back to where we're supposed to be," Ceara answered, wiping her eyes and drawing back. Maren nodded.

There was some agonizing over what she would write, but they finally agreed that Maren would address the paper as though it were a letter, printing her father's full name and mailing address at the top. Maren did so, pressing down hard with the sharp point of the pencil in order to make the letters as dark as possible. Then she wrote a personal message, short and to the point:

"Da, I am in the convent laundry. Please come and get me out. I love you and will wait for you. Cassán." She knew that by putting her nickname and not her given name, her father would know the message was really from her and was not a cruel joke, which doubtless he would think at first. The nickname was a personal thing between father and daughter, and not many beyond the walls she was imprisoned behind would know of the name.

She relaxed her tense shoulders with an uneasy sigh as she folded the letter back into its quadrants and looked up at Ceara. "I guess that's it," she muttered, lifting the paper for Ceara to see.

"Write his name on the front, too, now that it's folded," she urged. "Maybe no one will notice it if it's white. Remember, it's snowing out there."

"Good idea." Maren painstakingly printed Oran's name and address once again, in bold, stark letters. The point of the pencil snapped off just as she finished the last letter, and both girls jumped slightly, startled, as the tip flew into the air and disappeared behind the bed. They laughed nervously.

"Okay..." Ceara encouraged breathlessly. "Put it through."

Maren hesitated. "Should I push it all the way through or just wedge it in so it will stick out from the wall? Maybe it will be easier to see that way."

"See how far it will go and then just make sure no one can see it from this end. Then we'll decide if we need to push it all the way through."

Nodding in agreement, Maren rolled the folded paper so that it was a slightly elongated tube, the dark letters on the outside showing crisp against the whiteness of the page. She slid it into the hole and began to push it through.

"Wait!"

Surprised, Maren snatched the paper back from the hole in the wall and looked at Ceara, wide-eyed. "What is it?"

"Let's pray over it first." She reached for the paper and Maren consented, holding it out so that both girls had a grasp on the missive. Ceara bowed her head and Maren did the same. "Dear God, You have been watching over us all this while. You brought us together when we both needed a friend, and You have protected us and loved us even through the toughest times we've ever had to go through. Lord God, Father, this is Cassán's chance to go free, to be released from this awful place—"

"—*our* chance," Maren interjected, but Ceara ignored her and continued.

"—You have shown us the way so far, Father, and we place this letter in Your hands. Deliver it to the right people, and bring Cassán's father here so that she might be set free from the evil of this place."

"*Both* of us, Maelisa," Maren urged, and Ceara squeezed her fingers slightly as she continued, a slight quiver in her voice.

"Thank You that You have given us each other. Thank You for the true friend Cassán has been to me. I ask You, Father, that through this experience she will come to know You, that she will trust Jesus as her personal Savior and friend. Lord, You know that is all that matters to me. Bring Cassán to trust in You...please. We ask this in the name of Jesus Christ, Your Son. Amen."

The prayer touched Maren, and she gave Ceara a quick, gentle hug as soon as her hands were released. "We'll both get out, Maelisa; I know it." She rolled the paper into its tube once more as Ceara wiped her streaming eyes.

The note slipped easily into the crack and through the wall. Maren pushed it gently, afraid that it would suddenly break all the way through and fall to the ground, but it held steady. Soon she could push it only with one finger, and then it was beyond her reach. Maren sat back and contemplated it. "It looks pretty good," she commented. Ceara leaned forward and nodded.

"I can't see it at all, but there's no light coming through either. It's perfect, Cassán! It must be sticking straight out of the wall! Praise God! If someone comes this way they're *bound* to see it!" She gave Maren a tight squeeze and then stood up, brushing more cement dust off the bed and her smock. "We should go. I don't know how much time we've used up."

Backing away slowly, Maren scrutinized every inch of the wall above the bed. It was remarkable; she could see no hole, no paper, nothing. The wall looked as it had when they first walked into the room. She allowed herself a little smile and turned around to leave the room.

It was done. All that remained to do now was wait.

Chapter Twenty

It was an agonizing task to put the thought of the missive out of her mind. Maren returned to the laundry room and worked hard, but her mind was churning over the events of the morning. That girl with the long, shining golden hair! Who was she? Maren couldn't help but glance up as each girl passed by her station on their way to retrieve more filthy laundry or to bring a load out to the drying lines, waiting to see that girl again.

The more she thought about it, the more she realized how different the girl had been; her hair was shiny and clean, her eyes were cheerful, and her teeth were white and beautiful. She couldn't have looked like that for more than a few days after entering the laundries, and Maren knew of every new girl who had come to the convent. New girls were a fascination to the hardened, bitter internees of this place, and they stared and whispered and gossiped every time a new one was brought in. This girl had not been one of them, of that Maren was sure.

Then who had she been?

Maren thought about the mess on the floor. It should have taken that stranger a lot longer to clean up a spill of a washtub filled with water and dirty linens. Maren knew that she herself would have been there mopping for at least a quarter of an hour; she had added those precious minutes into her calculation of how long she would be away from Ceara. Yet Maren had taken only two steps before turning back, and the mess had already been cleared up and the girl gone.

Who had she been?

Then there was the question of the water. Maren had often scalded herself at the beginning of her shift, sometimes even from just leaning her wrists against the tub for scant seconds too long as she carried it to her station. The water was steaming, boiling as it splashed from the pumps into the metal basin. The metal conducted the heat, making Maren sweat before she even started washing the clothes. The fires that heated the water were kept going all day long, and the long laundry room was often suffocative from the billows of steam that often issued forth from the pumps and the washtubs all around the room. Maren remembered clearly the steam from her basin rising up into her face as she balanced it on her way to her post; she had to blow it away in order to see where she was going. Yet only a few moments later, the water in the tub had been only lukewarm as it drenched her. And by the time she had walked out into the hall, her clothes were completely dry.

The girl who had bumped her seemed to be the answer to all these questions. Maren shook her head as she scrubbed and mouthed her prayers, somehow certain that she would never see the mysterious stranger again, but feeling sure that she was the key. Without warning, that small voice rang out clearly in her head once more: *I **do** care about the small things, my little one...but mostly, I care about you.*

Shocked, Maren clapped a hand to her chest as she straightened up and looked quickly about. The voice had been so clear that it felt as though someone were breathing on her neck. No one was there, so she bent her head again, her heart suddenly beating rapidly in her chest. "Who are you?" she muttered into the steaming bubbles, terrified that she would hear an answer.

No answer came.

Maren tried again. "Who are You?" she repeated, this time directing her question solely to Ceara's God. *If You are truly a God of love, You will answer me and help me figure all this out!*

I AM THAT I AM.

Maren drew in a quick, shocked breath at the clear, loud voice and put her hands to her ears. Looking about, she realized that no one else had heard the booming answer and that all the girls nearby were looking at her curiously. Folding her hands in front of her, she tried to quiet her heart, which thudded loudly in her chest, and turned back to the washtub. "Are You...are You Ceara's God?" she questioned timidly, just under her breath. She knew that no one would question her mouth moving and would assume that she was reciting her Hail Marys.

The answer came clearly, but more gently than the last. *I am God. I am Ceara's God, and the God who created this world. I wish to be your God, Maren Bradigan...and I will wait for you to come to Me.*

Tears began to course down Maren's cheeks. "The girl...the girl with the long shiny hair...Can you tell me who she was?"

She is my servant.

"Was...was she an angel?"

There was no answer, and Maren began to panic. "Oh, please...please help me find the answers!" She looked frantically around and pleaded for the Voice to speak again, but it did not. She bowed her head over her laundry.

Her mind raced. She finally had to admit to herself that this God of Ceara's was a God that she wanted to know. He *wanted* her...He had asked her to come to Him, and she felt herself responding. *He loves me...and Ceara said He died for me.* All at once a picture of the tiny Bible that Sister Líadan kept in her office drawer formed in her mind, and an idea came to her. That Bible contained the answers, and tonight, Maren was determined to find them.

Chapter Twenty-One

After Maren and the other girls had finished their meal of dried beans and brown bread, they stood to move to their rooms, pushing the splintery wooden chairs back under the tables with the screech of wood against rough concrete. Maren's mind raced with trepidation, as did her heart. Never had she been so excited about a venture as the one she faced this moment.

Ceara had retired to bed after the Plan had reached its completion, and Maren knew that she would likely be asleep by the time Maren had made her way back up the stairs. Silently she pleaded with God that Ceara would awaken in order to help her decipher the answers to the questions that tormented her, and smiled ruefully as she realized that she was praying to the God she hadn't yet decided even existed. The thought came to her that she wouldn't have asked for His help if she didn't believe He was really there, or if she thought that this whole mission was unnecessary. *But I must know*, she thought. *I don't want to just believe because Ceara does. I want to find out for myself, once and for all.*

She made her way down the hall with the other girls, carefully watching the three nuns who were orchestrating the exodus. Sister Líadan was one of them, so she breathed a sigh of relief that the nun wasn't in her office. Her task would have been impossible to execute had Líadan been there as she stole down the long corridor to retrieve the Bible.

Still, she knew that she would not have much time, for Líadan could quite possibly move directly down the hall as well, as soon as the girls had all disappeared from sight. If Líadan caught Maren on her way out as she was entering, Maren would likely not survive the punishment. Líadan did not take kindly to finding anyone in her private space, as Maren and the other internees had discovered one day when Líadan encountered Sister Mary coming out the door of the office. The girls had snickered over their meals as Sister Líadan's loud, furious voice and Sister Mary's weak murmurs of apology rang down the hall. If even a fellow nun could be victim to Líadan's wrath, the fate of a penitent who dared cross the threshold of Líadan's chamber would be terrible indeed.

Keeping a wary eye on the three sisters, Maren waited for her chance. As soon as all three were looking in another direction, Maren broke away from the pack of girls and dashed stealthily down the corridor, keeping her hands against the stone wall and her knees bent in order to stay below the nuns' line of sight. She came to Líadan's door at the end of the hall and peeked in through the slight crack of the open door. No one was in sight.

Maren's heart hammered as she stepped through the opening, wincing at the slight creaking of the hinges. Glancing around to make sure no one was about, she crept around the heavy walnut desk on her hands and knees as quickly as she could manage, and pulled on the handle of the top drawer. It slid open easily, and Maren could see the shining edges of Líadan's small black Bible. *This is too easy*, she thought as she reached in to grab the little book, but memories of the last time Líadan had caught her trying to bring soup to Ceara made her cautious. She didn't have enough hair left for Líadan to cut off this time, and she didn't want to think of what an alternative punishment might be.

She closed the drawer quickly and smoothly and crept around the desk once more. Now came the hard part; if Líadan was on her way to the office there was no way that Maren could make it back down the hall without being seen. *Okay, here we go*, she thought. *I'm going to pray once more to the God I'm not sure of. Let this work, God.* She rolled her eyes at the irony of it even as she was making her way to the door.

Peeking out, she saw no one in view. Tucking the Bible into her apron pocket, she slipped through the door and tiptoed back into the hallway, streaking along the rough-hewn rock wall as fast as she could, striking her foot on a small outcropping of stone and letting out a muffled cry.

Suddenly seized with panic, she dashed to the stairwell and raced up the stairs two at a time, no longer caring how much noise she was making. Voices floated down the corridors and spurred her mad flight. She reached the top of the third flight and pounded her way to the room where Ceara was sleeping, opening and shutting the heavy door in one fluid motion. As the door closed, Ceara sat up in bed, startled.

"Cassán?" she cried out. "What's happening?"

Maren moved straight to her bed and immediately pulled the Bible out of her pocket and tucked it under the thin mattress. She stripped her dress and apron off and threw them in a corner, yanking her nightdress over her head as she leapt into bed and pulled the covers up to her chin. "Shhh!" she instructed Ceara sternly, then turned away from the door and shut her eyes, trying desperately to control her ragged breathing.

Not less than a minute later the door was pushed open again. Sister Dairíne stood framed in the light from the torch she carried to illuminate the dark room. Maren could hear other nuns moving hastily up and down the hall behind Dairíne. "Girls!" she snapped. "Have either of you heard anything amiss tonight?"

Ceara sat up and shook her head, her eyes darting to Maren questioningly. Dairíne caught the look and focused on Maren's shadowy form. "Miss Bradigan!" she barked. "Do you know anything about the ruckus we heard in the hall a moment ago?"

Maren turned and sat up slightly, blinking in the dim light and yawning. Her breathing had slowed somewhat, but she could feel her heart pounding in her chest from the exertion of running up the stairs and opening the heavy door. "No, Sister," she muttered, wiping her eyes with her hand. "I didn't hear anything until you came in just now."

Sister Dairíne looked at her suspiciously, then moved forward, holding the torch over Maren's bed in order to get a better view. "Pull down your coverlet, Miss Bradigan," she directed in a slow, threatening tone. Maren did so, exposing her nightdress, and prayed that her beating heart would not be visible through her chest. Sister Dairíne looked her up and down carefully as she moved her arm to shine her torch into the corner where Maren had thrown her clothes. "Is that your clothing, Miss Bradigan?" she asked icily.

Maren nodded. "Yes, it is, Sister."

Apparently Sister Dairíne was not quite satisfied that Maren had not climbed into her bed still wearing her work clothes, for she leaned so closely over Maren with the torch that she could feel its heat on her legs. Maren lay calmly looking back at her until she drew back with a sigh and turned to leave, closing the door behind her without another word.

The girls lay in silence for quite some time, listening carefully to the sounds in the hall outside their door. After a while, they heard the voices grow faint as the troupe of investigating nuns moved down the stairwell and back to their activities in the common room. Still, they lay quietly until they were sure no one had come back, and then Ceara pulled herself painfully up to rest on one elbow.

"What was *that* about?" she demanded in a whisper.

Maren crawled from the bed and reached below the mattress for the Bible. "I stole this from Líadan's office," she confided as she held the small, gilt-edged book out for Ceara's inspection. "I tripped on something at the bottom of the stairs and they heard me, so I raced up here as fast as I could. I didn't want to get caught with it. Líadan would have done something terrible to me, I'm sure." Ceara continued to watch her face, and Maren felt suddenly guilty for having unwittingly involved her friend. "I'm sorry you had to lie for me," she added regretfully, unconsciously winding a finger around a strand of her ragged hair. "But I just had to do it. I didn't know where else to find the answers."

Straightening up slightly, Ceara shifted herself to the edge of the bed. "What answers, Cassán?" she inquired softly, taking the Bible and leafing through its delicate pages. "What answers are you looking for?"

Maren thought before responding, sensing that this was an important moment. She wasn't sure how to express to Ceara all that was in her heart, but she knew that if anyone would understand, Ceara would. Never had Maren fully been able to trust anyone the way she trusted this young girl. "Before I came here," she began slowly, "I thought I knew who

God was, and what He wanted from me. I was taught about Him all my life, and my parents always told me what I needed to do in order to be in His favor." She paused, suddenly recalling her mother's stern words about Faolán Ó Ciarmhaic, and tears began to form in her eyes. "It seemed so simple; just follow the rules and don't mess up, and you will go to Heaven. Everyone in our village lived that way, and they all seemed so happy."

Ceara was listening intently, and her warm eyes, without saying a word, encouraged Maren to continue. A tear wrenched itself free from Maren's eye and she wiped at it self-consciously. "So when my mother told me that it was wrong to be falling in love with Faolán, I did what I thought was right, and I went to confess. That's how it's supposed to work, right? I confess my sin, say my penance and then all is forgiven. But this time it didn't work that way. Instead of being patted on the head and told that God still would have me as part of His kingdom, I was stolen from my school and they brought me here to be punished." She was crying now, and her words came out with difficulty. She could feel Ceara's eyes on her but refused to look up as she dried her face on her blanket, working hard to stop the tears. When she was slightly more composed, she looked up again.

"Suddenly I saw a whole new face of God, a God who punishes even if we're sorry and uses his servants to hurt us and beat us into submission. I couldn't understand it; what had I ever done wrong? All these other girls, if they went through what I did when they first came in, must have had to go through the Sacrament of Reconciliation as well, didn't they?" She paused and stared at Ceara for the answer. Ceara nodded. She had been through it as well. "Father Seanán said that I had been absolved of my sins. I can't understand how that could be if they still wanted us to stay here and work and be beaten and punished every minute of our lives. Isn't forgiveness total? If you did something to betray or hurt me and I forgave you, I wouldn't expect you to do anything for me in order to earn it. I already forgave you! So why do we still have to work for it if we are truly forgiven?"

Ceara looked as if she wanted to say something, but she closed her mouth and nodded in encouragement for Maren to go on. Maren suddenly gave a strange half-smile.

"And then I met you. I had never met anyone who trusted in God the way that you do, even in your worst pain. All through what you have gone through, you still love Him and trust that He will take care of you. I haven't been able to understand that! First you were raped and became pregnant. Then you were shunned by the community and your own family and brought here to this awful place. Then you were beaten, and stripped of all your dignity, forced to work even though you were ill and growing heavier with child every day. Then you—" Her chin trembled at the memory, her voice broke, and she dropped her face again. "Then you went through all that labor and only got to hold your precious baby for a few moments before her life was taken from her." She sniffled and pictured Treasa's tiny face, an image that would never leave her. Tears flowed down Ceara's face as well as Maren continued. "All this you have gone through, and I have never seen you lose your faith that God is loving you and holds you in His arms. How can you have such faith in a God who would put us here and torture us every day?"

She leaned forward and placed her hand on Ceara's, and felt her friend squeezing her fingers lightly. "Then I slowly started to realize that your God and the God I obeyed and thought I understood all my life may not be one and the same. If God loves us, He wouldn't command His servants to hurt other people. That didn't make any sense to me. But *your* God doesn't seem to do that. I trust that you would not trust in a God who demanded torture, for I can see that you are His true servant and I know that you would never do that if anyone asked you to. From the way you treat others, I think I've seen a little bit of how God treats you."

Reaching for the Bible again, she held it reverently. "I've never seen a copy of this close up," she confessed. "My parents always said that only a priest should be allowed to read the Bible. But after what has happened the last few days, I know that this Bible is my only way to find the answers. A priest can't explain it to me; I've talked to many priests and never heard anything like what I hear from you. I heard God speak to me, Maelisa! I *know* I did! And that girl...the one who spilled my washbasin...I thought – I *hoped* – that maybe she was an angel sent to help our Plan work that day." She opened the Bible and stared at its pages for a few silent moments, and then turned to Ceara with shining eyes. "I want to know your God, Maelisa. I want to know why you trust Him so much, and I know and trust that this is His Holy Word. I asked Him a question, and if I'm hearing Him right, He pointed me here." She held up the Bible again. "I've been so angry, and confused, and I feel like I'm starting to understand. I'm believing again. Tonight I finally want to *know*, and I would like you to help me."

Sensing that this was the moment for her to speak, Ceara smiled at her friend. "I would love to help you find the answers, Cassán," she responded in a voice that trembled with emotion. "And I think before we go any further, I would like to pray that God will be here with us now and reveal the answers to you so clearly that you will never again have any doubt of His complete love for you." They bowed their heads, but Maren wasn't listening as Ceara poured her heart out to her God. Her mind was swirling and her palms were wet. This, she knew, could be one of the most important moments of her life. Ceara closed the prayer and they sat back again. "What is the first question, Cassán?" Ceara invited gently, leaning back against her pillow and allowing the wall to support her weight.

"Has God forgiven us? Was He the one who commanded Father Seanán to bring me here?"

Ceara smiled. "That question could be easily answered. Here, let me see if I can find that for you." She reached for the Bible and flipped to a point somewhere near the middle. "Here it is: First John, chapter one, verse 9: 'If we confess our sins, He is faithful and just to forgive our sins and to cleanse us from all unrighteousness.'" She looked at Maren to see if she had understood the verse. Maren gazed at her blankly, so Ceara flipped back through the Book. "Let me show you this, in Ephesians, where it says 'even when we were dead in trespasses'. That means that we were so lost in our sin that it could be likened to being dead. We were so sinful that we might as well not even be living, but according to First John, He forgives us anyway, if we confess."

"But that wasn't me," Maren argued. "I wasn't sinful."

"But you were, Maren. All of us are. It's human nature!" At Maren's confused look, Ceara once again flipped forward through the tiny Book, keeping her finger in the place from where she had just read. "See here, back in First John again, right before the other verse I read. 'If we say that we have no sin, we deceive ourselves, and the truth is not in us.' And in Romans 3:23, it says, 'for all have sinned and fall short of the glory of God'. People sin, Maren, every day in every way, and it is just because we are people. If you lie, it's a sin. If you take an apple from a tree that doesn't belong to you—or a Bible from a desk that isn't yours,"— she winked at Maren—"it's a sin. You cannot look at me and tell me that you have never done anything like that."

Slowly, Maren nodded. "Of course I have. I just don't think of that as a sin."

"It *is* a sin, though, Maren. God sees things differently than we do. Do you think a holy, just God would ever tell a lie? Or even eat a piece of candy after His mother told Him not to? God doesn't do anything that is wrong. Only humans do." She watched Maren's face closely to see if she understood her words. Maren was suddenly looking very thoughtful.

"But you said that He forgives us, right? Like the priest does?"

Ceara shook her head. "Not exactly. When the priest forgives you, how long does it last? Forever? Or only for a while?"

"Until the next time you sin," Maren answered promptly. "Then you have to go and confess again. But isn't that the same with God?"

"In a way, yes. When we sin, we must go to Him and confess and ask His forgiveness. The difference is that God has already forgiven us, for everything we had ever done wrong and everything we ever *will* do wrong."

Maren looked astounded. "How did He do that?"

Ceara was flipping pages again. "Here. Read this verse," she encouraged, handing the book to Maren and pointing to the verse she wanted read. Maren took the small volume. "John 3:16," Ceara told her.

Hesitantly, Maren read aloud, "'For God so loved the world that He gave His only begotten Son, that whoever believes in Him should not perish but have everlasting life.'" She looked up at Ceara, confused. "This is talking about Jesus."

Ceara nodded. "God sent Jesus, His Son, to earth in the form of a man, to be a sacrifice for our sins. When Christ was crucified, He was being punished for every sin every man or woman in the world had ever done or would ever do. He took it all on Himself."

Mystified, Maren glanced back and forth from the verse to Ceara. "Why would He do that?"

"It says why right there," Ceara answered, pointing to the book. "Because He loves us. All we have to do is accept this free gift that Jesus has already bought and paid for. He paid the price already. There's no need for us to go to a priest to confess every week. The only One we need to confess to is Jesus, and He willingly forgives us. The debt is paid."

Maren stared at her friend. "I never could figure out why Jesus had to die. I thought that God was a horrible, mean God if He could kill His own Son. But now...I think I understand. He loved us so much that He was willing to die for us, and He did."

Ceara was smiling. "He still loves you, Maren. He's just waiting for you to come to Him and tell Him that you accept His wonderful gift. The people here—the priests and the nuns—they've never accepted it. We can tell because if they had, they would know Christ's love and their lives would reflect it. Once you accept God's gift of Jesus' death, He comes to live in your heart and you have newness of life. They are still bound to the wrong doctrine, but Jesus can set you free from a lifetime of untruth and uncertainty."

Grasping Ceara's hands, Maren felt her heart swell. Suddenly she understood it all so clearly! "Please, Maelisa; tell me how I can do this! Do I just talk to God and ask Him to help me?"

"Pretty much," Ceara nodded, laughing at her friend's elation. "Just pray to Him and ask Jesus to come into your heart."

Maren bowed her head immediately, and surprised both of the girls by bursting into tears. "Oh, Jesus," she managed in between gulping sobs, "You have sent such a wonderful girl to me to tell me about You. I know now what You've been trying to tell me for so long. I understand that You died on the cross for all of us—for me!" She cried harder as she suddenly realized how much she wanted a personal relationship with God. She didn't want him to just be Ceara's God; she wanted him to be *her* God. "Thank You, Jesus, for Your sacrifice. Please forgive all my sins and come to live in my heart so that I can be pure and clean, like Maelisa is. I want to be as content as she is. I want to *know* You. I want to trust You, like she does!"

She felt a great rushing peace flow through her body, and she clung to Ceara and laughed joyfully through her tears. Ceara's tears mingled with her own, and they hugged as Maren finished the prayer with an "Amen". Finally they moved apart, each girl wiping tears from her face and neck.

"So, Cassán," Ceara finally said with a big smile, "what was your next question?"

Maren grinned. "I don't have any more questions now, Maelisa. I know there is only one Answer." They lay back down under the covers and prepared for sleep, each girl mentally reliving the past hour. Maren felt such joy and understanding that she felt barely able to contain it, and finally knew why Ceara had been so peaceful throughout all her time here at the Laundries. She looked toward her friend, who was obviously exhausted and trying not to show the pain she was in. "Maelisa," she whispered, and Ceara looked over at her. "Thank you."

Ceara smiled again. "You're welcome."

Chapter Twenty-Two

Maren was fairly bubbling with excitement as the girls woke the next morning and clambered into their shifts. Ceara moved slowly and painfully, but Maren barely noticed as she dug out the prized comb and began to tug it through her disheveled curls. "Today's the day, Maelisa; I just know it. Someone will come and rescue us today, and we'll finally leave this awful place and go home to Mother and Da. I can feel it!" She clasped her hands together, and the sharp points of the wooden comb dug into her palm. "Ow!" Dropping the comb on the floor, she pinched the small cut between her fingers and moved her hand to her mouth to suck away the drops of blood. Distracted, it took her a few moments to notice that Ceara was sitting on the bed with her shift half on and half still hanging from her side, breathing heavily. Maren immediately forgot her hand and moved forward. "Maelisa! Are you okay?"

Ceara waved a hand in the air. "I will be," she whispered hoarsely. "I'm just feeling weak." Panting, she tried to pull the work dress over her arms. "Can you please help me with this?"

Maren hurriedly helped Ceara put her hand in the sleeve and draw her arm through the opening, noticing how thin Ceara's arms had become. "Are you sure you're all right?" she asked again, supporting Ceara as she stood up. Ceara nodded and stood for a moment with her eyes closed.

"I'm just a little weak from losing so much blood after Treasa was born," she responded. "I'll feel better in a moment." She prayed silently, standing with one hand still on the bed and her lips moving rapidly as Maren watched in concern. When Ceara was finished, she opened her eyes blearily and started to move toward the door.

Maren finally voiced her thoughts. "You're not still bleeding, are you?" she asked, taking Ceara's arm and helping her across the room. "I thought that all stopped soon after she was born!"

"No, it's not finished yet." Ceara blinked a few times to clear her head. "I guess it'll stop soon, but it's making things a little harder for me. I'll be all right, though; don't worry about me." She hugged Maren and smiled. "I'm so pleased about last night, Cassán. It's the start of a whole new life for you. Don't let worrying about me hold you back from your relationship with God." She walked down the steps, holding onto the wall for support, and Maren watched as she disappeared down the first flight of stairs. She was worried, all right; never had she seen her friend look so disoriented.

Maren kept a close eye on Ceara all through breakfast and as much as she could while they were in the laundry room. Ceara was paler than she had ever been, yet she moved determinedly through her regular routine, trying hard not to let the nun on duty see how little strength she had left. She had stationed herself next to Maren, for which Maren was grateful, for from time to time Ceara would lurch slightly to one side and Maren was able to quickly move to help her friend stay upright. Her tired eyes said a silent "thank you" for the concern, and her chapped, reddened hands trembled as she plowed through the basin of wet clothes. Maren wished the day would end so that she could help her friend eat some food and get tucked back into bed.

Halfway through the day, Maren was bringing a load of wet linens to the drying lines when she heard a commotion coming from elsewhere in the convent. Used to hearing shouts of protest from newcomers or disobedient internees, she ignored the sounds at first, but as she got closer to the hall, she heard a man's voice clearly shout, "I'll find her! I know ye've got my daughter here! Leave go of me!" Several nuns could be heard arguing feebly with the intruder, but it was obvious from their faltering tones that he was overpowering their arguments. The voices grew closer, and Maren stopped dead as she heard the man call out, "Maren! Maren Bradigan! Where are ye?"

"Da!" she shouted joyfully. Immediately she dropped the clean laundry on the floor of the laundry room and raced for the door just as Sister Sorcha moved to intercept her. The nun held her arms out to block Maren's way to the door.

"Wait, Miss Bradigan! You don't know who that could be! Perhaps it's someone who means harm to you! Now let's pick up the linens and get back to work." Sister Sorcha did her best to sound commanding, but the fear and anxiety in her voice caused Maren to press on.

"Don't you think I know my father's voice? Da! Da! I'm in here!" She struggled with the taller woman as the nun tried to push her away from the door. All the girls in the room were watching with open mouths and their hands hanging straight by their sides. Maren paid no attention to them. All that mattered to her was that she made her way to the source of that familiar voice.

The door burst open and Oran Bradigan raged through, a cluster of muttering nuns wringing their hands behind him. His eyes searched the room quickly, then came to rest on the struggling figures of the girl and the nun. At the first sight of Maren's face, joy lit his features and he rushed forward. Maren broke free of Sorcha's grip and was enveloped in her father's strong arms. "Da! You came! You found me!" She was crying now, pressing her face against his broad chest and breathing in the familiar scent of his hard work. Oran held her tightly, tears streaming down his weather-worn cheeks.

"Oh, my girl," he rasped, kissing the top of her head and stroking her ragged, matted hair. "I've been searching for you for so long. Never did I believe you would have ended up here! Father Seanán helped me with my search...I can't believe he wouldn't have known you were here." His tone was disbelieving and furious.

The nuns stood in a huddle, unsure of what to do. The girls around the room were focused on the reunion, their eyes wide and their shoulders shaking with emotion. Maren clung to her father and looked up at his craggy face. "The note—you must have found my note!" Her features were radiant, an expression of the wonder and joy she felt inside. She knew that no one could have done this but her newfound God, and she rejoiced in His gift to her. She realized that had her father come before this day, she never would have found the peace and joy in knowing her Lord that she had discovered with Ceara the night before. *His timing is perfect*, she reflected in wonder, then looked back up to her father as he answered her.

Oran nodded. "Your brother found it, just this morning. I sent him on to do the rounds while I took care of some other things on the farm. He came racing back home like his tail was on fire, babbling and yelling about going up to get you. I couldn't figure for the life of me what he meant until he showed me your letter." He squeezed her tightly. "My Cassán...how clever of you to think of such a thing! But how in the world did you end up in this place? Who did this to you?"

As Maren opened her mouth to answer him, there was a slight murmur in the crowd and most of the girls quickly turned back to their duties as Líadan entered the room. Her eyes were ice as she observed Maren with her father, and Maren's arms tightened around Oran's waist as the tall nun stepped forward to address them. There was no way Maren would let him leave her side.

"What, may I ask, is the disturbance here?" Her expression seemed to bore a hole through Maren, who wanted to shrink away, but Oran stood fast and glared angrily at the nun.

"I'm here to collect my daughter, who was brought here without my knowledge. I'll be taking her home now, if you'll excuse us."

Líadan took a step backward to block the door. "These girls are trying to do their work, Mr. Bradigan. I would suggest that we move this little—*party*—to my office. If you will?" She stepped aside and motioned toward the door, and Oran moved forward, still clutching Maren in his comforting arms.

"I don't think there's anything we need to be talking about, Sister," he growled, "so if you'll just be getting out of my way I'll be taking my daughter out of this hellhole and back home where she belongs."

Sister Líadan crossed her arms in front of her bony chest and glared at him. "I'm afraid that's not at all possible. You see, someone who was very concerned about her welfare brought Miss Bradigan here to be admitted. He did the right thing by bringing her here; she is dangerous and a menace to society and herself. She must complete her penance before we can allow her to leave. I am afraid she has become very belligerent and rude, and in fact has been caught several times sneaking out to meet boys." Maren opened her mouth in protest but shut it again, realizing it would not matter, as Líadan continued. "I'm sure you would much rather have her here under our competent supervision than bringing her home to have her running around with that stableboy of yours again."

Oran, sensing Maren's fear, grasped her waist and pulled her tight to his side. "It doesn't matter to me what you say about my little girl. I've looked for her for months, and I will not leave her here now that I've finally found her. You can rot in hell for all I care! And as for whoever brought her here, if I ever find out who he was, he'd better be ready to face his Maker." Furious, he turned and, pulling Maren with him, pushed past the astonished group of nuns, intent on striding down the hall and making his way to the door. Maren shrieked and balked as he went through the doorway. "Maelisa!"

Oran turned to glance at her. "What is it, my Cassán?"

She tugged at his shirt. "Da, we have to go back in and get my friend! Her name is Mae—er, Ceara MacAodhagáin. I promised her that you would take her out as well. We have to go back to get her! She's sick; she can't stay in here! Please, Da; please!"

Oran turned and looked at the nuns, then back into the vast laundry room as he gently put a hand on Maren's shoulder. "Which one is she, child?" he asked, his voice guarded.

Daring to risk Líadan's anger knowing that her father was here and would protect her, Maren ran to Ceara's station and grasped her friend's hand. Ceara was watching her, her eyes sad. "Come on, Maelisa! It's finally happened! Da is here to rescue us." She tugged at Ceara's hand

and started to walk, expecting her friend to follow, but Ceara pulled gently away. Maren turned to her, surprise on her face. "What's wrong, Maelisa? We can leave! God has brought us the miracle we prayed for."

Ceara shook her head, and a tear coursed down her cheek. "It's *your* miracle, Cassán," she said softly, smiling at her friend. "It's not mine."

Confusion wrestled with fear as Maren stared at her. "What do you mean? Da will take you with us; I'm sure of it! This is the chance we've been waiting for!"

Patience glowed on Ceara's white face. "I can't come with you, Cassán. I don't belong to your family, and I was brought here by my parents. The only way I can ever get out is if they come to get me out, and I know they won't." Maren started to protest, but Ceara shook her head, her voice thick with emotion. "This is the chance we prayed for...for *you*, Maren, but never for me. I knew I wouldn't be allowed to leave here."

"But we can ask the nuns! I'm sure if Da vouches for you then they'll let you go! I'm sure of it!"

"Are you really sure of that?" Ceara asked gently, and Maren turned her frenzied face to the door. One look at Líadan's hard features and her father's expression of sadness told the whole story. Maren would be leaving the laundries today, finally—and Ceara would stay...alone.

Desperation clawed at Maren's heart. "I won't leave without you, Maelisa! I won't!" She reached for her friend and clasped her thin body in a tight hug. Ceara hugged her back, both girls crying openly. "I love you, Maelisa! I love you!"

"I love you, too," Ceara answered, stroking her hair and her back as Oran stepped forward. He reached for Maren and started to lift her away from the other girl, who let go immediately and stood back. Maren, however, screamed and tried to grasp onto Ceara's hands.

"Maelisa!" Oran wrapped a strong arm around her waist and pulled her close, stopping her from getting any closer to her friend. Maren sobbed and buried her face in her father's neck, feeling as though her heart was breaking. This was not what she had imagined. Always she had pictured the two of them walking out together, hand in hand, and Ceara being nursed to health at the farm. This was wrong.

Over her father's shoulder, she saw Ceara's face through her tears, and stopped crying almost as suddenly as she had started. There it was again, that peaceful, serene expression she had seen on Ceara's face throughout her many ordeals here at the convent. A little voice whispered in her brain, reminding her that Ceara was in God's hand as surely as she now was. *Let her go...* the voice whispered. *You will see her again, if not on this earth, then in eternity.*

"You're right, Lord," she said softly, and Oran stopped trying to pull her away as he realized that she was no longer struggling. He straightened, allowing her to step back from him and move closer to her friend. She reached out her hands to Ceara's, and they stood facing each other, the fingers of both hands entwined. Maren looked into Ceara's deep, peaceful eyes, and felt the peace of God fill her spirit. Ceara touched the tips of her fingers to her mouth, and Maren melted at this last, silent communication. *You okay?* Ceara was asking.

She lifted two fingers and deliberately drew a small circle around her heart. *I can handle it.* Ceara smiled at the familiar sign and repeated the gesture. "If not on this earth, then in eternity," Maren said in a low whisper, and Ceara nodded.

"In eternity," she answered, her eyes and her voice full of tenderness.

They stood for one long moment, and then Maren nodded in determination. With one last deep breath, she pulled her hands from Ceara's, moved to her father's side, and walked out of the door without looking back.

Chapter Twenty-Three

Nova Scotia, Canada: August 5, 1994

Brigid sat back in silence as her mother finished her story. Her brow was furrowed, and two lines marked her face where her tears had run down. Maren sat and watched her daughter's reaction.

She was quiet for a moment, soundlessly shaking her head as she absorbed all she had been told. Finally, she reached over to grasp her mother's hand in a warm, reassuring grip. "I can't believe they did that to you, Mum," she said in a whisper. "How did you ever keep this from us all these years?"

"Oh, I didn't," Maren responded, placing her other palm atop their joined hands. "Your father knows everything, of course. Right after I arrived home, my father moved our family to Kilrush, which is in County Clare—all the way on the opposite side of Ireland. I think he felt that was as far away from the convent and the past as we could possibly get. I met your father two years after we moved to Kilrush, and we started dating—in a way—shortly after that. I didn't tell him anything at first; it was difficult to allow myself to remember my past, and I worried that if I told him that I'd been in a Magdalen institution, he would think that I was a wayward girl and not wish to be with me any longer. By that time, I knew I was falling in love with him."

She smiled wistfully, the far-away look that had been in her eyes as she told Brigid her story appearing again. "He never pushed, but he knew there was something I wasn't telling him. It wasn't until six years later, when we had both finished our schooling and he came to me to finally propose marriage, that I finally told him everything. I couldn't bear to keep such a secret from him. I told him that if he was to marry me, he had to marry all of me, my past included." She looked at Brigid, who was listening intently. "I remember telling him that it was his decision, that if he still wanted me after he knew all I had been through and where I had been, then I would marry him. And, if not, we could go our separate ways and he would never need to see me again." Maren wiped a tear from her eye as she continued, giving Brigid another smile as she squeezed her hand. "That was so hard for me, darling, because I knew that I loved him more than anything, and that it would kill me to be away from him. There was nothing I wanted more in the world than to be his wife and raise a family with him, but I knew that I could never completely be myself with him until he knew. I also knew that he was a kind man, and that he would listen to everything I needed to say. And he did. He held my hands and watched my face carefully, just like you've done today, and he listened to every word—and perhaps a few more that I'll save for you for later. When I finished, he just wrapped me in his arms and told me that he loved me, and that he wanted to marry me all the more now, to protect me from the demons of my memories." Her voice was fond. "He has been my support all these years. And now you know, too."

Brigid smiled at her mother, tears in her eyes as well. "I'll always support you, Mum, as well as I can."

Maren patted her daughter's hand. "You have been a great support, just by listening. Come on; let's make some more coffee. This stuff's good and cold by now."

Picking up their mugs, they stood up and walked across the kitchen, each in their own thoughts as they methodically went through the motions of grinding and brewing the coffee. Brigid retrieved the bag of coffee beans from the refrigerator and handed it to her mother, who ground them in silence as Brigid filled the coffeemaker with fresh Brita-filtered water and opened the cupboard to get the filters.

It had never occurred to her how privileged she was; how well she had grown up. She had always had everything she needed at her fingertips, had always known the love of the Lord, and had assumed that it had been that way for her mother as well. She knew that her parents had moved to the large brick house on the cliff a few years after immigrating to Canada from Ireland, and her father's job as a real-estate agent had given them the pick of the best houses that lined the sea. His earnings, combined with her mother's salary as a nurse, had allowed them to comfortably furnish the house before Brigid and Donal were born, and now, eighteen years later, they had it completely paid off. Brigid had grown up with every comfort and security her parents had been able to provide for her, and as she looked back, she realized why her happiness—as well as her brother's—had always been Maren's most important goal in life. She had wanted her children to have all that she had missed out on.

  As they sat back down, Brigid studied her mother as she rearranged the folds of her housecoat around her bare legs. She glanced up and her eyes met Brigid's. Maren smiled painfully, and Brigid could see that she was struggling not to cry.

  Brigid immediately reached across for her mother's hand. Maren clasped it and held on, squeezing her eyes shut momentarily as a few lonely tears found their way down her cheeks. Brigid allowed the silence to continue for a few beats before saying softly, "You've done a good job, Mum."

  The few simple words seemed to tear at Maren's heart, and her mouth quivered as she looked back into her daughter's sympathetic, loving face. "I'm sorry, darling," she said at length. "It's just…it's still so painful to think about. Even after all this time…thinking about it isn't the same as saying it out loud. The memories are still so strong for me."

  "I understand, Mum." Brigid waited until her mother seemed more ready to talk, then asked cautiously, "Did you ever see Faolán again?"

  Maren shook her head. "Only the one time, when my father first brought me home to the farm. He had left my father's employ and gone back to Dublin, but he happened to be there when I returned, just picking up a few of his things."

  "Did he say anything to you?"

"Not a word." Maren let loose a rueful laugh. "He avoided me like the plague, just giving me a disdainful glance and making his way back to the car, where my old school friend Orla was waiting for him. She even had the audacity to wave at me as they left."

Brigid gasped, "Oh, Mum; how awful for you!"

Maren waved a hand dismissively. "It's all part of growing up, Brigid. That's all it is. You'll go through the little hurts, too, as you grow. No one is immune. By that time, I had more to think about than boys. I had a best friend who would never drive off in a car and leave me behind."

"You mean Ceara," Brigid supplied, but Maren shook her head.

"No, Brigid. You know who I mean."

"Jesus," Brigid smiled as understanding dawned, and Maren nodded.

"I might never have come to know Him if I had not been sent to the Magdalen institution. All things work together for good for those who love Him. Ceara knew that; she worked very hard to help me realize it."

"It took a long time, though," Brigid countered.

Maren considered this. "I was in the institution for only five months. Although it seemed like forever, I don't see it as being a long time in the grand scheme of things. And, especially according to our Father, that five months I spent there was barely a drop in the ocean of my life. I've lived five months countless times over since I was there. I've known hundreds of people for *much* longer than five months each. Yet, isn't it interesting that such a small amount of time was all it took to have such an impact on my life? Ceara was the best friend I ever had, yet I knew her not even half as long as I carried you inside myself. And during those five months, I made a decision that impacted me spiritually more than any other decision could have, to accept Jesus Christ as my Lord and Savior."

She smiled at her daughter, and leaned forward to place a hand on each side of Brigid's face, cupping her cheeks in her palms. "I pray that you never have to go through anything like I went through in those months, my love. But should you ever find yourself going through a trial such as that, please, don't ever forget just how much good can come out of something so awful. If I had the choice, I would do it all over again." She raised her eyebrows, waiting for a signal that Brigid understood. "I *would*, Brigid," she repeated, and at her daughter's nod, she released her and sat back again, satisfied.

Brigid's mind was already far away, engrossed in her mother's memories. "The Magdalen institutions…that's what you called them, wasn't it?"

Maren nodded. "According to the nuns, we were representative of Mary Magdalen, sent there to wash ourselves clean as Jesus did for her. Only, they were never satisfied that we were clean enough. Many people call them the Magdalen Laundries, but it is a very hush-hush topic in Ireland."

"Are there…are there still Magdalen Laundries in Ireland?" Brigid asked in sudden horror.

Slowly, Maren nodded again. "The first one started in the mid-1800's, and as far as I know, they have yet to be shut down. Right at this very moment, Brigid, there may be girls and women suffering as I and Ceara did." The faraway look in her eyes had returned. Brigid couldn't believe it.

"But Mum, that's terrible! Can't we do something about this? Have you ever contacted the government? Told them your story? I'm sure they would want to shut them down – if there are still girls there, suffering like you did, you could do something to save them!" Maren watched as her mother seemed to shrink into herself, sitting with her eyes downcast, slowly shaking her head. As a question suddenly occurred to her, Brigid broke into her mother's introspection. "And Mum, what about Ceara? Is she still there? Did she survive?"

Maren looked at her, pain and regret evident in every line of her face, and Brigid, rigid with tension, waited. Her hands curled into fists as she looked wildly at her mother. She was not aware that her fingernails were cutting deeply into her palms until after Maren answered her question.

"I don't know, Brigid. I haven't seen or heard from her since that last day."

Late on the eve of her seventeenth birthday, Brigid Adair found herself alone in the kitchen, her fingers wrapped around a mug of warm tea as she stared out into the dark night. Donal was asleep, and her mother and father had gone for a walk on the beach before they settled in for their evening television show on the small set in their room. The moon was reflected in the sea, and scattered light danced on tiny waves as she watched her parents walk barefoot in the sand, a small echo of their laughter floating up through the air and in the open window. Brigid smiled as Maren reached up to tousle Garvan's dark red hair and dashed off across the beach, spraying sand up onto her rolled-up slacks and sun-browned legs. Brigid's father gave a shout and took off after her.

Brigid sighed as she gazed out the window. It seemed she had aged much more than just a year. Her mother's story had settled deep into her soul, creating a restlessness, a yearning to know more. All at once, Maren Adair was more to her than just a mom, a sometimes frumpy, getting-more-than-slightly-older housewife whose part-time work as a nurse lent her life some meaning. She was suddenly much more of a real person, a person who had suffered and been through things that Brigid herself could never have imagined before this day.

Brigid shook her head. *The Magdalen laundries,* she mused. As a thought occurred to her, she got up from the breakfast nook, casting another glance across the water before walking out of the kitchen and leaving her mug of still-warm tea on the table. Her parents were nowhere to be seen.

She wandered into the den, where her father had left the computer running when Maren had called for him to join her in a walk. It hummed in the darkness, sending an eerie glow across the room until Brigid switched on the desk lamp and settled herself into the comfortable computer chair. Reaching for the lever and reclining back an inch or two, she moved the mouse and started a connection to the Internet.

When the computer's high-pitched dial tone had ceased its noise and the flashing hourglass on the screen changed to an arrow, indicating that the connection had been made, Brigid sat forward and selected the menu for "Favorites", highlighting AskJeeves.com and waiting for it to load.

Enter a topic, the machine prompted. Picking at the keyboard and mentally cursing herself once more for never having taken typing classes, Brigid painstakingly typed in the keywords "the Magdalen laundries". Punching the *enter* key, she leaned back once more, her heart thumping within her in anticipation. She reminded herself that her mother had told her the convent institutions were an unsavory topic in Ireland, and tried to convince herself that she would not be disappointed if the search turned up nothing. The hourglass on the screen metamorphosed into a flashing arrow once more, and Brigid caught her breath as the search engine unrolled the results it had found on her topic: "*Baltimore Area Laundromats*"..."*Maytag announces plans for new front-loading washing machine*"..."*Facts on the Magdalene by Roman Catholic authorities*"—nothing seemed to be relevant to what she wanted. Frustrated, Brigid checked out a few of the websites, skimming the Catholic literature on icons and stories about Mary of Magdalene with some interest, but found nothing on the convent laundries.

She sighed in resignation and closed the open windows, bringing the screen back to her search engine. Slowly she added the word "Ireland" to her search, and hit the *enter* button again, watching with mild curiosity to see what the device would come up with. Hundreds of links to websites scrolled across her screen, and she lazily moved the mouse down the page, glancing through the titles. Her eyes searched frantically for any mention of the laundries, but there was not one to be found. "I guess it really is a hush-hush topic," she grumbled, clicking on one of the links.

The page brought her to the Ireland Information site, flashing a friendly welcome banner across the screen and listing a plethora of topics she might be interested in. She skimmed the titles, and noticed one that read, "Sign up for free weekly news emails from the Irish Journal!"

Brigid considered the idea. *Well, why not?* she thought. Even if she never found an article relating to the laundries, at least she could learn some useful and interesting information about her heritage. She had never learned much about Ireland, and to tell the truth, had never been much interested. Her mother's story had brought her curiosity to the forefront. She suddenly found herself desiring to know all she could about where her parents had come from. Decisively, she clicked on the icon.

Swiftly she was brought to an area where she could fill in her email account information and areas of interest, and half-heartedly she typed in her email address, skipping over the personal information that was not required. Her father's warnings never to give any private information over the Web played sotto voce in her brain as she passed over the spaces for her home mailing address and age, and she smirked as she placed a checkmark in the box after "male" where it asked for her gender. *There, Dad, no personal information given. They can't come racing through the modem wires and come and get me.* She gave the *enter* key one last jab and waited as the page refreshed itself.

"*Thank you for requesting the Irish Journal weekly email service. Now that you are registered, you will receive weekly updates of all the pertinent news on what's happening in Ireland, delivered right to your Inbox!*"

The computer went on to invite Brigid to sign up a friend or apply for special offers, and with a sigh she disconnected from the Internet and turned off the computer. Suddenly exhausted by the emotional rigors of the day, she dragged herself through the motions of brushing her teeth and washing her face, and went straight to bed.

Chapter Twenty-Four

Eight months later

"Mum!"

Maren turned from where she had been loading clothes into the dryer and glanced down the hallway. Brigid appeared around the corner from her bedroom and was dashing toward her, taking barely two steps inside the kitchen before bounding down the stairs to where Maren had been doing the wash.

"Mum!" she yelled again, and Maren chuckled to herself, shaking her head at her exuberant daughter.

"Yes, Brigid," she answered calmly. "What is it?"

Brigid thrust herself through the laundry room door and practically into her mother's arms. "Look," she panted, striving to catch her breath. "...Look...what I found..." Leaning heavily forward, her palms on her knees, she waved a piece of paper wearily before crunching it between her fingers as they found her kneecap once again. Maren watched in bemused bewilderment as Brigid struggled to speak.

"What did you find, Brigid?" she encouraged, laughing softly and reaching for the paper. Shaking her head, Brigid snatched it away.

"Nuh uh," she managed, wheezing, then straightened as she caught her breath at last. "You have to let me explain first." She stood at attention and held the paper out in front of her. "'Welcome to the Irish Journal,'" she trumpeted in a faux Irish accent. Maren grinned at the attempt and leaned back on the washing machine, folding her arms across her chest as she listened. "I signed up for this weekly email," Brigid continued in a rush, "and it gives all the news in Ireland, the major headline-makers anyway. I subscribed to it the day you told me all about the Magdalens." She took a breath and hastened on. "I just did it out of curiosity, mainly; I mean, I didn't expect to really find anything about the laundries! So I've been getting these emails every week, and I basically just scan them and read what's interesting. It's been very fascinating—I've learned a lot about Ireland, Mum, just not about the Magdalen laundries. But today—" she lifted the paper and shook it in the air, "—today there was something about them! Look!"

Her heartbeat speeding up slightly, Maren reached for the paper. Brigid had apparently hastily pulled the piece of paper out of the printer, for the last few lines were streaking across the page and virtually illegible, but there was no mistaking the headline at the top of the printout. **MAGDALEN MEMORIAL TO BE ERECTED IN GLASVENIN**, the large black print screamed. Maren, eyes wide, scanned the article and gasped.

"It says here this is about Sacred Mercy convent," she said in disbelief, glancing at her daughter for confirmation. Brigid nodded.

"I know; that's the first thing I noticed. It's in Dublin." She waited eagerly as Maren stared at the name, then looked up at her daughter.

"Brigid, that's the convent I was in." Her eyes were filled with fear and something akin to anticipation.

Brigid's cheeks flushed with excitement. "Are you kidding? Mum, look at this." She snatched the paper out of Maren's hands again and scanned it, finally pointing with her finger. "There; see?" she asked, moving the paper so that Maren could see the words, and they each held a corner of the paper as Brigid read aloud and their eyes moved in unison over the page. "'Early this year, the Sisters of Mercy, the owners of Sacred Mercy Convent, sold it to the government for development, stipulating that the bodies of one hundred and thirty-three girls buried on the convent grounds must be exhumed before further work could ensue. The bodies were those of girls who died at the convent while working in the convent laundry. Recently, these bodies were exhumed, cremated and buried in a double grave plot in Glasvenin Cemetery with several other "Magdalens" who have died in the convent. Today, with little ceremony, a marker is to be erected at the site, listing the names and dates of death of all the girls buried in the mass grave.'" The article went on to briefly give the story of the Magdalens. Brigid stopped reading.

Maren dropped the corner of the page that she had been holding and sat down heavily on the floor. Her head in her hands, she squeezed her eyes shut and shook her head slowly. Feeling suddenly drained, Brigid folded the paper and stood watching her mother, waiting patiently for Maren's mind and heart to assimilate the news. "I can't believe it," Maren finally said softly, staring into space. "One hundred and thirty-three bodies...buried in the grounds..."

Brigid moved forward and crouched down to look Maren in the eyes. Gently reaching for her hand, she whispered, "This is it, Mum. It's your chance to find out what really happened to Ceara."

Maren's eyes filled with tears. "You mean...go back there? To relive it again? I can't do that, Brigid. You must understand." She sniffled and wiped the back of her hand across her eyes. "I can't go back."

She looked terrified, but Brigid gently pressed on. "You said yourself that you would do it all over again if you had to, Mum. Isn't this something that you need to do? You have to be able to put it to rest. Who knows; maybe you'll discover Ceara walking down the street with her seventeen grandchildren and a smile on her face." She grinned as Maren laughed softly at the image, then lowered her eyes briefly. "To tell you the truth, Mum, I'd kind of like to see it for myself as well."

"Ireland?" Maren asked, drying her face on a towel from the wash basket.

Brigid nodded. "Yes; Dublin, the convent, and your village as well. It all feels so close to me now. I want to see it all in person." Her voice rose in enthusiasm. "Let's go, Mum. Let's get Dad and Donal and go right now!"

Maren laughed tersely and got to her feet. "It's not as easy as that, Brigid, but...I'll talk to your father and see what he says." Brigid clapped her hands in delight, and Maren shook her head as she grabbed the basket full of clean, dry laundry and moved toward the stairs. "I'll see you later, love. I think I'll just spend a little time in my room right now." Her voice was shaky, and she turned away so that Brigid could not see the tears starting once more.

Nodding again in understanding, Brigid watched her mother move up the stairs and close the door behind her, knowing that she would need some time alone.

Soon, though, Brigid thought, glancing again at the printout. *It's going to happen soon, and then Mum will be able to put her past to rest, once and for all.* She sent a silent thank-you to the Lord for answering her prayers, and opened the door to head for her own bedroom.

One month later — June 1995

Brigid put a reassuring hand on her mother's shoulder as they walked through Heathrow Airport, working hard to stay together as they passed through the thousands of people rushing to board planes or racing to find their loved ones after deplaning. They had decided only to spend one day in London before catching the connecting flight to Dublin, and although Brigid was disappointed that she hadn't been able to see more of the sights of England, she knew how important this trip was to Maren, and she could tell that her mother would not feel relaxed until after she had been back to Dublin and dealt with her past. Each moment that they spent in preparation for the visit to the cemetery and the convent was another moment for Maren to gain anxiety, and as she patted her mother's shoulder, she could feel the tension emanating from her in fierce waves. Brigid smiled, knowing how difficult this had to be, but she was proud of her mother for facing this challenge head-on.

They managed to find the correct departure gate after fifteen minutes of wading through people, and eventually boarded the plane along with many other passengers. The route from London to Dublin was the busiest international air route in the world, having just recently surpassed the routes from London to Paris and London to New York. The plane was painted a pleasant green with the bold lettering on its side spelling out "Aer Lingus", the official airline of Ireland, and Brigid struggled not to get separated from Donal and her parents as they were jostled by the many other people boarding the plane. They made it to their seats, and each settled in for the short trip to Dublin.

Maren had thought she was prepared for the trip. Nothing, however, could have made her ready for the rush of terror and emotion that accompanied the first squeak of the plane's wheels as they touched down on Irish ground. Maren turned instantly from where she had been staring out the rounded window of the plane to Garvan's side and buried her face in her husband's shoulder, tears of loss, regret, and grief streaming unchecked down her face. As the plane slowed to a stop near Dublin Airport, he held her wordlessly until her silent crying slowed, then took her hand in his and smiled into her eyes.

"It is over, Maren," he stressed, his face tender as he looked at her. "Nothing can harm you now."

She had nodded against the silk of his shirt. "I know it is," she replied, "but she's still with me, in my heart, and being here again brings back the pain we both went through. I've wondered for thirty-four years what happened to her." Her voice broke with fervor. "I should have gotten her out of there. To think of her in that place... it just seems like her life was such a waste."

Garvan nodded in understanding, but then he shook his head. "No, Maren, it wasn't a waste at all. If she hadn't existed, do you think you'd be here now?"

Maren thought a moment, then answered her husband with a reluctant grin. "No. I know that I wouldn't. Maelisa touched my life in so many precious ways, and she gave me the most wonderful gift of all." Silent for a moment, Maren let the memories swirl through her mind, and the lines on her forehead were a testament to her sorrow. "I just wish I didn't feel that I traded my life for hers. I would give everything up to know that she were safe, and here with me now."

A smile creased Garvan's forehead. "That doesn't speak too highly of me, then, if you'd easily give up me and the children for her." Maren stole a quick glance at him to see if his expression held the same hint of teasing that was in his voice. When she saw the twinkle in his eyes, she let loose a quick laugh and elbowed him in the ribs.

"You know what I mean, Garvan. I just want an answer. I want nothing more than to see her walking down the streets of Dublin, her handsome husband beside her, and children flocking behind them. You understand that, don't you?"

"Yes, I do." He hugged her tightly for a moment, as the flight attendant at the front of the plane unbuckled herself from her jump seat and stood, smoothing her wrinkled Aer Lingus uniform into submissive flatness over her stomach and hips.

"Ladies and gentlemen," she announced in her heavily Gaelic-accented English, "thank you for traveling with Aer Lingus. Passengers in rows one through fifteen may now exit through the front door, and passengers in rows sixteen through twenty-nine may file out through the back door, which is located on your left." She pointed toward the back of the plane, where another smiling attendant had opened the rear door and now stood beckoning and waving. "Please be courteous of other passengers when leaving the plane, and retrieve any baggage stowed under seats or in the above compartments as quickly and carefully as possible. Again, thank you for flying with Aer Lingus, and welcome to Ireland." Her microphone was shut off with a loud click, and Maren and Garvan stood up from their seats in row fifteen, grabbed their travel bags from the overhead compartment and made their way with the other passengers slowly off the plane, joining Brigid and Donal where they had been sitting a few rows forward.

Maren led the way out of the airport, pointing out the baggage carousel for Garvan and Donal to retrieve their bags, and walked with Brigid a few feet further to the *bureau de change* to exchange their Canadian money for Republic of Ireland pounds. She was quiet as she counted out the money, and Brigid stayed silent as well, though she was curious about the exchange rate and eager to see what Irish currency looked like. Maren, abruptly looking up, noticed Brigid's curiosity and was sensitive enough to cater to it. She gave her a few five- and ten-pound notes to look over, as well as several 10- and 50-pence coins. Donal, having left the baggage retrieval to his father, came up behind them excitedly and had to examine them as well.

They stopped by Avis Rent-A-Car and shelled out some of their newly changed Irish money for a rental car to drive into town, and although Garvan complained about the price and the twelve and a half percent rental tax, he knew that Maren was happier to be traveling in a private car rather than on public transportation. The Airlink Express Coach was inexpensive and ran directly to the center of Dublin, but if they had been on foot in the middle of the city it wouldn't have been easy for them to visit Somhairle, where Maren had grown up. A nagging fear at the back of Maren's mind convinced her that she would run into someone she had known from the old days, and she gave everyone they passed such strange, suspicious looks that Garvan was doubly glad they had decided not to travel by bus.

They didn't immediately head for the monument. Maren had instead chosen to keep as far away from familiar places as possible, preferring to visit the decorative, quaint parts of town that she had only heard of as a youngster and never had the chance to see. Brigid was thrilled with the Temple Bar area, with its trendy shops and pubs, but Maren steered her clear of the less reputable places carefully. They admired Christ Church Cathedral, and walked leisurely north to cross the River Liffey by way of Ha'penny Bridge, where they noticed two statues of women, bronze shopping bags littered by their feet, sitting on a park bench. "The hags with the bags," Maren murmured, a tiny smile crossing her face, and Brigid laughed.

"Why do you call them that?" she asked her, wondering if that was what the statues really were called or if her mother was just poking fun. Maren grinned.

"Dubliners have their own unique way of giving the statues they really hate—or really like—names, usually rhyming ones. I'd heard about the 'hags with the bags' for years, but this is the first time I've actually seen them."

"You didn't spend much time in Dublin, then?" Brigid asked in curiosity. "I mean, apart from in the convent?"

Maren shook her head. "No, not at all. In my own way, I'm as much a tourist here as you are. But, my father did grow up here, so I heard a lot about it while I was growing up." She gave her daughter's hand a squeeze, and they continued on.

They stayed in a cozy bed-and-breakfast close to the River Liffey, which divided the city north and south. Their hostess was a kind, plump lady who had lived on her own and run the bed-and-breakfast herself since her husband had died several years before. Maren and Garvan found her quite hospitable and were grateful to return to the cheery little house at the end of each day of their stay.

It was three days before Maren was able to take the first steps inside the tiny village where she had spent her youth, and showed her curious children around its sights, still familiar after nearly thirty years away. She was silent for periods, jovial for others, and Garvan watched her closely as she moved easily around the little, diamond-shaped town, stopping to look around the meat market, the general store, and the dairy that her father had once owned. At one spot on the crowded main street, Maren had stopped suddenly, standing stock still in the midst of the dozens of pedestrians who milled around her without taking much notice.

She stood staring at a church a few feet away, planted tidily on a corner and dwarfing the tiny businesses that surrounded it. Its spire stretched tall into the air, and rows of gaily waving flowers of every hue surrounded the stretch of steps that led up to where its double oak doors stood open in welcome. Brigid watched her carefully, with a guarding possessiveness more suited for the mother of a young child, and Garvan stayed a few paces behind and let his daughter do her mothering. Maren was expressionless, and then she had taken a deep breath and turned to where her family was waiting. "I'm ready now," she whispered. "Let's go see it."

Chapter Twenty-Five

They were all silent in the car ride back to Dublin, the air heavy with anxiety and expectation. Garvan drove down Parnell Street, occasionally asking for directions from Brigid, who sat in back with the map and guidebook, and pulled to a stop outside the gates of Glasvenin cemetery. Many tall crosses and high stone monuments were visible over the edges of the walls, and Maren took a deep breath as Garvan found a place to park. Steeling herself, she closed her eyes and muttered a brief prayer, then jerked on the door handle and threw herself out the door before she could change her mind. Her family followed at a slight distance, wanting to give her the space she needed.

Maren walked around the cemetery for a long time until she saw it: a large gray stone memorial that marked an oversized double grave. Hesitant to approach it, she stood back for a moment, her heart pounding. She could smell the blossoms from the nearby magnolia tree; their scent carried on the air and wafted past where she stood stiffly, her back erect against the pain and memories from thirty years earlier. With a glance toward where her family stood nearby, she took a deep breath. Brigid nodded at her. "Go on, Mum," she said softly.

Her husband nodded. "It's time, Maren," Garvan agreed. He stood quietly with Brigid and watched as his wife took a hesitant step forward. Donal watched with the mild curiosity of a twelve-year-old unaware of the importance of what is happening around him, then returned his gaze to the ground, where he plucked blades of grass one by one to suck on their sweet white roots.

The face of the stone was unremarkable, but the names were carved in bold relief and were slightly damp from the early morning dew. Maren closed her eyes as she inched forward; this moment had been a long time coming, and she wasn't sure if she felt quite ready for it yet. For twenty-five years she had kept herself safe in Canada, away from the haunting memories and the pain of her past. She had tucked it away, telling no one but her closest family of the horrors she had endured here, and now it was time to bring it all back to the surface.

And now she was here, standing only inches from where the only acknowledgment of the torment she and many others had gone through had been placed. This was the only way that many would know of the girls of the Magdalen laundries, and Maren needed to see the names, to know for certain what had happened to her best friend. With one final deep breath filling her lungs, she opened her eyes and took her first look at the words on the gray stone.

"In Loving Memory Of The Magdalens of Sacred Mercy" was etched starkly at the top of the slab. And underneath, name after name was listed. Maren felt tears in her eyes as she scanned the list of young women. As she read them quickly, her heart filled with emotion for the many lives these names represented. Several of the names she recognized, and faces long forgotten sprang into her mind as she scanned the list.

Gavriela Collins...Anya, the beautiful girl whose head had been shaved because she was too pretty, who had stood tall and proud in the room with Maren and the other girls as Líadan had demanded proof of their menstruation. *Maxime Naeve Donegan*...Maxime, the girl Ceara had told her about, whose baby Kathleen had been taken from her arms just moments after her birth. *Nessa Vaughan*...the young girl who had died of a hemorrhage after she miscarried while working right next to Maren during her first few days at the laundry. So many girls who, even though some had grown older, never had the chance to become women, girls whose lives and souls and children had been taken away from them unfairly. There were one hundred and seventy-five names and dates of death scrawling across the monument, and Maren tried not to think of them all, cremated into one little pile of ashes beneath the soil. *Patricia Kiley*...Étain. So she had not escaped.

She continued scanning the list of names. *Echna Laoise Sullivan*...*Lasarina Farrell*... And then there it was. Neatly printed on the stone was a name that Maren had held dear to her heart for thirty-three years.

Ceara Brigid MacAodhagáin—December 7, 1962.

Emotion swelled up inside Maren's heart. The trees waving softly overhead disappeared from her peripheral vision; all she could see was the name before her as she struggled to fight back her tears. Maren fell to her knees in front of the memorial. "Oh, Maelisa," she cried out, her hands reaching out to grasp the cold stone before her. "Why did it have to be you? How could you, of all people, end up here? It isn't fair." She bowed her head until her blond bangs, slightly dulled now with age, touched the name she cherished. As her family stepped forward to lay comforting hands on her back, she began to cry again.

So she had seen it. There, in the simple name boldly printed on the gray stone, was a declaration that Maelisa had indeed lived and breathed, had walked on this earth and smelled the same flowers that now grew abundantly around the memorial. Many visitors would walk this same path and read these names, and know that Ceara Brigid MacAodhagáin had been a victim of the laundries, a system that had seemed to work from the outside, while inside it was destroying girls and young women in the name of God. Maren looked up again at the date of death that was inscribed next to Ceara's name: *December 7.*

One week after she had left the laundry. Ceara had lived only a week longer than Maren had known her. How could she have died so soon?

Maren looked up to the bright sky and remembered a conversation from many years earlier: "*I think I know what I'm here for, Cassán,*" Ceara whispered with a tiny smile, "*but I have a feeling that it might take you your whole life to figure out what it is.*" Maren smiled as she finally realized the truth; Ceara had indeed had a purpose in her life, and now she finally knew what it was. "The Lord sent you to me, Maelisa," she whispered to the breeze. "He sent you to me that I would know Him." Lifting her face to the sky, she offered a prayer to her Lord and Savior. "Thank You, Father. Thank You for sending Your Son to die for me, and thank You for sending Ceara to me to teach me of you. Thank You for rescuing me from the Laundries, and most of all, thank You that I will one day see Maelisa and Treasa again, at Your side."

She glanced around, seeing that Garvan had moved Brigid and Donal down a few rows, looking over the intricately carved gravestones and monuments. Grateful for his sensitivity, she stood up, wiping the tears from her eyes, and noted a slight movement out of the corner of her eye.

A tall, thin elderly woman, swathed in a warm woolen coat and with a scarf wrapped around her neck and the lower half of her face, was walking slowly and deliberately toward her. Maren furrowed her brow; there was something familiar about the way this woman moved, but she couldn't place her. After so many years away from Ireland, she thought it unlikely that anyone she had known was liable to be in the very place she was, but she couldn't shake the feeling that she knew this old lady. For a moment the woman stood back, then hesitantly took a step forward.

"Excuse me, miss," she said in a voice that, though rusted with age, was also recognizable. Maren stepped toward her as well.

"Yes?" she said politely, her mind racing as she tried to decipher who this person could be. The stranger looked uncertain, and although Maren still couldn't see much of her face, she could tell that the woman was struggling to decide what to say. Finally she spoke again, in that hauntingly familiar voice.

"Did...did I hear you say the name *Maelisa* just now?"

Maren's heart jumped and her right hand immediately reached up to clutch at her chest. She had rarely said that name herself in the past thirty years, and to hear it from someone else's lips was a shock. Barely recovering in time to seem aloof and natural, she tried to relax as she forced her hand back down to her side. "Yes, I did," she answered in as normal tones as possible. "I...had a friend who died at the Convent of the Sisters of Sacred Mercy." She gestured vaguely to the gravestone and stared at the woman's face as she waited for her reply.

The woman took a deep breath, and as she reached her hand up to touch her scarf, Maren saw that she was trembling. Long veins traced the contours of her thin hands, and her fingers were bony. Maren's eyes narrowed...she knew those hands...

"Miss Bradigan?" she asked, and Maren's eyes leaped to those of the stranger. Her mouth dropped open and her heart would not stop its incessant racing in her chest.

"Who are you?" she demanded, falling back against the monument. "How do you know me?" But even as she asked, she knew the answer. The moment the woman had spoken her name, she recognized her voice and dozens of memories flashed through her head. The long, bony hands pulled at the scarf, revealing a face lined with age, but the eyes were the same. Maren forced the name out in a harsh whisper: "Liadan?"

Liadan took a step back, aware of how much she was upsetting Maren, but she was determined to talk to the woman who, though older, still looked remarkably youthful and just like the girl she remembered. "Yes, Miss Bradigan – Maren – it is me," she said softly. She fumbled with the words, not wanting to frighten Maren more, but unsure of how to proceed. "I—I heard you say her name, and I...I had to say something." She paused uncertainly. "You look just the same," she offered, but Maren was searching frantically for Garvan. Many times she had imagined standing up to Liadan if she ever faced her again, but now that the time had—incredibly—come, she found herself without words, and full of that old fear. Her feet felt frozen to the ground.

"What do you want?" she whispered. Liadan's eyes dropped to the ground.

"I had to tell you, Maren. I—" Suddenly she leaned forward, her hands in front of her in supplication. "Please, Maren, don't be frightened. I'm not the same person I was then." Her dark, familiar eyes probed Maren's, beseeching her to understand.

Maren suddenly saw Liadan as she was now: not an imposing, black-clad nun with the power of death at her fingertips, but an old woman, skinny as a twig and looking to be as easily snapped. Slowly her heart rate slowed, and she drew herself up to her full height. *I am no longer her slave,* she reminded herself. *I am a grown woman, and a free one. Never again will she have me under her thumb.* She felt a sudden warmth surrounding her, and she closed her eyes to listen to the voice of the Lord as He spoke to her. *Forgive,* she felt Him urge her. *Listen to her.* She opened her eyes once more to look at the feeble elderly woman who stood waiting in silence, her expression open and her eyes pleading.

"Yes, Father," she thought. "I will listen." Aloud she said, "What do you wish to say to me?" Her voice was gentle, and she moved slightly toward the other woman.

Líadan let out a breath. "It's about your friend…Ceara," she said softly. "A few days after you left…we spoke. I was angry at her, for what I can't remember, but she was so calm and peaceful, like she always was." Her eyes dimmed as she retreated into memory, and a tear started to form in the corner of her eye. Maren couldn't believe what she was seeing. Sister Líadan…crying?

The nun stared into space as she continued. "I…beat her…I beat her until she was lying bleeding on the floor, unable to get up." The tears were rolling down her face uncontrollably now, and Maren's own eyes started to flow. Remarkably, she could find no animosity in her heart toward the nun for what had happened so long ago, but the image of Ceara once again lying on the cold stone, bleeding, cut her to the core. She forced herself to listen to Líadan's next words. "I told her to get that smirk off her face, and she told me that she couldn't. 'Why not?' I yelled at her, and I kicked her and kicked her as she lay there, but she just kept smiling. Finally…finally she answered me. 'I see my Lord coming for me,' she said. She lay there, covered in blood, and her eyes were clear and open, and she looked me right in the eye. 'I forgive you, gray lady,' she said, 'and Jesus will too… if you ask Him.'" Líadan looked at Maren with tear-bright, sorrowful eyes. "And then…she died."

Maren shook as a sob escaped her. So Líadan had succeeded in killing Ceara after all. She wrapped her arms around herself and squeezed her eyes shut tight, an image of Ceara's shining, smiling face appearing before her. When she opened them, Líadan was standing a few steps closer, and a smile appeared on her wrinkled face. Maren didn't shrink back as Líadan reached toward her and put a gnarled hand on her shoulder. "So I asked Him," she whispered, "and He forgave me."

The warmth of the Lord suddenly enveloped them both, and Maren gasped with unexpected joy. Líadan had come to know the Lord! "When?" she managed, unable to keep the smile off her face. Líadan's face shone as she answered.

"It was only a few days later. I finally opened the Bible, and read it...for the first time, really read it. I devoured the Gospels and found so much in there that I had never understood before. After I finished reading, I lay down on the floor right there and prayed, asking the Lord to forgive me for everything I had done wrong, and I asked Him to come into my heart and change me." Her eyes sparkled. "Right there, I felt it. He...He filled me, completely. And soon after that, I left the convent and forsook my calling as a nun."

"You're not a nun anymore?" Maren asked incredulously. Líadan shook her head.

"Not for many years. I moved to Knowth in County Meath and immersed myself in the Bible. I read everything I could and prayed every night that God would someday give me the opportunity to ask forgiveness from all the girls—all the *women*—that I had hurt so badly. I tried to help...I wrote letters to the government; I tried to tell anyone who would listen, but because I had left the Church, no one in authority would listen to me. When I heard that Sacred Mercy had been sold and all the bodies were exhumed, I praised the Lord that the secret was revealed and the horrors ended. My trip to Glasvenin today was to visit the monument and ask these girls for forgiveness in the only way I can, now." She clasped Maren's hand in hers. "And when I saw you kneeling there, with your beautiful hair just the way I remembered it, and heard you say that name—I knew, I just knew that Jesus had presented me with a wonderful opportunity, an opportunity that I will never have with any of these girls." Her eyes moved to the gravestone with an expression of sorrow that Maren knew she would never forget. She reached with her other hand to place it over Líadan's. Líadan looked at her with such earnestness that Maren's heart nearly broke. "Please, Maren, can you ever forgive me for all I've done to you, and to Ceara?"

Maren's tears broke forth again. "I forgive you," she replied brokenly. "I forgave you many years ago." She realized as she said the words that they were true; she had forgiven Líadan years earlier, as she had grown in her walk with God and became conscious of the facts of Líadan's spiritual blindness and that she walked in ignorance. She felt a joy in her heart and knew that her journey to find peace had ended here, in Glasvenin cemetery. Prompted by the Holy Spirit, she reached out to pull Líadan into her arms and held her tightly.

Líadan gave a glad cry and returned the embrace. "Thank you, child," she sobbed into Maren's neck. "Thank you."

"*Go mbeannaí Dia duit,*" Maren said to Líadan, and the old woman cried harder at the gentle words. *May God bless you.* Maren looked up into the sky and felt that gentle breeze pass over her again.

The woman who had once been a young girl with golden curls stood holding her old archenemy in her arms, cradling her as her sobs died down. With a smile, Maren lifted her right pinky into the air and made a subtle slashing motion, their old sign meaning *Thank you.* Picturing Ceara looking down on them, Maren whispered into the air, "If not on this earth, then in eternity, my dear friend."

THE END

Author's Note

The Magdalen Laundries is a novelization of true events. It is not the story of one girl, but many: every event in this book has been documented as occurring to countless young girls, teenagers, and women. These often innocent girls were taken or barred by their family from their homes, put to work for long hours in an unforgiving environment. They suffered fatigue, loneliness, malnutrition, miscarriage, physical abuse and even death under the guise of atoning for their sins. It is a devastating chapter in Ireland's history that has come to light over the past three decades.

I first came across the story of the penitent women's laundries in Ireland in the late 1990s, when I saw a feature on television show *60 Minutes*. Horrified to learn of the way these young girls had been treated, I delved into research and began writing that night, and Maren and Ceara sprang to life fully-formed almost immediately. Their experiences spoke to my heart, and I told their story as I learned of it. Eventually, I completed *The Magdalen Laundries*, a book that has taken me two decades to put forth.

The Laundries first began in the mid-1800s as a place for "wayward girls" – presumably, prostitutes, hence the name "Magdalen" or "Magdalene", for Mary Magdalene in the Bible – to symbolically cleanse themselves of their sins by washing the dirty clothes of others. Throughout the years that the convent laundries were in effect, young girls were brought in for the crimes of pregnancy outside of wedlock; fornication; getting too close to someone of the opposite sex; or simply being too attractive and considered a temptation to men. They were abused, neglected, and overworked. Many girls lived there, watching their babies grow up in an adjacent orphanage and not knowing if family members would ever come to rescue them. Too many died there.

The last convent laundry in Ireland did not close until the mid-1990s. In 1993, the discovery of a reported 133 bodies – it was later confirmed to be 155 – buried in grounds of a convent up for sale led to an exhumation and investigation into the penitent women's laundries. In 2009, an inquiry into child abuse allegations produced a 2,000-page report including testimony from hundreds of Irish residents who had been victims of the laundries. In 2013, the Sovereign State of Ireland officially apologized to the victims. Currently, the last known laundry in Ireland is for sale, prompting an outcry from those who want just recompense for those who lived and died there.

When I started my research, the Internet was new. These days, a simple Google search – and I encourage you to do so – will give you much information about the Magdalen Laundries and what was endured by those who lived within the high stone walls. Justice For Magdalenes, especially (www.magdalenelaundries.com), established in 2003, works tirelessly to ensure that the survivors of the laundries are treated with respect and given both the apology and the compensation they are due. This remains a story that needs to be told, not only to give the lost girls some recognition for the horrors they endured, but to attempt to show that the actions of some – purportedly in the name of Christ – should not be held as representative of those who love and act in actual service to their Lord. There is hope in Christ, not despair, and I hope that Maren and Ceara's story shows that this hope can sustain even under the worst of circumstances.

Thank you for reading.
Go mbeannaí Dia duit.

Lisa Michelle Odgaard, May 2017

Pronunciation Guide

As this novel was written in order to tell readers outside of the UK about the events that took place in Ireland over many years, The Magdalen Laundries was written in North American vernacular and is not an accurate portrayal of how Irish people speak to one another. However, most of the names in the book are intended to be authentic Irish names, and may therefore be difficult for the intended audience to pronounce. Here are some (hopefully!) helpful hints for pronunciation of the names in The Magdalen Laundries – and, of course, given Ceara's great interest in the meanings of names, those as well.

All name pronunciations and meanings, unless otherwise specified, are from http://www.namenerds.com/irish/

Ailbhe: AL vyeh – "white king" or "world king" (m/f)

Anya: AWN ye – "splendor, radiance, brilliance" (www.babynamesofireland.com/anya)

Bodhrán: BAO rawn (as in "taking a bow") – a drum; an iconic Irish instrument

Brigid: BRIJ it – "exalted one; high goddess; noble"

Cassán: CAS awn – "little curly-haired one"

Ceara: KYAR a or KA ra – "fiery red"

Céilidh: KAY lee – a traditional Irish or Scottish social event

Conall: KUN al – "strong as a wolf"

Dáirine: DAW rin yeh – "fruitful, fertile"

Deirdre: DAIR dreh – "perhaps 'chatterer', or could be derived from a name beginning with *der-* meaning 'daughter (of)'"

Donal: DOE nal or DUN nal – "world mighty"

Étain: AY teen – "jealousy"

Faolán: FWAY lawn – "little wolf"

Garvan: GAR vin – "rough"

Gobán: GUB awn – "smith"

Gormghiolla: GURM yu la – "grey servant"

Grania: GRON ya, GRAW nya – "grain" or "inspires terror"

Líadan: LEE a din – "grey lady"

MacAodhagáin: mək-EE-gan – Irish Gaelic form of Keegan (www.surnames.behindthename.com)

MacCeallach: mac KEL lee – "bright-headed"

Maelisa: mal EE sa – from Mael Íosa meaning "servant of Jesus"

Maren: MAIR in – "of the sea" or "bitter" (www.namemeaningsdictionary.com)

Maxime: max EEM – "greatest" (www.thinkbabynames.com)

Naomh: NAV, NEV – "saint"

Ó Ciarmhaic – O KIR bee – "descendent of Ciarmhaic" – anglicized to Kerwick or Kirby

Oran: OR an – "dun-colored"

Orla: OR la – "golden princess"

Rian: ree AN – "little king" (www.thenamemeaning.com/rian)

Saraid: SAR ad – "excellent; best"

Seanán: SHAN awn – "old; ancient"

Somhairle: SO ar leh – "from Norse: summer wanderer"

Sorcha: SUR a ka – "bright; radiant"

Treasa: TRAY sa – "strength"

Ultán: UL tawn – "Ulsterman"

Uillean pipes: ILL un or ILL EEE un pipes – the national bagpipes of Ireland

Printed in Great Britain
by Amazon